Carbet de la ⸺⸺ ⸺ ⸺ ⸺⸺ Prize (2012)

WINNER
Insular Book Award (France, 2012)

'Suárez applies chaos theory to Cuba, starting with the events of 1959 and expanding to take in ideas about the relationship between science and literature, in the vein of Queneau and Sábato, Calvino and the Oulipo group.'
Le Temps (Switzerland)

'A brilliant, joyful and beautiful novel that unfolds to the precise, musical and harmonic rhythm of finely chiselled chapters that betray the author's training as an engineer.'
Leer (Spain)

'Equal parts historical novel, comedy of errors and detective story, Suárez portrays with extraordinary voluptuousity and suggestiveness one of the toughest periods of this Caribbean island whose future still hangs in the balance.'
El Mundo (Spain)

'The characters move between romantic relationships and simulations, in search of a chimera that perhaps is nothing more than an attempt to prove that life in Havana has not come to a complete halt.'
Télérama (France)

'The original plot, narrated like a mathematical conundrum, and the apocalyptic portrait of Havana in 1993 are two of the great attractions of this novel.'
La Libre Belgique (Belgium)

'With incisive and restrained language, Suárez portrays a country ravaged by the economic crisis, where Cubans must struggle and dream every day to make life a little more bearable.'
Le Matin d'Algérie (Algeria)

'Her writing is rich in the ingredients typical of the best literature: a good story, with rhythm and flow, but also sensibility, elegance, intelligence and a sense of humour.'
Duas margens (Portugal)

HAVANA YEAR ZERO

First published by Charco Press 2021
Charco Press Ltd., Office 59, 44-46 Morningside Road,
Edinburgh EH10 4BF

Copyright © Karla Suárez 2011
Rights managed by Silvia Bastos, S.L., agencia literaria
First published in Spanish as *Habana Año Cero* by Quetzal (Lisbon)
English translation copyright © Christina MacSweeney 2021

A CIP catalogue record for this book is available
from the British Library.

ISBN: 9781913867003
e-book: 9781913867010

www.charcopress.com

Edited by Robin Myers
Cover design by Pablo Font
Typeset by Laura Jones
Proofread by Fiona Mackintosh & Fionn Petch

2 4 6 8 10 9 7 5 3 1

Supported using public funding by
**ARTS COUNCIL
ENGLAND**

Karla Suárez

HAVANA YEAR ZERO

Translated by
Christina MacSweeney

CHARCO PRESS

For Alexander León

Some people pay no attention to a speaker
unless he offers mathematical proof.

Aristotle

It's not you, it's screwed-up everyday luck,
the door to delirium, murky reality,
the narcos, inflation, the odd solution,
the switched-off gods, disabled fantasy,
Berlin, Fidel, the Pope, Gorbachev and Allah.
It's not you, my love… it's everyone else.

Santiago Feliú

Margarita, I am going to tell you a story.

Rubén Darío

1

It all happened in 1993, Year Zero in Cuba. The year of interminable power cuts, when bicycles filled the streets of Havana and the shops were empty. There was nothing of anything. Zero transport. Zero meat. Zero hope. I was thirty and had thousands of problems. That's why I got involved, although in the beginning I didn't even suspect that for the others things had started much earlier, in April 1989, when the newspaper *Granma* published an article about an Italian man called Antonio Meucci under the headline 'The Telephone Was Invented in Cuba'. That story had gradually faded from most people's minds; they, however, had cut out the piece and kept it. I didn't read it at the time, which is why, in 1993, I knew nothing of the whole affair until I somehow became one of them. It was inevitable. I'm a mathematician; method and logical reasoning are part and parcel of my profession. I know that certain phenomena can only manifest themselves when a given number of factors come into play, and we were so fucked in 1993 that we were converging on a single point. We were variables in the same equation. An equation that wouldn't be solved for many years, without our help, naturally.

For me, it all began in a friend's apartment. Let's call him... Euclid. Yes, if it's all right with you, I'd prefer not to use the real names of the people involved. I don't want to hurt anyone's feelings. So Euclid is the first variable in that damned equation.

I remember that when we arrived at his place, his mum greeted us with the news that the pump had broken down again and we'd have to fill the storage drums using buckets of water. My friend scowled, I offered to help. So that's what we were doing when I recalled a conversation that had taken place during a dinner a few days before, and I asked him if he'd ever heard of someone called Meucci. Euclid put down his bucket, looked at me and asked if I meant Antonio Meucci. Yes, of course he knew the name. He grabbed my bucket, poured the water into the drum and informed his mother that he was tired and would finish the task later. She protested, but Euclid turned a deaf ear. He took my arm, led me to his room, switched on the radio – his usual practice when he didn't want to be overheard – and tuned in to CMBF, the classical music station. Then he asked for the full story. I told him what little I knew, and added that it had all started because the author was writing a book about Meucci. An author? What author? he asked gravely, and that irritated me because I didn't see the need for so many questions. Euclid got to his feet, went over to the wardrobe and returned with a folder. He sat down next to me on the bed and said: I've been interested in this story for years.

And then he began to explain. I learned that Antonio Meucci was an Italian, born in Florence in the nineteenth century, who had sailed to Havana in 1835 to work as the chief engineer in the Teatro Tacón, the largest and most beautiful theatre in the Americas at the time. Meucci was a scientist with a passion for invention who, among other things, had become interested in the study of electrical phenomena – it was known as galvanism in those days – and their application in a variety of fields, particularly medicine. He'd already invented a number of devices and was in the middle of one of his experiments in electrotherapy when he claimed to have heard the voice of another person through an apparatus he'd created. That's the telephone, right? Transmitting a voice by means of electricity.

Well, he took this thing he called the 'talking telegraph' to New York, where he continued to perfect his invention. Some time later he managed to get a kind of provisional patent that had to be renewed annually. But Meucci had no money, he was flat broke, so the years passed and one fine day in 1876 Alexander Graham Bell, who did have cash, turned up to register the full patent for the telephone. In the end it was Bell who went down in the history books as the great inventor, and Meucci died in poverty, his name forgotten everywhere except in his native land, where his work was always recognised.

But they lie, the history books lie, said Euclid, opening the folder to show me its contents. There was a photocopy of an article, published in 1941 by the Cuban anthropologist Fernando Ortiz, which mentioned Meucci and the possibility that the telephone had been invented in Havana. In addition, there were several sheets of paper covered in notes, a few old articles from *Bohemia* and *Juventud Rebelde*, plus a copy of *Granma* from 1989 with that article I just mentioned.

I was fascinated. In spite of the fact that, so long after the events recounted in the documents, I was still unable to enjoy the advantages of a functioning telephone at home, I felt proud just knowing that there was a remote possibility that it had been invented in Cuba. Incredible, right? The telephone, invented in this city where telephones hardly ever work! It's as if someone had come up with the idea of the electric light, satellite dishes or the Internet here. The ironies of science and circumstance. A dirty trick, like the one played on Meucci, who, over a century after his death, was still a forgotten figure because no one had managed to prove that his invention had preceded Bell's.

A dreadful historical injustice, or something like that, was what I exclaimed the moment Euclid finished his exposition. That was when I learned the other thing. Euclid rose, stepped back a few paces, looked me in the eyes and said: Yes, an injustice, but one that can be righted. I didn't understand. He sat down again, clasped my hands and, lowering his voice, added: What can't be demonstrated doesn't exist, but the proof of Meucci's precedence and, ergo, its demonstration, does exist, and I know because I've seen it. I can't even imagine the expression on my face; I only remember that I made no reply. He freed my hands, never taking his eyes from mine. I guess he was expecting a different reaction, waiting for me to jump up, perhaps, cry out in surprise or something, but my only feeling was curiosity, and that's why, in the end, I simply asked: The proof?

My friend sighed, stood up and began to pace the room. Years ago, he told me, he'd met a marvellous woman whose family had once been wealthy, and so she still possessed items that the ignorant might consider old junk, but which intelligent beings would appreciate for their artistic or historical value. In addition to those items, many of them real heirlooms, the woman had old documents, ancient birth certificates and property titles that would make any historian's or collector's mouth water; and among that bundle of papers, Euclid had one day discovered an original document in Antonio Meucci's handwriting.

I thought he must be kidding, but you should have seen Euclid's face. He was euphoric. Some ancestor of the woman had lived here in Havana at the same time as Meucci and had kept a sheet of paper with diagrams of his experimental device. It all still seemed a bit weird to me, too much of a coincidence, but Euclid swore that he'd held that document and was absolutely certain of its authenticity. Can you imagine it, an original scientific document? That's what he said, opening his eyes wide. I tried to imagine it. Making such a discovery public would undoubtedly raise the prestige of any scientist. And, naturally, he'd done everything in his power to persuade the woman to give it to him, but she'd refused. Apparently it was the sentimental value of the document that mattered to her, not its content.

In principle, Euclid could understand this; she had no desire to part with things that had been in the hands of her family and, in some way, retained their finger-prints. She'd even carefully taped some of the documents, including Meucci's diagrams, onto sheets of white paper to prevent them from getting creased, torn or dog-eared, or just disintegrating from sheer old age. What began to torture Euclid was that, despite the strength of her desire to hold on to all her belongings, she'd been obliged to sell some of them – a silver dish, a gold crucifix, things like that – at the time when the government launched a campaign to recover precious metals and gems, which could be exchanged for the right to buy a colour television or designer clothes from what were known as the 'Gold and Silver Houses'. Euclid understood the heartache of a woman who had no other option but to use her heritage to survive. What he didn't get was that she was capable of swapping her grandfather's silver ashtray for a stereo tape deck, but couldn't see that the Meucci document rightfully belonged to international

5

science. That was why, in a moment of desperation, he even offered her money. It made no difference, she stood her ground: her grandfather's ashtray could go to hell, but not Meucci's manuscript. What really did it for Euclid was that, after so much discussion about that damned sheet of paper, and even though she was aware of his interest in it, she decided to give it to someone else. But he was determined. Years later, he was still on the trail of the document. That was why, when he saw the piece in *Granma* in 1989 about the invention of the telephone in Cuba, he began to feel uneasy; the article might stir the waters or set alarm bells ringing. And now that I'd told him other people were talking about Meucci, he heard those alarm bells getting louder. If the person in possession of the document understood its importance, it would be extremely difficult to get his hands on it. But the greatest problem was that he didn't know who that person was.

As I watched him pacing back and forth across the room, his excitement began to infect me and I felt that something needed to be done. *We* had to do something. The time had come to work together again and make our voices heard; they had been silent for too long.

Euclid, like me, was a mathematician. Our friendship was based on a passion for science and on the deep affection that comes from having shared so many things over the years. We'd met in the eighties, when I was studying at the university. First he taught me and then became my supervisor. In those days all the female students were half in love with him because he spoke slowly, in a quiet voice, and so sweetly that it aroused instant attraction. I wasn't immune to that attraction. There's no getting away from it: I really like older men. Our affair began in a seminar room one wet day. We were alone. It was late. My thesis topic was complex and the rain was pouring down outside. We found the solution to those problems on top of a table. And that was the beginning of something that lasted for the rest of the year. He was married with three children, but we never mentioned that. What would have been the point? We were lovers and my thesis was beginning to take shape. Everything was fine until, following the theory of errors, he committed one that could be defined as 'random'. One evening he announced that it was his fiftieth birthday and he wanted to celebrate it with me at Las Cañitas, the bar of the Hotel Habana Libre. What a surprise! Thrilled, I accepted his invitation and we had a wonderful evening. The difficulty arose later. I wasn't able to see him during the following weeks and when we did finally meet, he was in the midst of a full-blown family crisis. Someone had seen us together and had told his wife. Disaster. We decided to limit our meetings to professional encounters. I was due to defend my thesis in July and I heard no more from him until I returned to the university in September. By then our affair had gone off the boil but, thanks to the amazing success of my thesis, I got a job in the Maths faculty. We became colleagues and then friends.

The opportunity to work with Euclid was a great piece of luck. He was at the peak of his career; everything about him was science, passion and method. I was his apprentice. It was a very intense period. A shame that when my two years of social service came to an end, there were no vacancies at the university and I had to wave goodbye to the faculty. That's when things started to go downhill for us.

I began teaching at the CUJAE polytechnic, but got into the habit of visiting my friend at the university. One day I noticed that he was behaving strangely. He said he needed some fresh air. We went to the Malecón and there, sitting on the wall, he explained that his wife wanted a divorce and he didn't know what to do: he felt old, was afraid of how their children would react, was at the end of his tether. The following month he had no choice but to accept the separation and move back in with his mother. What else could he do? There have always been housing problems here; you can't just up sticks and change your address. Euclid's options were close to zero. He didn't say much about the reason for the divorce and I preferred not to ask. I was afraid that the crisis provoked by our affair might have influenced his wife's decision, and when the reasons behind things are murky, it's almost better to know as little as possible. That's what I think, anyway. As for their children, the eldest ones took their mother's side. According to Euclid, it was just a matter of initial reactions that time would smooth out. But in fact, after a few months, only the youngest showed the least interest in him; the others didn't even phone.

And then the year 1989 rolled around. *Granma* published the article on Meucci that, like I said, I didn't read and Euclid never mentioned. The truth is that we both had much more concrete issues to deal with than the invention of the telephone. Do you remember when the Berlin Wall came down? Well, it wasn't the only thing to collapse that year; we were buried in the rubble. Cuba was dependent on aid from the Soviet Bloc, so the economy did a nosedive, taking everything down with it. The last thing Euclid needed during his inner crisis was an external one, but that was inevitable, given the state of the country. We didn't meet for a while and the next time I visited the university, my friend was so thin that I hardly recognised him. As public transport was in such a mess, he had to walk from the university to his mother's place at the other end of the Malecón tunnel. I decided to accompany him. After a while, he stopped, hugged me and began to cry. Right there, in the middle of the street. I was at a loss for what to do until I finally grabbed his hand and led him to a park, where he told me that, in the intervening three months, his eldest children had left the country. Logically, this had nothing to do with him; it was the result of the impending collapse, the profound economic crisis that was expected in Cuba and the prevailing sense of hopelessness. Despite the fact that his youngest had decided to stay, the departure of the others hit him like a bomb, and Euclid refused to accept the consequences of that impact. It was so devastating that he developed clinical depression and had to resign from his job at the end of the academic year. He spent a lot of time undergoing treatment and taking pills. And that was how I gradually lost my tutor.

When Euclid told me about Meucci in 1993, the worst of his depression had passed, but I can honestly say that I hadn't seen such a glint in his eyes for a long time. That might be why I allowed myself to be carried away by his enthusiasm.

As for me – I'm not going to tell you my real name either, so let's say it's Julia, like the French mathematician Gaston Julia – my fall from grace was simpler. From my very first weeks at the CUJAE, I knew something wasn't right. I wasn't easy in my skin. My dream had always been to do research; becoming a lecturer was something I found hard to accept because I hated teaching. See the problem? I was meant to be a great scientist, receive invitations to international conferences, publish my discoveries in prestigious journals, but all I've managed to do is endlessly repeat the same old formulas. I know that in the early days I put all my energy into doing something great, but little by little that energy was transformed into a sense of dissatisfaction I was unwilling to define. It was Euclid who found the words for it: What's happening is that you feel frustrated, he told me one day. And he was right.

I can't tell you how often I thought about leaving the CUJAE. I was sick of the students, the poor food, the working conditions, the commute to and from the campus. If you think about it, as the crow flies the neighbourhood where I live, Alamar, is at the exact opposite end of the city from the CUJAE. Maybe in other parts of the world that would just mean a longish commute, but in the Havana of those years, it was almost a safari.

I made my mind up one morning in 1991. I'd finished a class and had gone to the toilets, but just before coming out of the cubicle I heard two students enter and mention my name. I stayed in the cubicle to listen. There was no way they could know I was there. One of them said it was true, I was grouchy, and you could have knocked me over with a feather when the other replied that everyone was saying I was starved of it; that's to say, according to my students, I was not only grouchy but wasn't getting any sex either. At that time I was seeing a physics professor, but my dumb students were trying to make me a laughing stock. Maybe you think it wasn't such a big deal, but the thing is that I was fed up, my whole life seemed to be mocking me. It was the straw that broke the camel's back. Enough was enough! Those people weren't worth the effort. There and then, I made my mind up to leave my job, and that's just what I did at the end of the year. And where was I going to find work? I ask you, just what the hell does a mathematician do in a country that's in crisis? Fuck all. I had no option but to accept anything that would at least cut down my daily commute. Through a colleague, I found a post at the technical college in El Vedado, right in the centre of Havana. After teaching undergraduate classes, it was a comedown, but times were hard and my choices limited. I thought of it as something to tide me over. The situation would change, I told myself, and I'd regain my former status.

And it's true, the situation did change: for the worse. So in 1993 I was still there, telling myself to be patient, trying to explain basic formulae to kids who had absolutely no interest in anything.

So, when Euclid told me about Meucci and the unpublished document he wanted to find, I immediately felt that things were looking up. My former tutor was pacing back and forth across his bedroom, telling his story, while I looked on, enthralled. An original scientific document. That was definitely something to hang on to, the lever capable of moving our small world, as Archimedes would put it. I was at a loss for words. But then I too stood up and began to think aloud. Something like that couldn't be left in just anyone's hands, the document was a piece of scientific heritage and belonged to mankind. But are you sure it's genuine, Euclid? Yes, he said, it was signed, and the woman had proof that a member of her family had worked in the Teatro Tacón at the same time as Meucci. It's authentic, Julia, I swear on my grandmother's grave. I'd never in my life seen an original scientific document, but now it felt like it was there before my eyes. Have you any idea what this means, Julia? Euclid asked. And I began to have ideas. The document was a tangible, material reality; it was a sheet of paper with a particular significance. It could be offered as proof of a forgotten truth and so vindicate a great inventor. And what's more, whoever succeeded in doing that would go down in history. And that person could publish an article in a prestigious scientific journal, give interviews on foreign TV channels, speak at international conferences and acquire a reputation in her or his field. That simple piece of paper might have the power to raise us out of anonymity and give meaning to each day of that Year Zero.

Something has to be done, Euclid, I eventually said, and he smiled, confirming that something indeed had to be done because who knows what might happen to that document if it fell into the hands of some idiot, especially now, when we were all suffering hardship. Here in Cuba, Julia, there are people capable of selling their own mother given half the chance. He was right; it was just that I didn't know where to start the search. He said he had a few vague ideas he needed to think through, but for the moment the main thing was not to mention the subject to anyone. The fewer people who knew about the document the better. Euclid put a finger to his lips and I did the same. We smiled. Once again, we were sharing a secret. We could work out what to do later, but that evening I was certain that something did have to be done. It was our duty as scientists.

2

I believe that everyone in this country remembers 1993 because it was the most difficult year of the so-called Special Period, when the economic crisis was at its worst. It was as if we'd reached the minimum critical point of a mathematical curve. Imagine a parabola. Zero point down, at the bottom of an abyss. That's how low we sank. There was even talk of the Zero Option, having to subsist on the absolute minimum, or even less. A Year Zero. Living in Havana was like being inside a mathematical series that never ever converges on any point. A succession of minutes going nowhere. It was like waking up each morning on the same day, a day that branched out and became small portions replicating the whole. Hours without electricity. Food shortages. Rice and split peas every day. And soya. Soya hash. Soya milk. In Europe that might have been some kind of fancy dietary choice, but here it was our daily bread: and we were only allowed one stick of bread a day. It was awful. The split between dollars and local currency. The streets empty at night, bicycles replacing cars, shuttered shops, mountains of trash. It was also the year of the 'storm of the century', when the sea reached so far into the city that in some areas people used snorkels to fish for goods the water had washed from hotel storerooms. Manic! And then the calm. The country devastated, but at least calm. The return to the feeling of going nowhere, our trusty sun beating down like a punishment on the backs of people getting up each day, trying to live life as normal.

In the middle of all that, Meucci's story had come to me like a glimmer of light in the darkness, so that evening, when I left Euclid's, I was turning over the whole thing in my mind as I walked. I couldn't make sense of that woman giving away something so unique after guarding it jealously for years. It was clear that she'd sold the document at a high price when things began to go downhill, because my friend wouldn't have been able to offer much. I had no idea what we'd do if we were lucky enough to find the new owner since neither of us had two cents to rub together. But we could cross that bridge when we came to it. What mattered to me was that I was walking along, feeling like a new person. I scanned the faces of the passers-by, wondering if one of them had the document. Maybe even had it in their pocket. Would they suspect that I also knew about it? I can tell you, it was a weird feeling. Have you ever seen a hologram? Those three-dimensional pictures recorded using lasers? When I was having an affair with the physics professor, we used to meet secretly in his lab and he once showed me a hologram. There was a photograph illuminated by a beam and the image rose into three dimensions before our eyes, like any physical body occupying space. It was so beautiful that I couldn't resist the temptation to move closer and touch the image, but my hand passed through the projected body and I was unable to grasp it because, of course, it didn't exist. It was right there in front of me, but it didn't exist. I'd often felt that way in the Havana of 1993, like a hologram, a projection of myself, and I sometimes feared that if anyone reached out their hand to my body, they'd discover I didn't exist. However, the day I learned about Meucci, it suddenly seemed like other people, the ones walking along the street around me, were the holograms.

Do you get it? I knew a story that would interest the whole scientific community, people from other countries, and that made me solid, in some way important. It really did. A week before, nothing much had been happening in my life. But things began to change on the day I first heard the name Meucci in the conversation I recounted to Euclid. Why was I at there? I'll make it short.

Not long before the dinner I met the second variable in this story. Let's call him... Ángel. Yes, that's perfect. Everything always happened by pure chance with him. I was walking down Calle 23 one evening after work when suddenly an extremely strong motive force knocked me to the ground. I was dazed, only able to watch the wretched cyclist disappear with my briefcase. Then I heard a voice behind me and discovered my guardian angel. He helped me to my feet, gathered up my belongings, told me he lived nearby and kindly asked if I wanted to clean my scratches.

That damned cyclist would never know how grateful I was for his act of aggression. Although I must have seen Ángel hundreds of times, I'd never actually met him before. And he was so beautiful. Slim, but with clearly defined muscles. Fair-skinned but with a nice tan. And he wore his hair long. There's no denying it: I love guys with long hair. I used to see him around there, always walking with a sort of weary gait, as if his head were full of things that weighed him down. When I was a child, Mum used to say that Anthony Perkins looked like he was walking on eggshells. I never understood that phrase, but in my mind Anthony Perkins became the eggshell man. And the truth is that when I came to analyse Ángel, I realised that he walked on eggshells too. He walked slowly. Cautiously. I went back to his apartment that day. There was no one else there, so I was able to take my time washing my hands and knees. Before I left, just to keep the door ajar, I told him that if he dropped by to see me at work, I'd buy him a coffee. He also assured me that I could call around any time. Bye, bye.

I spent the following days on the lookout for him at work. Euclid was amused to see me so anxious, but insisted that a woman had no business getting herself into a strange man's home. According to him, it was the man who should take the initiative. That's what he said until the three of us met by chance in the street. Euclid and I were chatting as we went along, and when I raised my eyes I saw Ángel walking towards us; there was no time to warn my friend. Ángel smiled in recognition. I did the same. But when we stopped, I had a surprise. Ángel commented on the coincidence. He kissed my cheek and held his hand out to my friend, saying, Euclid, how are you? Euclid reciprocated the gesture. I looked at them in confusion. You two know each other? Ángel nodded and Euclid explained that he was a friend of one of his children. When we parted, Ángel promised to come and see me at work.

A few days later, I found him waiting for me outside the Tech, and that was the beginning of the very slow process of getting closer to one another. Euclid had told me that Ángel often used to drop by his home in the days when he still had a family. He said that Ángel was a good sort and what's more... I remember that he paused there and looked at me with a mischievous smile before adding that, as far as he knew, he lived alone and maybe it wasn't such a bad idea to visit him. That bastard Euclid was perfectly well aware of my housing problems and, while I liked Ángel from the first, I can't deny that the lack of a flatmate was another point in his favour. And not only did he live alone, but also in El Vedado, in a marvellous apartment with a balcony overlooking Calle 23 – a street I love – and a huge living room containing books, paintings, a television set and even a video player. In this country, especially at that time, having a video player set you in a class above everyone else. That stuff about us all being equal just means that we have to mark the differences in small ways. You can take it from me.

As I said, my relationship with Ángel developed slowly. He was a complicated sort of man, but I'll get on to that later. What's relevant now is how I discovered all the variables, and it was in his house that I met one of them. Ángel and I had seen each other a few times and, although I thought he was great, we hadn't got any further than little glances and smiles. One night we'd arranged to go out together. I was in his living room having a drink, waiting for him finish dressing or something like that. So I was alone when the doorbell rang. I opened the door and saw a bespectacled mixed-race man whom I'm going to call Leonardo. That's right, like Leonardo da Vinci.

I have to admit that the first time I saw Leonardo, while he didn't strike me as exactly ridiculous, I couldn't help but laugh. I can tell you don't know him. He was so polite, apologising for turning up unexpectedly, as if anyone in this country ever announced their intention of calling around in advance, but as soon as he spotted the bottle on the table, he said: Shit, Havana Club. Brilliant! After I'd poured him a couple of fingers, he sat down in the armchair, sipped his drink and started babbling all sorts of rubbish about the nectar of the gods and what have you. It was clearly some time since the poor guy had seen a bottle of real rum; in those days, you could only buy it with dollars, and dollars were still prohibited.

I discovered that he was an author, had published a number of books and had a lot of projects in the pipeline.

By the time Ángel appeared in the living room, Leonardo was on his second or third drink and I remember that he got to his feet, explaining that I'd been very kind, but that he needed to talk to Ángel about something. Ángel replied straight out that it wouldn't be possible right then. I wasn't sure if I'd put my foot in it by letting him enter; Ángel must have noticed my concern, because the expression on his face softened and he said they could talk some other time. They clinked glasses. When the author left, Ángel apologised, explaining that people who turned up out of the blue and never left until they'd finished the bottle drove him crazy. He gently stroked one finger along my cheek and then I believed him.

I didn't see the author again until the night I met the next variable. It's like one led me to the next, isn't it? Ángel had invited me to a party in the house of an artisan friend. He knew a lot of people there, I knew nobody, and that's why it cheered me a little to spot Leonardo. Ángel was chatting with our host when a hand rested on his shoulder, and there was the author: a familiar face. The artisan smiled at Leonardo and raised the bottle he was holding, saying: Make yourself at home, you fools of the shadows. Then he left us. Leonardo turned slightly to allow the woman standing behind him through, and then, with a flourish, he introduced the penultimate variable in this story. Barbara Gattorno said *ciao* with a grin that wasn't just ear to ear but stretched all around her head, taking in on its path her whole body, and perhaps, while it was at it, even managed to squeeze her boobs into her bra, because that was definitely at least one size too small. She's an Italian friend, but speaks perfect Spanish, Leonardo informed us.

That night we all drank, smoked, talked and danced. Ángel and Leonardo disappeared for a while and I was left chatting with Barbara, one of those women who exude self-confidence and seem to have an opinion about everything. She said that it was her first time on the island, that she was a journalist, writing about Cuban literature, that she'd only just started reading Leonardo's stuff but it was an experience, Cuba was an experience, the smells, the people, the way they look at you and express themselves, she was dying to read all his manuscripts and live through all those stories. Leonardo was right, she did speak Spanish well; with a comical accent, but well.

I remember that at some point I changed from rum to water because I'm not a big drinker; that Ángel and Barbara got into a debate about Italian cinema; that Leonardo and I chatted for a while. And that, late in the evening, Ángel came up to whisper a request in my ear: could I help get him out of there because the Italian woman talked nonstop. When we were making our departure, Barbara suggested that the four of us should have dinner in a *paladar*, one of the island's homespun restaurants, the following evening. It would be on her, naturally.

And that was how we arrived at the famous dinner and the moment when my life began to change, although of course I didn't know that then. *Paladares* were still illegal in those days, so the restaurant kept a very low profile. We had a great night, eating well, laughing and drinking a lot of beer. Somewhere along the line Leonardo started to talk about his work. His most ambitious project, he told us, was a novel about Meucci, the inventor of the telephone. I immediately interrupted to say that Alexander Graham Bell had invented the telephone, but Barbara in turn interrupted me to insist that the true inventor was Meucci. Leonardo continued his account, adding that, as a mathematician, I should know things are only true until the contrary has been proved, and the contrary in this case was that not only had Meucci invented the telephone, but had done it in Cuba. I didn't have the first idea what they were talking about and, given the quantity of beer we'd consumed, I didn't think they did either. Apparently Ángel shared my doubts, because he didn't utter another word during the rest of the tale until, seemingly unable to bear any more, he rapped his can of beer on the table twice and said: Barbara, have you any idea how long it is since I've had a beer? She replied with a smile and ordered another round. In that way, the conversation moved to Ángel explaining our national shortages to Barbara, but the name Meucci had been spoken. And that was how I became the final variable in that story and, without realising it, found myself mixed up with them. The truth was that the only thing I was interested in around that time was Ángel: how to make him mine once and for all; how to break out of that circle of dead-end conversations and little glances.

That night, when we left the *paladar*, a wind that presaged rain had sprung up. It was pleasant. Barbara proposed we go on somewhere else, but I had to work the next day so couldn't. Ángel said he'd help me find a taxi. Leonardo looked at Barbara and said: If you want... We said goodnight. During the day, I'd usually try to hitch a ride home, but at night I preferred to go to Capitolio, where there were taxis that took local currency. As Ángel had decided to come with me, he chose the route. We started along Calle G. He made me laugh; every few minutes he stopped, opened his arms and his shirt billowed out. He said he was a balloon and that if I didn't hold on tight to him, he'd float away. The streets of Havana are wonderful in the wind, they have a strange, magical, somehow angelic charm. He stopped once more, his arms open, and shouted: I can't hold out any longer, I'm going. I laughed and he took my hand as if to continue walking, but instead pulled me tightly to him and looked deep into my eyes. Then he freed me and very slowly his hands reached my face, I felt the heat in my cheeks and heard that 'I can't hold out any longer' whispered in a grave tone. I wasn't laughing either. And the wind continued to blow and Ángel's shirt continued to billow, the only difference was that he moved his lips close to mine and kissed me. And I kissed him back. We kissed. And the wind went on blowing, and I finally sunk my fingers into his long hair, and Ángel went on kissing me, my face between his hands, his tongue in my mouth, his hands passing from my cheeks to my neck, until one of my earrings fell out. That's right, in the middle of all that I felt an earring fall out, but it was the sort of thing you don't want to feel, but you do and you say: One of my earrings's fallen out. At which point he diligently bent down to look for it. I told him not to bother, it was nothing special, but he insisted that he wasn't going to let me lose an earring. I couldn't believe it. I'd been longing for that kiss for over a month. I got the urge to put my hands round his throat, but what I did was to cry out: I'm the one who can't hold out any longer. Then he straightened up, smiled idiotically and said: I'm an idiot, right? And he went on kissing me so the wind wouldn't carry me away. Just after we got back to his apartment, it started to rain. Even though we scarcely slept, the next day my dense students seemed ultra-likeable and we had the most beautiful class of the whole year.

Euclid was very pleased when I told him that I'd finally tasted the flesh of angels. The truth is that I still couldn't say for sure if we were a couple; Ángel was a complicated guy. I suspected that we were still in the first chapter of a long novel, but the main thing was that I was happy. Euclid made a joke about the glint in my eyes and, with a hilarious expression on his face, said that you had to admit the guy had good taste. Then he laughed before adding that he and Ángel now had a common denominator. That phrase seemed ingenious, which is why I haven't forgotten it. And I couldn't help but laugh with him, because he was right: he'd just made me the common denominator between the bodies of two men.

That conversation took place as we walked to his apartment one day. A short time later, after we'd carried buckets of water to top up the drums, Euclid told me Meucci's story and I learned that someone in Havana had the original document related to the true inventor of the telephone. It should be no surprise to you then that when I left, the world felt like a different place. As I said, nothing much had been going on in my life but, without warning, everything had changed. Absolutely everything. Get it?

3

Can I ask you something? Do you mind if we use first names? It's just that I'm telling you very personal things and surnames create a distance. So it's first names then. OK? Then I'll continue.

As I said, Euclid had recovered from his depression by then, although he never put all that weight back on. The only problem was that he was bored. It can't be easy to get used to hanging around the apartment with nothing to do after years of intense activity, which is why he decided to reread his science books and research new areas. According to him, his job at the university had taken up a lot of his time. He'd always maintained that scientific knowledge feeds the soul, and with a well-nourished soul the brain functions better and the body ages less quickly. Of course, he had to modify this theory in 1993, and then he asserted that scientific knowledge feeds the soul but the body also needs food. A well-nourished body and soul provides the necessary conditions for good brain function, which then positive consequences for everything else. In order to nourish his body, he set himself the task of finding students in need of private maths classes to top up his retirement pay and his mother's pension, which, even taken together, weren't enough to live on. As for the soul, he had the idea of starting a study group composed of him, me and two other colleagues, who would meet in one of their homes to discuss scientific issues. We started with fractal geometry, the implications of chaos theory, Mandelbrot, the Julia set. Yes, that's the Gaston Julia who provided me with my pseudonym. In short, maths stuff. We didn't expect to get very far, but at least we meant to avoid brain death during that terrible year. Euclid made me laugh. He used to claim that alcohol, crosswords and park benches for sitting and chatting with the elderly had no place in his life. He'd only admit words that began with M (for example, mathematics and mating).

Meucci begins with M.

A few days after hearing his story, I returned to Euclid's. On my previous visit he'd been downright in his refusal to lend me the notes in his folder, had said that there was no way they were leaving the apartment. So my only option was to examine them there. And I was anxious to do that.

In his bedroom, after I'd finished reading, Euclid tuned the radio to CMBF and said: The other day you mentioned an author. What else do you know about him? He thought that Leonardo might be an interesting lead to follow; if he was working on Meucci, he'd probably already gathered quite a bit of information, and some of it might even be useful to his own search. But this isn't *your* search, Euclid. It's *ours*. It's our duty as scientists to find that document, I insisted. He looked me straight in the eyes and asked if I really wanted come aboard. Of course I did. I loved the idea that he was the captain of the ship and that we could return to our former roles as tutor and pupil. My friend smiled his satisfaction. We must act like real scientists, he said, taking into account even the smallest details, because everything was important, even things that might seem trivial at first. The author's an interesting lead, he reiterated, but we need facts.

All at once his bedroom had become our old maths seminar room. I stood up, stating that we'd have to start from scratch, and as I paced I began to recall everything I knew about Leonardo: his physique, the way he dressed, the few things Ángel had told me about him. But the most important fact of all was that I knew where to find him. At the party, when Ángel and Barbara were having a heated discussion about the development of Italian cinema, Leonardo had come over to chat. He told me that he worked in the human resources department of a company in Old Havana, near the cathedral. It wasn't a great job, he'd said, mostly just tedious paper pushing, but it meant he could write. That was when he told me I could drop by his office if I was ever in the neighbourhood. Nothing would be more natural than to take him up on the offer. What do you think? I asked Euclid and he smiled, saying that I'd always been his best student. He wanted to meet Leonardo too, but for the moment there was no justification for that. Luckily, I'd been presented with an opportunity on a plate.

That said, Euclid also began to pace the room as he spoke. I'd have to visit Leonardo and somehow bring up the subject of Meucci. Getting a writer to talk about his work shouldn't be too difficult, he added with a smile. Then I'd have to gradually strike up a friendship with him, not hurrying things, so that later it would be natural for Euclid to meet him too, as a friend of mine. If he knows anything about the document, he won't tell you straight out, Julia. We have to be patient.

Euclid had me in his spell. Seeing him there, designing our strategy, it was as if he were solving one of those differential equations that used to be such a headache at the university. We had to be very cautious and shouldn't just take everything Leonardo said at face value since he might be hiding something. But I can take care of that later, Julia; for now, just try to attract him, win his confidence. That shouldn't be hard for you. Euclid gave me a little grin that instantly took me back years: to the maths seminar room where a slightly younger version of him smiled in exactly the same way as he unbuttoned my top. That won't be too hard, I said. And we both laughed.

So, Euclid and I had a pact. Leonardo was now our number-one objective, the lemon we had to squeeze every last drop of juice from. It's weird, but sometimes when you think things are totally fucked, some tiny detail changes everything. It must have to do with a lack of objectives. Having no objectives in life can be soul destroying, and if the soul is destroyed, the body hasn't got a chance. You just die, you fall to pieces, vanish. I've always feared having no objectives, but at that moment I had two: one Ángel and the other Meucci. Do you see?

When you have concrete objectives, all other problems shrink to next to nothing, become infinitesimal. My classes at the Tech still lacked any interest, but that no longer worried me so much. The situation in the country was still a disaster, but that didn't bother me either. Or the shortage of food, or the power cuts, because I had concrete objectives. Blaise Pascal said that the last thing one knows is what to put first, yet the only thing Euclid and I had clear was where to begin. Pythagoras said that the beginning is half the whole. If that's true, we'd already covered a lot of ground. The beginning was Leonardo.

I went to visit him that same week, on an afternoon when I finished early and hadn't arranged to meet Ángel. Leonardo was surprised to see me standing in the lobby of the building where he worked. I told him that I was in the area doing some errands at the Ministry of Education, needed to make a few phone calls, and remembered that he worked nearby. No problem, come on. He led me to his office, where I did in fact make some phone calls, but to non-existent numbers, and then complained about wasting my time. It was almost five, and there was no way I was going to find anyone at their desk. I'd had a lousy day, nothing had gone right, and I was dead on my feet. Did he know where I could get a coffee? Leonardo said there was a small stand not far away; the coffee wasn't great but if I wasn't in a hurry and could wait for him, we could go together. I'm finished for the day, I told him, and sat by his desk to wait. That was when he asked how Ángel was.

It was a perfectly normal question, given that we'd met through him, but it honestly took me by surprise, because none of the questions I'd imagined had included references to my lover. That's why I hesitated for a moment before replying: He's fine, I haven't seen him for a couple of days. Leonardo said he hadn't seen him since the night at the *paladar*, but wanted to call him. He liked Ángel. And how's Barbara? I asked to change the subject. Fine, I haven't seen her for a few days either, he replied. We left the building just after five. Leonardo collected his bicycle, which was chained in the parking lot, and we walked together to the stand. He bought me a coffee and as I still wasn't in any hurry, suggested that we sit in the Plaza de Armas for a while to get some fresh air and chat.

Leonardo was one of those people who need no encouragement to talk; in fact his words seemed to be permanently stationed just outside the door, waiting for a moment of carelessness to barge in. That evening he told me many things. I discovered that he was divorced and had a son he couldn't see as often as he wanted because he lived with his mother in Santa Fe, which was a long journey; Leonardo had returned to live with his parents in Cerro, where he'd converted the garage into a small studio apartment. Cycling all the way to Santa Fe was no easy feat, so he had the child once a fortnight and visited him occasionally in between. I learned that he'd published a few books of poetry and short stories; but the Special Period had entailed a crisis in the publishing world, with the shortage of paper and the corresponding reduction in the number of new publications, so he hadn't seen his name on a front cover in quite a while. I told him I loved poetry and he promised to lend me his books. They're good, he assured me. Or at least that was what the critics had said. I learned that he'd had a few other jobs before his present one. A writer, he insisted, is a complex being who is capable of perceiving things that are invisible to others, can find beauty where others see filth, and that's why writers need to mix with the world without allowing it to swallow them whole. Do you see what I'm getting at? he asked. And without waiting for a response, he explained that the only reason he worked in the company was because he needed frequent contact with other humans but couldn't handle a job that would take up too much of his time. That was my window of opportunity to ask about his new literary project. Leonardo smiled; he took a pack of cigarettes from his pocket, offered me one, and I told him I didn't smoke. Then he leaned back on the bench, lit a Popular, inhaled deeply, turned to me and said: My new project is a bombshell. I smiled and, of course, wanted to know more.

It was his first novel and a highly complex, ambitious project. A novel that could be called historical, in inverted commas. Umberto Eco had had the audacity to incorporate Latin into *The Name of the Rose* and that work was a bestseller. Leonardo wanted to incorporate science, but in a different way. He was thinking of a work where there was hardly room for what we understand as fiction because the whole thing was based on real events. Naturally, he assured me, everything that's written, absolutely everything, even history books, because it's all rooted in the writer's interpretation. Do you see what I'm getting at, Julia? I nodded and he went on: For example, if someone were to ask us separately what we'd talked about in the square that afternoon, we'd both tell a different story because we were different people and had different points of view. We wouldn't recount what had actually been said but the fiction our minds created. Interesting, I said. But Leonardo was too fired up to listen. In fact I don't even think he was actually seeing me; he was observing something far off. The difficulty, he said, and this was what made the project so ambitious, was to make real life read like fiction; for readers to settle into their sofas, convinced that they were once again dealing with literary deceit, and then wham, in a flash the reality would suddenly come crashing down on them, because each and every tiny detail in the book was justified by demonstrable historical data, and then the fictional space they were so comfortably inhabiting would become unstable and readers would unexpectedly discover that they were in History with a capital H. Don't you think it's amazing? he asked, actually looking at me this time. I thought for a moment before blurting out that whatever the case, the story would also be fiction because, as he'd said, it depended on who was telling it. I don't think Leonardo liked that comment because he twisted his mouth in a strange way and finally replied: No, not if the things you narrate are fully demonstrable.

I laughed, saying that instead of writing he could have taken up mathematics, an area where demon-strating the truth was a fundamental activity. But even in maths, what is shown to be true today may be revised tomorrow, because demonstrations depend on the state of our knowledge at any given moment. For example, I added, Euclidian geometry (I was, logically, referring to the original Euclid and not my friend) could never have solved the problems posed by fractal geometry because they correspond to different periods of our knowledge of the natural world. Leonardo opened his eyes wide and I, fortunately, paused, because the minute I mentioned the word *fractal*, my friend came to mind and I realised that, in my enthusiasm, I'd forgotten that my mission that afternoon was to extract information from Leonardo; I'd forgotten all about the lemon and the objective and was getting tangled up in Leo's arguments. He smiled, saying that maths wasn't his strong point, that it had been the bane of his schooldays, what he knew about was words, and... I'd have to forgive him because he tended to rattle on. There's nothing to forgive, quite the contrary, I replied and insisted that I was loving everything he said, it was really interesting. And what was that Italian man's name? The one with the telephone. He's a character in the novel, right? Leonardo lit another cigarette and continued: Antonio Meucci, prof, get that into your head and forget about Bell... Then he added: Are you hungry? I know someone nearby who sells pizza. Are you up for it?

Pizza. Pizza is from Meucci's native land, and with that Leonardo concluded his disquisition on the novel for the afternoon. I know, it was my fault; instead of channelling the conversation towards the things that interested me, I'd allowed myself to be swept away by him and everything he was saying, which did in fact seem interesting. That's always happening to me. I don't know why, but when I start talking to a man, I lose myself. And anyway, my objective was to strike up a friendship, and exhausting the topic at the first meeting would limit future possibilities.

Leonardo led me to a place where, at the end of a long passage, we found a window framing a head, and he bought two pizzas. He commented that I was in luck as I'd turned up on a day when he had cash; he'd just won the Nobel prize, he said with a laugh, then explained that one of his short stories was going to be included in an anthology in Spain, and he'd been paid twenty-five dollars; he was rich. But I'd better not get my hopes up because he had a son to bring up and that money had to last a long time. Twenty-five dollars wasn't much, but they were dollars and could be used to buy goods only sold in that currency, basics like oil and shampoo. And since Leonardo's salary was in local currency, he was feeling wealthy. I bit into my pizza, then leaned back to stop the grease from staining my dress and, before I could reply, he said he was kidding, he loved treating people, it was just that he hardly ever could. That's why he was happy that I'd visited on that particular day. I smiled: Thanks, next time it's on me.

That debt was a guarantee of a next time. After finishing our pizza, we set out towards the Malecón, where I could hitch a lift home. At one point Leonardo asked me to stop so that he could look at me for a moment. I did as he requested, a puzzled expression on my face. He began walking again and explained that I reminded him of someone. He said that the evening when I'd opened the door of Ángel's apartment, he'd thought I was a girl he'd known years ago in Barcelona: her face was very similar to mine, and there was even something in the way I moved that made him think of her. You've been to Barcelona? I asked in amazement. Yes, Leonardo had visited the city a few years ago and said it was beautiful, a place where anyone would want to stay forever.

Leonardo had a way of speaking that, with your eyes still open, transported you to wherever he was describing.

It was something I discovered that day. Each of his words was like a fragment building up a picture of the city so that, little by little, I found myself in Barcelona. I haven't been lucky enough to travel, I've never left the island, but I swear that the city Leonardo constructed for me as we walked the dirty streets of Havana – he pushing his Chinese bicycle – is indelibly imprinted on my mind.

That evening, when we parted, Leonardo invited me to a *tertulia* he hosted in his home. A few friends usually met there whenever the electricity was down and they'd spent the blackout reading aloud, drinking, playing dominoes and badmouthing the government. It's fun, he said. The only condition was that all the participants had to bring something – a candle, a bottle, a stick of bread, a pack of cigarettes, anything at all – because however much he'd like to do otherwise, he could only offer his small room. But women just have to contribute the pleasure of their company, he added. I felt it was good that Leonardo was viewing me as an independent person and not someone who was attached to Ángel. It was fundamental to my plans that he considered me as a woman he could meet up with. That way, we could establish a bond, an exclusive bond.

I gratefully accepted his invitation and reminded him that I still owed him. We exchanged telephone numbers. He gave me his work number and a neighbour's, just in case. I gave him mine at the Tech. I promised to call him about the *tertulia* and added with a smile: Clear debts make good friendships. And then we parted.

When I phoned Euclid to update him, he was glad to hear that there would be a second meeting. After I'd rung off, I stood, playing with the telephone dial. I was in the school office, but suddenly I felt like a secret agent, a 007 of science. The thought amused me.

4

Perhaps because it seemed easiest, Ángel and I had established the routine that I'd phone him in advance to arrange where to meet. One day we'd agreed that he would come to the Tech after running a few errands, and then we'd have dinner at his place. When we arrived there, I discovered a girl, all in black, sitting at the door to his apartment. The moment she saw us, she jumped to her feet, hugged Ángel with tears running down her face and said: Angelito, please, let me move in with you. He put an arm around her shoulders and kissed her hair, murmuring calming words, with some difficulty, he groped for the latchkey in his pocket. She was quite young, was wearing a t-shirt, a long skirt, military boots and armloads of bangles. I stood a few steps behind Ángel, unsure of what to do, until he managed to open the door and enter the apartment with her hanging around his neck, still crying and repeating her plea. A few seconds later, I heard Ángel's voice: Julia, come in.

When I entered they were still in an embrace. I closed the door behind me, but clearly not as quietly as usual because the bang caused the girl to raise her head. Her woeful face was marked by two black lines descending from her eyes. Ángel stretched out a hand toward me: This is Julia. Then he pointed to her and said: Julia, meet my sister Dayani. She wiped her nose with the back of her hand, said hello, moved away from Ángel, threw her bag onto the armchair and disappeared down the hall. I was still standing in the same spot. Ángel moved closer and explained that this wasn't an uncommon occurrence. His sister was eighteen and whenever she had an argument with their father she came to stay with him. I still hadn't said a word. He put a hand to my cheek and stroked it: Julia, my Julia, are you listening to me? I sighed and raised my head. Of course I was listening, and maybe I should give them some space. He nodded sadly, but did ask me to call him the following morning. Don't stop calling, he insisted.

The next day was May 1st, a detail I remember well because of what happened afterwards. I called, but things were going badly and it wasn't possible for us to meet. Ángel was going to accompany his sister to their father's house. He said he was tired. What he really wanted was a quiet Sunday. Why don't you come around tomorrow at midday and stay over? I've got used to you being here. I bit my lip and replied that I'd be there.

I read somewhere that Einstein said, 'At first, all thoughts belong to love. Later on, love belongs to all thoughts'. That's true. In the beginning, I was fascinated by Ángel. He was a vulnerable sort of guy and, as you must know, vulnerability in a man inspires incredible tenderness in women. It's probably the maternal instinct. But who knows?

I'm not sure just how far Ángel suffered from what's called abandoned child syndrome, and of course I never dared ask. When he was very young, his mother left the country but couldn't take him with her because his father refused to give his authorisation. However, some time later, the father remarried and went to live with his new wife, with whom he had Dayani. Ángel was left with his maternal grandmother, who raised him and remained with him until her death. It was from her that he'd inherited the apartment.

From the very beginning, Ángel's stories had entranced me. He'd been married and claimed it had been true love. They were so close that his father, who at the time had an important post in the tourism industry, had interceded and found them jobs in a Cuban-Brazilian company. The problem was that, after she'd been working there a while, Margarita – that's his ex's name – had built up close contacts on the Brazilian side of the corporation. As a consequence, when they'd been married for only two years, she left him to move to São Paulo on an indefinite contract. My angel was heartbroken. Later, he was sent to São Paulo on a short training course. It was a chance to see Margarita and an attempt to win back her love. But she wasn't interested, and in fact had already found someone else. Ángel returned to Cuba, his world shattered, and couldn't even bear to go on working in the same office. So, despite the fact that a job in a joint enterprise company was something everyone longed for due to the advantages it offered, Ángel handed in his notice and became unemployed. As far as I can remember, he told me that story the day I first met Leonardo. Yes, that's it – in the evening, after the author had left, Ángel apologised for seeming a little brusque, and explained that Leonardo was more his ex-wife's friend than his own. Then he told me about Margarita. Later, I learned that he'd only had casual affairs since then. He'd never been able to forget her and she had gradually become a ghost who haunted his home. That was why Ángel liked to define himself as 'a solitary soul, forever alone', as the song he loved to sing goes: 'If I could only find a kindred soul.'

So you see, that's one of the reasons why it took so long for us to get together: the ghost of 'Margarita, the sea is beautiful, and the wind carries a subtle scent of orange blossom'. Sometimes, as a joke, I used to recite that poem, although I couldn't have imagined then how much I'd come to detest it.

Ángel was a mix of a child in need of protection and the man I wanted to get into bed. My mathematical brain firmly believes that small results lead to final outcomes, so from the first I suspected that things would move slowly. It had taken me over a month to get between his sheets, and I had no idea how much longer it would need to break through his solitary-person shell. I sometimes wondered which of us was really the mathematician. Which of us was calculating the moves.

As we'd arranged, I arrived at his door at the stroke of twelve on Sunday. I tried the bell but it made no sound, so I had to knock until he opened up. He'd only just got out of bed. His hair was tousled and there was alcohol on his breath; there's no disguising the smell of rum. I followed him into the kitchen and, while making coffee, he told me that he'd taken his sister home but as their father even worked on May 1st, he'd got home at some unearthly hour. Ángel paused there since nothing happened when he turned on the gas. There was no electricity or gas and he wasn't one of those handyman-Cubans who'd installed a kerosene stove or any other kitchen gadget. Fortunately, his father had given him some money and a bottle so we went out to a nearby house selling cartons of takeaway food.

The night before, Ángel and his father had had a long chat over drinks. In the end, it seemed likely that he'd have to take Dayani to Cienfuegos one weekend to stay with her paternal grandmother until her stress levels descended.

Ángel thought it odd that the passing years had turned him into the family mediator. Fate was playing a trick on him. And like I said, after his mother left, his father didn't stay single for long. He was a lucky man, he'd always worked in tourism and had never lacked for anything: he had his professional skills and his women provided the domestic comforts. First Ángel's mother had invited him into her home in El Vedado and then his second wife had opened the door to her place in Miramar. Except that in the new arrangement, there was no room for his son. Ángel grew up spending occasional weekends with his father and vacations at the beach. His sister was born when he was thirteen, in mid-adolescence, with a seething mass of hormones and a declaration of war on the father. All the things that usually happen during teenage years, Ángel experienced in triplicate due to that little girl who gradually supplanted him in the non-starring role he'd already accepted, reducing him to a mere extra. And that was why he'd learned to hate her early on, although the hatred diminished with time, until he came to feel a deep love for the girl. She loved him like crazy.

Dayani had been a spoilt child. When they holidayed in Varadero, she always had the best room and was allowed to leave the table if she didn't want to eat. That wasn't the case for Ángel; he was a boy and the oldest, so he had to respect his father's rules. But then she too had reached adolescence, as we all do, a seething mass of hormones, declaration of war on the father, and that's when the problems really began. Once, for example, she'd dyed her hair half red and half green and went to school like that. She'd hardly set foot inside the building before she was sent to the principal's office, and from there back home, with an appointment for her parents. And what did Dad do when he returned from the meeting? He grabbed his daughter's arm and told her that if she was trying to attract attention, well, he was going to make sure she did. They went to a hairdresser's and he asked them to shave her head. Dayani was in tears during the whole time it took her hair to grow back. Ángel and Margarita, who were married by then, were shoulders to cry on, particularly Margarita, he stressed, because they got along so well.

The thing was, Ángel explained, battling with their father had become his sister's favourite sport; but their father couldn't have cared less, he insisted there had been too much pampering when she was a child, and all that had come to haunt her. Ángel suspected that she and her friends were taking drugs, because she'd once or twice turned up at his apartment looking pretty wasted, asking for a place to sleep. Dayani knew better than to go home in that state, and Ángel couldn't bear that she was harming herself, was in open rebellion against herself. Now she's obsessed with getting enough money to leave the country, he sighed, and he felt powerless to help. However much he'd have liked to, all he had to offer was affection, because he had nothing else; certainly not cash. He lived by occasionally renting one of the rooms on an informal basis and with assistance from his father, who sometimes gave him money or stocked his pantry shelves. That said, he invited me to share a 'slap-up' dinner he'd cook himself.

That evening, as was the case of so many others later on, we sat on the sofa drinking rum, 'courtesy of Dad'. Me sitting, Ángel stretched out with his head in my lap. From above, Ángel looked very beautiful. He raised a hand to stroke my hair and asked if I wasn't tired of his stories. No way, I said. Listening to him was a means of entering his world and beginning to belong there, even though I formed no part of his past. He smiled and enquired how things had been for me since we'd last seen each other.

I met Leonardo, I said. I wanted him to hear it from me before blabbermouth Leo could mention it. Ángel stopped stroking my hair and asked: Leonardo? I smiled and told him that I'd passed by his office to make some phone calls. Ángel twisted his body around to pour himself another rum while saying that he'd never really felt sure about the guy. He says he likes you a lot, I assured him. He took a sip of his drink, settled his head in my lap again and rested his glass on his abdomen, cupping it with both hands. According to him, I should watch my step when it came to Leonardo; they had known each other for quite a while but had never been friends because there was something about the guy that didn't ring true. He didn't know how to explain it, it was just a matter of intuition, so he was polite but didn't feel like trusting him too far and, from his point of view, neither should I.

It suddenly occurred to me that Ángel was the sort of man who was jealous of his girlfriends' male friends. He was jealous that I'd met with the writer, and this pleased me. Look, the thing is, I said, Leonardo invited me to a *tertulia* in his home. Ángel gave me an irate look and then, after a few moments, said that Leo never ceased to surprise him. He was invited too; in fact, he'd been meaning to tell me about it, but their host had got in first. I was overjoyed to have confirmation of his jealousy. The knowledge that we both had invitations made the evening a simple get-together rather than an opportunity to develop my friendship with Leonardo, but I'd find another moment for that. In any case, it wasn't such a bad thing that Leonardo, in addition to being my number-one objective in the search for Meucci's document, could be used as a threat in my quest to make Ángel mine and mine alone. I bent to kiss his lips and murmured: Could the reason you don't like him be that he was a friend of

Margaritatheseaisbeautifulandthewind? He grinned and stuck out his tongue to pass it quickly over my lips. Then he said: Witch... He added that his ex and the writer were already friends when he met Margarita, that he knew Leonardo had been up for it, but she'd preferred him. That last phrase was said with great pride and I smiled. I leaned over, took a sip of rum and, without swallowing, returned to his lips so that the liquid would run into his mouth and then disappear down his throat, mixed with my saliva, the taste of my mouth. I felt the urge to ask him when he was going to boot Margarita's ghost out of the house, but I restrained myself. What was the use? I suspected that she was one of those stories that just get in the way, like when you lay a rug in an awkward place so that every time you pass, one corner curls over and trips you up, and you think about moving it somewhere else but then you forget until the next time you trip over it.

You know, Margarita *is* leaving the apartment, Ángel said when we'd done with kissing. I froze. It was as if he'd read my mind. Then I straightened up and took a sip of my drink like someone who hasn't heard anything special so that he wouldn't notice my curiosity. He added that I should be grateful because she was feeding us. I raised my eyebrows. I'm selling her clothes, he said. He told me that she was an unresolved problem, something beyond his control, a cycle that had been violently aborted.

When Margarita left Ángel to go to Brazil, he was still in love with her and so hadn't believed the separation was permanent. He thought she was going through a crisis and needed to be alone, nothing more; to spend some time alone and regain her inner balance. They had always been very close, too close. Margarita needed to prove herself as an independent being, and what could be better than a trip abroad to a place where you can be by yourself and everything you do depends on your own personal and professional abilities. That's what he'd imagined was going on. But when he went to São Paulo, she told him that she had no intention of coming back to him, that in fact she was truly happy to have put such a distance between them. The way the brain functions is incredible, he said. It really is, because even though she'd rejected him, he hadn't wanted to admit it to himself, hadn't wanted to accept the break up. For him, it was just a matter of time. Margarita was the love of his life and she couldn't just vanish in that dumb way. So he was very low when he returned to Havana, but still hoping to receive a letter announcing her return.

It goes without saying that the letter never arrived. Margarita wasn't going to come back either to Ángel or to Cuba, which was by then in the early stages of its major crisis. And she even had a local boyfriend, which is the first step anyone takes when they're thinking of staying in a place. It had all happened very quickly. One night they were in that living room where he was telling me the story, when suddenly they started arguing. That had been happening quite regularly but the dispute was more bitter that night, and they went from one thing to the next until they found themselves going over their life together as a couple. The argument came to an abrupt end when Margarita announced that she was leaving him and that she would soon be leaving Cuba too.

Ángel paused to pour himself another rum. She left carrying a small suitcase the same night, as if she would be back soon. That was why he'd decided not to change anything in the apartment, leaving her clothes and shoes in the wardrobe, her books on the shelves, even her toothbrush in the bathroom. Everything was ready for her return. And that was how he'd lived for years, until time made him understand that, even before she'd left him, Margarita had been thinking of quitting the country.

Ángel sighed and gave a sad smile before adding that he'd recently begun to dispose of her belongings. It was a good decision because selling things was bringing in money and, besides, it was as if Margarita were slowly beginning to fade, to leave him in peace. But he had to be the one to close the cycle in order to finally exorcise her ghost. I've got a plan, he said. Do you want to hear it? I nodded; of course I did. Well, he'd begun with the clothes and shoes, then the books, followed by their romantic mementos, and finally the most personal things, which he was going to send to Brazil with a letter that said just one word: goodbye. While he was speaking, I wondered if it wouldn't be better to sell anything that would bring in some cash and bin the rest, but Ángel had made a plan and that had to be respected. I merely smiled. He said that the whole process was really important, that it wasn't simply a matter of forgetting and writing off his marriage as a failure. No, the thing was to close the cycle, keeping what was beautiful, acknowledging what he'd learned and locating Margarita in her proper place in his memory. I liked what he was saying, as I liked the faraway look in his eyes. Ángel sat up next to me, finished his drink in one gulp and said that it was important to preserve the past so we knew who we were.

Preserve the past, those words sounded good. Ángel needed to close the cycle of his past in order to preserve it. That day I understood that our relationship wouldn't be able to really start until Margarita was in her proper place in his memories. That's what he'd said. And I had to do something to ensure that happened, although I wasn't sure what. Not then.

5

The following week, a number of things happened that I was only able to understand much later. As we'd arranged, I phoned Leonardo to confirm that the *tertulia* was going ahead and asked if I could join him a little before the others because I finished work early that day. He said it was no problem, the electricity cut out at eight and people began to turn up soon after that; and with any luck, he might even be able to offer me some rice and split peas. And then I'll still owe you, I replied. You should worry more about the interest than the debt, he responded with a laugh. Nice one, Leo. That day Ángel was supposed to be visiting his sister, so we planned to meet at the author's place, which had the advantage that I could arrive alone. Leonardo lived in a garage, a small space containing a bed, a worktable with his Remington typewriter, a cabinet stacked with vinyl records and cassettes, several bookshelves and a kerosene stove. Plus, in one corner there was a tiny bathroom. As soon as I turned up, he heated up the peas, set out a folding table, two plastic chairs – also folding – and we sat down to eat.

Leonardo had grown up in his parents' house, but when he started university, given that the garage was only used to store junk, he'd decided to clean it out and convert it into his den. You can't imagine the things these four walls have seen, he said. Then he married and went to live with his wife in Santa Fe, where he'd spent almost two years constructing a small house in his in-laws' yard. His son was born there but, in contrast to what they say in fairy stories, he and his wife didn't live happily ever after. They divorced and Leo returned to Cerro. After lying empty for so many years, the garage-room was a mess, but he was too old to be living with his parents. There was nothing for it but to revamp the place. He installed the pipes and electrical cables, added the bathroom, made bookshelves, managed to find a mattress, whitewashed the walls, and he was set. He had a den again. His mother usually did the cooking, so he only had to prepare his breakfast and heat up food. The only problem was the lack of a fridge. But then what was the point of having one when there was hardly ever any electricity. It wasn't a mansion, he added, but he'd built that lair with his own two hands.

I looked around. I'd have loved to have a place like that but my situation was different. I grew up in Alamar, a district on the northeast edge of Havana, fifteen kilometres from the centre. Identical, rectangular buildings. Our apartment is on the fifth floor and there's no lift. The view from the balcony is the back of one building, and from the bedrooms you can look out on the balconies of another. The most depressing thing is that, although the sea is nearby, it isn't visible. You can smell it but not see it. As a child, I didn't use to mind living there, but when you grow up and the paint begins to peel because it hasn't been renewed since the place was built, things start to look different. Alamar is like a huge beehive that produces nothing. Life goes on elsewhere.

My parents divorced when I was young, having discovered that they weren't in love and, moreover, that they each had a lover. Since they were still very fond of one another and had two children, they decided to separate in the least dramatic way possible. Papi went to live with his lover and Mami's lover moved in with us; he's been like a second father. To be honest, neither my brother nor I have ever lacked parental care, quite the opposite. Not long after the break-up, a whole new world opened up to us. At weekends Papi usually visited with his new wife and her two daughters from a previous marriage. The women cooked. The men drank rum. And we kids played, thinking how wonderful it was to have such a big family with two fathers. I'm not lying when I say that I've only ever seen my papis argue over dominoes. The rest of the time it's pure harmony. Enough to make you sick.

So my childhood in that two-bedroomed apartment was a happy one. My brother and I used to sleep together when we were small, until Mami said we were too grown up to share a room. My brother didn't understand, but it was his fate to be relegated to the sofa in the living room. And that's the way it was for years until he decided to get married. And where were he and his bride going to live? In the family home, naturally. A reallocation of space ensued: one bedroom for the new couple, another for the older couple and me on the sofa. This happened after Euclid's divorce; I remember it well because first I was consoling him when he had to move back to his mother's, then he had to console me about the sofa. Euclid at least had a room of his own and even a telephone. I couldn't make a phone call without having to ask a neighbour on the second floor, and his was often out of order. It's just as well that I didn't read 'The Telephone Was Invented In Cuba' at that time because I'd have pissed myself laughing, and I knew exactly what use I'd have put the newsprint to. Well, given my living conditions, you won't have any trouble understanding what went through my mind when I heard that Ángel lived alone.

It was different with Leonardo. His refuge provoked healthy envy. Nothing more. He was a pretty organised man; apart from the wastepaper bin on the table, everything seemed to be in its allocated place. The bed was made, there was a mat outside the bathroom, ceramic ornaments on the bookshelves, a poster for the film *Memories of Underdevelopment* on the wall and, surrounding it, several children's drawings. Did your son do those? I asked. He nodded, standing up to clear the plates, and said it was better not to mention him; the boy was a little brat, and was definitely in his bad books. Leonardo's son, like almost all children his age, had taken up painting and whenever he visited, he'd grab the first piece of paper he saw to draw on. That night, Leonardo had meant to read one of his latest poems, but although he'd searched high and low the blessed verses were nowhere to be found. He was certain that the child had used the sheet of paper for one of his drawings. What's to become of me if my own son is trying to sabotage my career? he concluded as he put a saucepan of water on to boil for the lemongrass tea.

The space in the garage was incredibly flexible; that night a dozen people met there. The early arrivals bagged the folding chairs. Then Barbara turned up with her big smile and, more importantly, two bottles of Havana Club rum, which were greeted with a general round of applause. I was pleased to find her there, and she soon came to sit next to me, asked how I was, said it was such a surprise to see me, and commented on how nice it was to have a candlelit gathering. It was like being at a funeral or in the Middle Ages, she loved it, so romantic. We're very romantic people, I responded without much enthusiasm.

By the time Ángel arrived, Leonardo and his friends had already been reading their work for some time. In addition to the candles, there was a lantern, which was passed around to whoever was going to read next. If they go on like this, I thought, those writers will end up like Borges: blind, if not exactly literary geniuses. Someone was in the middle of a reading when Ángel came in, and he merely waved at the company so as not to interrupt, then slowly made his way forward until he found a space on the floor, just in front of Barbara and me.

It was a long session. With so many poems and short stories being read, the truth is that I was slightly bored. So when Ángel appeared, I switched off my listening apparatus and turned my attention to him, whose listening apparatus was obviously broken. He spent the whole time drinking rum, absorbed in his own thoughts. When the readings finally came to an end, two of the guests pulled a table from under the bed and set it up, while someone else announced that the game of dominoes was starting outside. I seized the opportunity to move closer to Ángel. How's Dayani? I asked. He replied that she was no better. He'd felt like staying home but as he knew I was expecting him had made an effort. Even so, he wanted to leave early. He'd tell me what had happened later, this wasn't the right moment. And it definitely wasn't, because as soon as the words were out of his mouth, Barbara reappeared to say hello, bottle in hand. Other people gathered round to greet Ángel and hold out their glasses to Barbara. She poured drinks with a smile. Ángel returned that smile as he accepted his rum. I decided to stick to the lemongrass tea.

A little later Leonardo came along to ask me if I played dominoes, because he didn't have a partner. I gladly accepted his invitation and took his arm, moving away from the others to tell him how much I'd enjoyed his poems. I also added that I was interested in reading his other works. Leonardo was clearly gratified and thanked me warmly. Then he went to the door to ask one of the guests to tell him when his turn came around and, picking up a candle, led me to a set of shelves. Here you are, he said, handing me a book and explaining that it was his first. He would lend me all his publications, but one by one so he didn't bore me. In exchange, I was formally obliged to give him feedback when I'd finished each book. Debts, debts and more debts were just what I needed. Perfect.

When our turn came at the dominoes table, Leonardo was surprised to discover how good a player I am. My parents and my stepfather spend their whole time playing the game, so I learned it at a very early age and, without bragging, I'm sensational. If there's one thing men can't stand when playing dominoes – which, logically, amuses me – it's a woman winning. That night, I got the double nine and they all called me *bota gordos* for dumping my high tiles, but when we won the first game, one of the men who was sitting out looked at me askance. I took no notice. He'd already tortured me with a very long short story, so it was the perfect moment to take my revenge. We won and won again. Leonardo was over the moon, the others were much less pleased, and even conspired to destroy us. The Havana Club had run out and they were drinking some filthy homebrew, but the very last of the good rum had been reserved as a prize for whoever managed to beat us.

I'm not sure how long we played, but the game was still in progress a good while after the electricity came back and some of the guests had left. I was getting sleepy. I looked at my watch and saw that it was nearly one in the morning. I had to work the next day so I announced that the game was over. The others protested, demanding revenge; Leonardo got proudly to his feet, kissed my cheek and calmly poured himself the last of the Havana Club. I looked around and found that he and I were alone.

Inside, someone was sleeping on the bed. Barbara and Ángel were sitting on the floor, talking. When they spotted me, he smiled and said: You swept the board, right? He added that he'd come outside for a moment but I was too focussed on the game to even notice him. Ángel's eyes were red and he was holding a glass. I said that it was late and I had to leave. Barbara asked where I lived. At the world's end, I replied, and Ángel stood up, saying that I was staying over at his place, it was very late and the transport was awful. He helped Barbara to her feet and she informed us that there was no problem since she too lived in El Vedado and could get a taxi for the three of us.

We didn't speak much on the return journey, Ángel dozed in the front seat and Barbara and I were in the back. The taxi left us at the corner of Ángel's building. I kissed Barbara, he said bye from the street and, almost before we'd reached the stairs, he flung an arm around my shoulder, saying that he was dead beat, had been longing to leave for ages but I'd just kept on playing, and that he'd drunk all the shit alcohol the shit poets had brought. It was true, his breath didn't so much smell as reek. Once inside, he flopped onto the bed and I struggled to undress him. He hugged me, asking me to stay with him, not to leave him alone. I held him until he went to sleep, then I got up, took off my clothes, set the alarm and returned to bed with my back to him, so as not to smell his stinking breath. In the morning, I left a note and went to work. He was still out for the count.

Ángel was sleeping off his hangover. Everybody drinks in this country: when they're sad, they drink because they're sad; when they're happy, they drink because they're happy; and when they're neither happy nor sad, they drink because they don't know what's wrong with them. If they have good rum, they drink good rum; if they don't, they make moonshine and drink that. The important thing is to drink. All the time. You get it? All the time.

Fortunately, Ángel was conscious of this and the next day he came to the Tech to apologise. We decided to take a walk. His sister's situation was really bugging him. Dayani wasn't speaking to her father and was accusing her mother of always taking his side. According to her, Ángel was the only one who came anywhere near to understanding her, but he still wouldn't let her move in with him. She was alone, she said, and that's why all she wanted was to leave the country and disappear. Ángel told me that he could make an effort and bring her to the apartment for a few days, but that might lead to more problems, because once she was through the door, it would be very hard to return to the way things were.

How would he ever get her out? No, it wasn't an option. She wasn't moving in, full stop. What worried him most of all was Dayani's obsession with leaving the country. He wanted to put the thought out of her head, and so he'd suggested that they look for a room to rent so she could spend some time away from home. Of course renting meant money, and at that time it also meant dollars, and Ángel had no idea how to get his hands on dollars. But at least Dayani had liked the idea. Their father, however, refused to get involved: his daughter was an adult and she could do whatever she wanted outside the home, but they shouldn't count on any help from him if she intended to go off and live any old how. In the meantime, Dayani had promised her brother that she'd try to find some money. He'd also do his best and, to help ease the tension at home, he'd decided to go to Cienfuegos with her for a few days. A change of scene and a bit of pampering from her grandmother would do the girl good. It's all so complex, Julia dearest, he concluded, and the word 'dearest' was music to my ears.

That evening, he also told me about an idea he'd had when we were at Leonardo's: he could rent Barbara a room in the apartment. Not that she was looking for a place, but maybe if he didn't charge too much, she might agree. Part of the money could go to Dayani and the rest would be for him. What do you think? he asked. I was still hearing the music of the word 'dearest' and, as if that weren't enough, my angel was including me in his decision-making. It was all too beautiful, so beautiful that I replied yes, it sounded like a good idea. A brilliant idea. He kissed my cheek and said that he'd ring Barbara as soon as he returned from Cienfuegos.

We didn't see each other again until he came back to the city. I missed him, missed his skin. The days without his body seemed longer than before, immensely long. It was as if they started off down a hill until it got to noon, and then the slope turned upward, because at twelve o'clock there was a sort of hole through which the day dripped and escaped. Something like that.

So I decided to take advantage of his absence to concentrate on Objective Leonardo and rang him after I'd carefully read his book. To my surprise, the author told me that he wanted to hear my impressions in person, and invited me to go to the theatre with him. There was very little to do that year. The energy crisis left us living in the shadows, so cinemas and theatres only opened their doors at weekends. It was, I imagine, like being in a country at war, but without the bombs, because the bomb had already exploded somewhere else and we were left with the penury, the lack of choice, the desolation. Going to the theatre with Leonardo seemed like a magnificent idea and I don't have to say that Euclid agreed. That Saturday, after the study group meeting, I went to my friend's house for a shower and something to eat. Before I left, he kissed my forehead and wished me luck.

When we came out of the theatre, Leonardo suggested we go to the Malecón. He freed his bicycle from the three chains that bound it, invited me to sit on the back carrier and pedalled me to the sea wall that forms the city's frontier with the rest of the world. If the Malecón wall could talk, I know there would never be enough time for it to tell all its stories because it has witnessed everything: couples getting together and breaking up, confessions, suicide attempts, readings, scandals, pleas, actual suicides, inseminations, farewells, laughter, tears... The wall has witnessed it all. And that night it witnessed Leonardo and I in conversation. We first spoke about his poetry collection, because that had been my justification for meeting him. Then we discussed his next novel, because that was my real objective. Leo was one of the most fascinating conversationalists I'd ever known. I mean it. Sometimes when he was speaking his glasses would begin to slide down his nose due to the sweat; he'd keep talking, peering over the frame instead of looking at me through the lenses, and it was only when he came to what he considered the end of a paragraph that he'd raise an index finger to push the glasses back up. An endearing habit, I thought.

That night he began to tell me about Meucci; not in terms of the novel that was going to revolutionise the genre but as a historical personage. As Euclid had rightly suspected, Leo was a bookworm who had been consulting documents for some time. It had never before crossed my mind, but literature can, in certain situations, be like science. Leonardo hoped to write a novel, but first he had to do research, collate his findings, analyse hypotheses, verify sources, demonstrate proofs. The novel was based on an intuition; that, however, and particularly in this case, was just the beginning since the story he wanted to tell was directly related to a real person. I thought it was wonderful: intuition is just a starting point. According to Poincaré, mathematical discoveries aren't spontaneously generated but presuppose a solid, well-nourished base of preliminary knowledge. Something similar was occurring with the novel Leo wanted to write: before he could create it, he had to amass and nourish a knowledge base. That night, as he spoke, I wondered whether he'd find greater pleasure in the actual writing or the research that preceded it, because his eyes – either when viewed directly or through the lenses of his glasses – expressed extraordinary enthusiasm.

In terms of Meucci, I only knew what Euclid had told me, but Leonardo had a great deal more information. We talked long and hard that night until he finally offered me a lift to Capitolio, where I could find a taxi. On the way, he said, we'll pass the Teatro Tacón or the Gran Teatro, as it's now called, and maybe we'll encounter Meucci's ghost still haunting the streets. As he pedalled, Leonardo told me stories about the theatre from its opening to the present day, and I could see the sweat drenching his shirt. Take my word for it, he was a really likeable guy, and the better I got to know him, the more comfortable I felt about my mission to become his friend. He was the sort of person you might not notice at first, but just let him open his mouth and you were all ears. He was a snake charmer. And, of course, he knew it.

6

A few days later, I went to see Euclid to report on my meeting with the author, but he was busy teaching when I arrived. His son, who was paying him a visit, opened the door to me and announced that the family had a new member. He led me to the bathroom, where I found Euclid's mother on her knees by the tub in which I saw a poor, scrawny, grey excuse for a dog, its coat soaked and its eyes wide open. The young man, who they called Chichí, had found it near a rubbish bin, but according to him, it was a poodle that had been abandoned and, just as soon as it was dry and groomed, would show its true lineage. That year the streets were full of stray dogs with frightened faces.

After the bath, Chichí carried the dog out into the sun and began to towel it down. The animal appeared to be grateful, shook itself and contorted its body to scratch all over. It was a pitiful sight, but one that also made me laugh. That poor animal is a blot on the landscape, I said, and as if by magic it raised its head and barked for the first time since its arrival. Chichí smiled at me and, turning again to the dog, putting a hand on its head, pronounced: That's what we'll call him. Blot. So I was responsible for naming the dog, and Blot really was its name; I'm not inventing that one. But as the dog is dead now, no one's going to recognise its owner. Or at least that's what I hope.

In relation to dog's owner, it was, in theory, Chichí, but as his mother was allergic to animal hair he'd decided to bring it to his father's home. He knew that Euclid would initially protest but end up adopting the animal. Which is exactly what did happen. Chichí was Euclid's youngest son, the only one remaining in the country and, although his father was sometimes annoyed with him, he inevitably came to understand his son's decisions. Children are a headache you don't want to go away, he used to say. Chichí had dropped out of university because he wanted to write and, according to him, university was a dead loss. So, while he was trying to become a writer he earned a living selling foodstuffs. He'd managed to hide this activity, which of course was illegal, from Euclid until the night two steaks were served up for dinner. Beef was a luxury and, although Euclid had devoured his like someone who's just survived a famine, it didn't sit well with him. Imagine, a retired university teacher who gave private classes to support his mother, with a son involved in illegal trade and, to top it all, whom he had to thank for the food. Chichí's grandmother claimed that he was only trying to help his father. Euclid maintained that the boy was already a man but had no sense of responsibility. Chichí, for his part, never said a word, but continued to supply food, which his father eventually came to accept without protest.

The day Chichí turned up with Blot, Euclid was unsurprised to find his son no longer in the house and the dog sleeping placidly on a cushion. Children are a headache you don't want to go away, he repeated before inviting me into his room so we could discuss our business undisturbed. He knew I had a great deal to tell him.

Settled in his bedroom, I started to recount everything Leonardo had told me about Meucci. Euclid already knew some of it but, following our research methodology, no detail was to be omitted. I therefore began at the beginning. Antonio Meucci was born in 1808 in Florence and studied design and mechanical engineering there at the Academy of Fine Arts. But given that he was interested in everything, he also expanded his knowledge of chemistry, physics, acoustics and what was then known about electricity. Euclid confirmed each datum with a nod of the head. As a young man, with all that study behind him, Meucci began working as a stage engineer at the Teatro de la Pérgola where, among other things, he built machines to assist in everyday operations. According to Leonardo, the theatre still possessed, at least until lately, one of his inventions: a sort of speaking tube connecting the stage with the upper levels, where the scenery-shifters worked. An apparatus like that might seem very basic nowadays, but you have to bear in mind that we're talking about the early nineteenth century. An inventor's genius sometimes lies in discovering the simplest use for a very basic object. Don't you agree?

Meucci lived in Florence for many years, but eventually left the city because his interests weren't limited to the world of science. It seems that his liberal, republican ideas proved problematic and that led him to accept the offer of a job in Havana. He was already married to Ester, who worked in the costume department of the Teatro de la Pérgola, and the two of them reached this island in 1835, alongside an Italian opera company. The Teatro Tacón had yet to open its doors to the public, but the couple had been offered contracts in what would become the continent's most important theatre: Ester in charge of costume and Antonio as technical director.

I stopped for breath. Euclid heaved a sigh and after a few nods, shakes of the head and various barely audible sounds, finally said: So where the hell did that guy get so much information? My friend was surprised and, I believe, also a little irritated. It was as if it pained him to discover that someone shared his obsession. But Leonardo was an author and his interest in Meucci wasn't purely scientific; he was fascinated by the personage and his biography, his childhood, his love life, the milieux he'd moved in, and so it was natural that his research would cover so many areas. While, for instance, he was telling me about the Teatro Tacón – him pedalling his bicycle, me observing the sweat on his back – I'd been gradually transported to the location he evoked, a place so beautiful, so elegant that it would have dragged words of praise from our first female author, the Condesa de Merlín. I knew the theatre in its present-day incarnation, but Leonardo's words had the yellowing tinge of old paper. Do you get me? In my mind's eye, I was able to contemplate the nineteenth-century opulence of a newly opened theatre and admire the brilliance of the crystal chandelier suspended over the stalls. Leonardo said that the chandelier, which had been imported from Paris, became an iconic symbol of the place, but sadly, some years later, had been broken during a botched restoration job. He told me about the masked balls held there during the Carnival festivities that coincided with the inauguration of the theatre in 1838, injecting his speech with such gusto that you could almost believe he'd been present to enjoy them. He didn't know what Meucci and his wife had been doing before that date, but he'd discovered that, once the Tacón was up and running, the couple had moved into a suite of rooms in the theatre itself, which served as both their living space and laboratories. It was there that Meucci set his ingenuity to the task of improving the acoustics and stage machinery.

While Leonardo was speaking, I attended performances of Italian opera, listened to Enrico Caruso, watched Sarah Bernhardt, heard the sound of Brindis de Salas's violin. I witnessed the tribute to the Cuban-born author, Gertrudis Gómez de Avellaneda and it was as if I were the person crowning her with the laurels. Leonardo spoke and I regretted never having even once attended a performance by our National Ballet, not even to see Alicia Alonso, who is part of the contemporary history of the theatre, but the author had indeed seen her dance and I could almost hear him applaud her *Giselle*. So while I travelled on the back carrier of a bicycle, dodging potholes in the darkened city of 1993, I learned of the transformations and name-changes that the theatre underwent before becoming the Gran Teatro de La Habana. It was a journey through time that took us to the actual front of the building, where Leonardo stopped pedalling; we dismounted, me with my butt shredded by the metal tubes of the carrier, him wiping the sweat from his face with his forearm. Just look at it, Julia. It's as beautiful as ever, he said. And yes, even though the dim light scarcely allowed a glimpse of the architecture, the Teatro Tacón was still very beautiful.

Euclid scratched his head when I recounted all this and gave another sigh before stating that the importance of the theatre lay in the fact that Meucci had invented the telephone there. He wasn't the least interested in the history of the place or any of the stuff Leonardo evoked in his portrait. What he cared about was that right there, in that location, Meucci had written the document that we now had to find. All that history, all those fancy words might impress me but they were nothing more than stage props, the froth on the coffee. In short, information available to anyone who wanted to find it. The details of Meucci's life were another matter, and the realisation that

Leonardo knew more than he did sparked his curiosity.

But he's always got his head in a book, I pointed out. According to Leonardo, he's been researching Meucci for years and can't even count the hours he's spent in the National Library scouring the contemporary newspapers – *Diario de La Habana*, *Diario de La Marina*, *El Noticioso*, *Lucero* – until he finally found references to Meucci. Thanks to those old newspapers, Leonardo had been able to build up a reasonable idea of Meucci's years in the Teatro Tacón and also of his departure from Havana; but those articles were insufficient, they were barely a chapter in the research, a tiny pearl indicating that it was worth continuing. Other information, as he told me, had come from different sources: articles published in Cuba or abroad... Euclid interrupted me to comment: Abroad? Yes, abroad. Leonardo had mentioned reading some articles written outside Cuba and although I'd enquired where, his response had been: Here and there.

Here and there. I agreed with Euclid that it was a pretty vague answer, but I honestly hadn't had the impression that Leonardo was trying to hide anything; it was more as if he was unwilling to stray from the main topic. That's what I said to Euclid, and he shook his head, telling me that my reasoning was incredibly naive.

From his point of view, the fact that Leonardo had access to information from outside the island was dangerous, to say the least. As you know, things are different now; we have tourism, Cubans travel overseas, many live in other countries and come back on holiday. But in 1993, that kind of coming and going was in its infancy. Words like 'abroad' and 'foreign' signified something strange, beyond our experience. What's more, a sort of spectre that haunted society, from the highest to the lowest spheres, triggered a sense of reserve or wariness in relation to anything that came from outside. And that was particularly true in those years, when the friends from overseas, the Soviet Union and almost the whole socialist bloc, had disappeared off the map, leaving us practically alone, floating in mid-ocean, and with the United States just ninety miles away. So those words were never neutral, although their meanings might vary with the age of the person who spoke them. For some of us, 'abroad' was the Devil incarnate; for others, it was salvation. For my friend Euclid the word was undoubtedly closer to the Devil than to salvation. His sons had gone abroad and he would never see them again: abroad was an unknown, foreign land, a place located in some distant, inaccessible part of the planet.

I understood all that and completely agreed that Leonardo's access to information was strange, even suspicious, but what I couldn't tolerate was Euclid saying that my reasoning was naive just because I claimed that the author didn't seem to be trying to hide anything. If his aim had been to conceal information, he could have just failed to mention where the articles came from. Right? But, in fact, he made no fuss about mentioning them. Which meant he felt comfortable talking with me and, therefore, I'd gradually learn more details, find out where the articles came from and if he knew anything about our document. My objective was to squeeze the lemon dry; I just had to do it in my own way. I swear, I can put up with a lot, but one thing I'll never allow is to have my intelligence undervalued. Never ever.

I remember that I stood up and, making it clear that I was annoyed, looked my friend straight in the eyes and told him that if he thought my reasoning was naive, maybe he should find someone else to help him, someone capable of reasoning more effectively. Euclid first gazed at me with a very serious expression, but then a smile slowly began to break across his face, a twitch in one corner of his lips that broadened to take in his whole mouth: You know something? I adore you, was what he said, his eyes fixed on mine. He then added that he hadn't meant to offend me, even if the way I behaved when I was offended was incredibly sexy; he knew he was getting old, but that didn't mean he'd stopped admiring my intelligence and my flesh. That's exactly how he put it: my flesh. And he begged my forgiveness if he'd treated me like an innocent.

I smiled back, ducking my head to avoid his eyes. There are things we only become conscious of with the passage of time. The body changes, loses its firmness, signs of ageing appear, but what puzzles me is that inside, or at least inside that increasingly less hairy thing we call a man's head, it's as if nothing's altered, as if he were still the same person. It's my belief that if there were no mirrors, the verb 'to age' wouldn't exist either. True, you might notice a decrease in stamina, but if it weren't for mirrors, that would be hard to explain and you'd go to the psychologist and say: I don't know what's wrong with me, I often feel tired. And the psychologist, who has never heard the verb either, would look you over, note that you're not physically the same as a twenty-year-old patient, and conclude that the change is undoubtedly due to relationship problems. That would be it; something wasn't as it should be in the patient's love life, hence the fatigue. There was no other explanation. A middle-aged man, moved by this reasoning, would return home happy, thinking that it wasn't really anything to worry about, that those sorts of problems have solutions, and to prove, or attempt to prove it, he'd start flirting with younger women. Funny, right? The body ages and thought is trapped inside it. The risk is that sometimes, what with being locked up for so long, thought becomes its own trap, begins to rot, and then, as a logical reaction, the process is reversed. Aged thought takes control of the body. To my way of thinking, that must be the start of death, which of course isn't necessarily linked to physical age.

Euclid had always been pretty seductive, and there was no reason why he shouldn't continue that way because both his mind and his eyes kept carnal desire alive. That day my annoyance was short-lived. As Euclid gazed at me, I felt a sort of tenderness. How can I explain it? I felt as if something were moving in waves through my chest. Do you get the idea? It was years since he'd been male eye candy for me, but it wasn't a matter of age; it was a habit, the friendship that united us; yet for him, in addition to being his friend, I was still a body worth looking at.

I raised my eyes, saw Euclid standing there gazing at me and realised that he desired me, but also that, in some way, he was alone and I was important to him. Many of his illusions had gone down the drain, he had no partner, was retired, living with his mother and slowly but inexorably sliding towards a state of inertia in which dreams have no place. But Euclid wasn't going to take it lying down. My Euclid was clinging tightly to the walls so the slippage would be as slow as possible. And for that task he had his science books and one great dream: finding Meucci's document. Another thing I understood that day was that he needed me; he was depending on me to get to Leonardo, I was the linchpin connecting him to the writer, and he wasn't going to learn everything Leonardo knew without my help.

I gave a heavy sigh and finally said that if Leonardo knew anything about the document, he'd tell me in his own time, that there was no need to worry, I knew what I was doing. Euclid smiled without adding another word and then, faced with his silence, and for absolutely no other reason, I placed my lips on his and kissed him. It was a short kiss, more of a peck, but still a kiss. When I pulled away, he was still silent and it was me who grinned and said: You know I adore you too, don't you?

7

I didn't meet my Ángel again until a few days after his return from Cienfuegos because my work schedule was crazy. He told me over the phone that he was longing to see me and proposed that we spend Friday night at his place because he wanted to take me to a marvellous, 'mystical' plance on Saturday. Naturally, I accepted the invitation. Ángel had a gift for inventing alternative realities: slap-up dinners in the middle of the crisis; evenings spent lying on the floor, things that helped me escape from everyday reality.

On the Saturday, we left the house very early, and no matter how hard I insisted he refused to tell me where we were going. After crossing half the city in packed buses, cursing the public transport and the long waits, we finally reached the Botanical Gardens and walked to the Japanese Gardens. They're miraculous, out of this world, mystical, exactly as he'd said. We arrived around noon, just in time for lunch in the eco restaurant. That was another surprise for me because when Ángel told me it served vegetarian food, I had my doubts. I've always been a second-generation veggie, by which I mean that the cow eats the grass and I eat the cow, but at that time cows were only to be found in the same place as dinosaurs: books. Considering that my daily fare consisted of rice with split peas or beans, cabbage and soya, the restaurant's speciality didn't at first appeal. But there was my guardian angel ready to explain that all those wonderfully colourful vegetarian dishes weren't just grass but natural, balanced foodstuffs, combinations of flavours, with no preservatives and brimming with healthful qualities.

After lunch we walked in the gardens. According to Ángel, they gave you the sense of having fallen into a story or a place that only existed in someone else's imagination, so that we were part of their dream, like the characters moving through the pages of a novel. I found that idea appealing. And strolling along the path bordering the lake, looking at the plants, hearing the sound of the water and breathing in the tranquillity really did give me the impression of being somewhere else, as if the city and its crisis didn't exist or were far, far away; in a foreign country, for example. Not that I had any clue what a foreign country was like!

We finished our stroll, sitting together near a clump of pine trees, and he told me about his trip to Cienfuegos. It had gone well, had been the ideal occasion for talking with his sister. But despite what I might imagine, my angel had felt troubled rather than serene. Dayani was still in low spirits, and the torrent of her sadness washed over everything within its reach, including Ángel. His only consolation was that she was still thinking of looking for a place of her own. The trouble was that he still wasn't sure what to do for the best. It occurred to me to say that his sister should visit a psychologist. There's no getting away from it, I'm a practical person: if you have a problem, you try to find a solution; if you can't, then you seek help. That's what psychologists are for, right? It seemed to me that Dayani had lost her bearings, and maybe a specialist could set her back on the right track. Ángel burst out laughing: if he wanted his sister to see a psychologist, he'd have to drag her there in chains, and even then she'd be capable of biting her own tongue off to avoid speaking. The only person who'd ever been able to get a word out of her was Margarita, who, by coincidence, had studied psychology.

To tell the truth, I hadn't counted on an appearance of Margarita's ghost in the Japanese Gardens, so I rested my head in my hands and said: 'A princess as fair, as exquisite as you, Margarita' in a tone that must have been ironic because he looked ashamed and muttered that he didn't want to discuss her with me. Then he moved his face close to mine and, with an expression I'd never before seen in his eyes, asked me to forgive him, saying he was all mixed up, that coming to the gardens with me was doing him good, I gave him a sense of calm, and he felt he could talk about anything with me, I was the only person who knew about his private life. I gazed at him for a few seconds and then put my arms around him. Don't worry, I murmured softly, and we stayed like that for quite a long time without speaking, listening to the water and the birdsong.

At some point we began to talk again. As I said, the Japanese Gardens are mystical, a physical invitation to ecstasy and revelations. And that afternoon, I had a great revelation; not the divine sort: I learned something extremely important. After a few jokes and kisses, I swore that it didn't bother me to hear him talking about Margarita, in fact, I was pleased that Ángel would share his inner life with me. He said he felt a little idiotic, but that it did him good to talk normally about his ex, it helped to close the cycle. He lay down next to me, resting one elbow on the grass with his chin in his hand. Do you know what fascinated me about Margarita?

he asked. Naturally, I didn't. Then, without raising his head, but opening his eyes wide in an expression somewhere between comical and perturbed, he told me that Margarita knew exactly where she came from, she carried her whole personal history around with her, but it wasn't just a matter of memories; it was something tangible. Tangible, he repeated.

Due to a tradition handed down from generation to generation, Margarita was the custodian of her family history. It had all started with the birth of a child called Margarita, the daughter of two Spaniards who had arrived in Cuba in the nineteenth century. Ángel told me that it was the birth of the girl that underlay the couple's decision to settle here, and so that initial Margarita had marked the beginning of something. She was the first Cuban in the family, and her parents wanted to make something extraordinary of the event, something that could be passed on to their descendants. So they created a tradition. Traditions are formed by repetition, sometimes voluntarily, sometimes from obligation, but at the end of the day, repetitions. Well, when that original Margarita married, her mother gave her what became a legacy: the first family photo, a piece of jewellery and some of her parents' mementos. To ensure the tradition was perpetuated, the newlywed Margarita had to pass on her name to her eldest daughter. Incredible as it may sound, Ángel continued, the custom had become so deeply rooted in the family that every Margarita had been determined to keep it alive by having a daughter. So from generation to generation, on her wedding day, each Margarita received the legacy, which expanded over the years as the family tree grew, with the addition of more photos, the stamps of each period and significant souvenirs of the respective parents' lives. And that was why, when she married Ángel, Margarita had been given the family history, the names and faces of her ancestors from her first namesake born in Cuba, the map of her whole family.

That seemed to me a very beautiful story: many of us know little more than the names of our grandparents and great-grandparents. After that, the trail generally fades out, our past might only survive a few generations before forgetting sets in, oblivion, ignorance of who came before, not knowing that some person you don't like shares your blood, is part of your extended family. Ángel put such passion into his narrative that, although I hate to admit it, I somehow envied Margarita. There was no way a woman who carried her family history with her could be just anybody, he stated: she knew exactly where she was, possessed her entire past without any chance of alteration. He was obsessed by that notion. Do you get me? Ángel had a great weakness for what he called 'women with history'. At least that was true back then. Sometimes I thought he was crazy. I once turned up at his place and found an enormous heap of videos on the floor. When I offered to help him to put them in order, he pounced on the cassettes and wouldn't even let me touch them. Afterwards he told me the story of his 'unknown favourite', saying that he was the custodian of a stranger's past.

Before going to Brazil, Ángel had visited Margarita's mother to pick up the letters the family wanted to send her. As you can tell, all his stories have to do with Margarita. What's more, given that he intended to win back her love, he'd managed to record practically the whole repertoire of Benny Moré, a musician she adored. Letters, cassettes, and all the rest of her things went into a FAPLA military knapsack, the kind that was all the rage after the war in Angola. Ángel added a padlock and sent it as checked baggage. What happened was that when he got to his hotel in São

Paulo and tried to open the knapsack, he discovered that he'd claimed the wrong one at the airport. When he succeeded in breaking the lock, he found women's clothing, various items of craftwork and a package containing videocassettes. The worst of it was that there was nothing to help identify the owner of those precious belongings. And however often he apologised, Margarita had never believed the story of the mistaken knapsack, much less that he'd managed to tape Benny Moré's repertoire. In fact, she accused him of not even being capable of bringing her family's letters. She was furious. Ángel most definitely had no luck when it came to Margarita. He got rid of the clothes and the craftwork but decided to hold on to the videos. They showed a little girl taking her first steps, attending a Young Pioneers party, celebrating her birthday and going on family holidays. According to him, there had to be some hidden meaning to the mix-up, and he was certain that if he ever found the girl in the videos, who of course would be a woman by then, something was going to change in his life. He'd been obsessed by that idea for a long time. By then, he rarely watched the videos as he knew every moment of them, but he enjoyed playing them when he was feeling lonely or when something turned out well. It wasn't the images themselves that fascinated him but the fact that they contained the history of a woman, and that she travelled, carrying her life story with her, not in her memory but in something tangible. Tangible.

Did you ever hear anything so crazy? That afternoon, I know I felt jealous of both Margarita and the woman in the videos, because something marked them out as different. I told him so, of course, and clearly recall the glint in his eyes as he sat up to move closer to me. Then he bit his lip – a habit of his – before saying that I had my history written on my skin. He glanced down at my belly and whispered: Go on, let me see it...

Years ago, I had my appendix removed. Nowadays those operations scarcely leave a mark, but that wasn't the case way back then and so I have a scar, and Ángel loved it. Sometimes, when I was lying on my back, he'd slowly stroke its length. I'd feel the touch of his finger and then his tongue. He really used to adore passing his tongue over my scar. He said it was an important mark, not like having an ear pierced, or getting a tattoo, or wearing necklaces or rings. It was quite different from all that. A window to my interior. Something all too personal. A scar comes into being without our having the time or prerogative to make the decision. He'd slide his tongue along it, murmuring such phrases. He asked me if I realised I'd once been naked before a lot of people. I was unconscious. The doctors opened up my body, surely very slowly, and viewed my insides as I would never be able to, put their hands inside, cut, extracted and sewed up. When I came round, my body was apparently the same, except for the presence of a scar that would be with me for the rest of my life. Ángel said that it was like waking from the sort of dream that seems very real and then experiencing the disorientation of not being sure whether or not it was; but I only had to lower my hand to my abdomen, and there was the scar to remind me that it wasn't a dream. My body had its history written on it. When he asked me to show him my scar in the Japanese Gardens, I knew that I was someone special for Ángel, a woman who carried her past with her. A tangible past. Get it? I was like Margarita and the girl in the videos: I was special.

In fact, I believe it was then that I developed the habit of touching my scar when I'm feeling low. If

71

something goes wrong, if it's one of those days when I look in the mirror and nothing's the way I want it, I feel fat, greying, and the wrinkles are starting to show on my face; if I discover that I don't have the answer, that there are things I don't know, that my neurons are losing their edge and my feet aren't set firmly on the ground; when all that happens, I only have to touch my scar to feel that everything's going back to its proper place, that the equations are coming out positive and two and two make four. Or at least until there's proof to the contrary.

All that was what you might call a personal discovery, but the really great revelation of that afternoon was still to come. After Ángel had kissed my scar and removed his head from under my blouse, he lay back and continued talking. He told me I should feel lucky because, come what may, my body would always have its scar, and so it was unlikely that I would ever lose my history.

The case of his unknown favourite was completely different, since a random Ángel had, by virtue of a muddle, become the custodian of her past, a past that didn't belong to him, and so he was awaiting the day when, perhaps again by virtue of a muddle, he could return it to its true owner. Can you imagine just how miserable that loss must make her? he asked, before adding that her sadness must be as great as Margarita's, because she'd lost her past too. That's right; Ángel told me that Margarita no longer had the family legacy. He'd learned this the last time he'd seen her, during that same trip to São Paulo, when he'd hoped for a reconciliation but found her living happily with her Brazilian boyfriend. After an extended encounter, during which he'd attempted to convince her of his love and had ended up convinced of her lack of it, they eventually regained enough calm to talk of the future, the past, and then Margarita had suddenly burst into tears, saying she didn't have the legacy and so was guilty of breaking the family tradition. Ángel used her tears as an excuse to embrace her, but although there was pleasure in that physical contact, he felt great sorrow. Remember my plan to exorcise her ghost from my life? he asked. The point was that Ángel had dreamed of being able to recover some part of the legacy, package it up with a one-word goodbye note and send it to Brazil so they could both find the peace they needed.

Ángel really was an angel. He said that I was definitely lucky because I carried my history on my body, and not just my own, since any personal history is also the history of a time now past. For example, the videos belonging to that unknown woman, who was a little younger than us, contained all those years, that black-and-white childhood, the objects, the way people moved, their habits. And in Margarita's case, it mushroomed: there were so many generations involved. I could have no idea, he insisted, how proud she was to be the custodian of that legacy. To give me an idea, it contained the first family photo taken in one of the city's first photographic studios, the same studio where the child José Martí had later had the portrait we all know so well taken. It also contained a document that, according to family tradition, had been written by the Italian who supposedly invented the telephone.

When I heard the words 'the Italian who supposedly invented the telephone', I felt like I'd been kicked in the guts. Are you talking about Meucci? I asked. And he said, yes, that was the name. The family legend was that the first Margarita had worked with him in the theatre and they'd somehow acquired this document belonging to him. Ángel wasn't certain whether or not the guy had invented anything, but the important thing was that it had been written in that era; so the paper, ink and handwriting belonged to another time.

I swear I was dumbfounded. Ángel was referring to Meucci's document. He'd seen it but had no idea of just what it was. That was why I stopped listening. I know he continued speaking because I could see his lips moving, but all I could hear was the phrase 'the Italian who supposedly invented the telephone'. Then my mind, my neurons – like I said, I'm a mathematician and mathematical brains are in constant ferment – sprang into action, making connections. I recalled Euclid's words, the story of the marvellous woman who had owned the document, and then came the image of the day Euclid and I ran into Ángel in the street, and Euclid's surprise (it was only then that I realised it was surprise) at seeing Ángel, his haste in explaining that Ángel was a friend of his son's, the change in his behaviour, the fact that he knew Ángel lived alone. Somewhere between Euclid, Ángel and the Meucci document was a woman called Margarita. I could see it all so clearly. Euclid, my great friend, Euclid, a man who loved women so much, had an affair with Ángel's wife. And that made her the 'common denominator'. When he'd smiled as he said that there was a common denominator between him and Ángel, I'd thought he was referring to me, but no: it was Margarita. So that bitch Margarita was the owner of Meucci's document. You think that's incredible? Well, imagine how I felt. Of the two million inhabitants of this city, I knew two who had seen the document. Unbelievable. It was clear that Euclid was aware of who Ángel was, but not so certain if Ángel knew exactly who Euclid was, and I thought it might be better not to ask him, at least not at that moment.

There's no doubt about it: the Japanese know how to design gardens. They are places of meditation, but I was incapable of sitting still. I wanted to write everything down so that I could go back and analyse it with a cool head. When Ángel nudged me and asked if I was listening, I kissed him and suggested we continue walking. I needed to move.

8

I believe that euphoria is exactly the right word to describe how I felt after the revelation in the Japanese Gardens. I was like Archimedes, longing to shout 'eureka', even though I hadn't actually discovered anything yet, because knowing that my friend had had an affair with Ángel's wife didn't actually add much to our knowledge; it was just another datum.

Among the things that the mathematician Poincaré said, I love: 'It is by logic that we prove, but by intuition that we discover.' I'd simply intuited something, and then I had to apply logic. I didn't spend that Sunday with Ángel. After our marvellous afternoon in the Botanical Gardens, I slept over in his apartment and returned to Alamar in the morning. Sundays tend to stretch out slowly, as if the day was bored with itself. Added to that, everyone who lived in the apartment was present. That Sunday was definitely a classic: my brother was making a fishing net in his room; my stepfather was hammering away on the small front balcony, repairing something; Mum was cooking lunch, coming out into the living room every so often to watch television; my sister-in-law was picking over the rice in front of the TV, accompanied by a friend who lived next door and who, in turn, was painting her toenails; the pressure cooker was whistling and in the rear, glass-enclosed balcony our ten chicks were pecking grain: Mum was determined to keep them, despite my stepfather's protests about turning our home into a henhouse. What the heck, our home was always like a henhouse. So whenever I wanted to work, I had to shut myself up in Mum's bedroom. That day, I put on Roberto Carlos, one of my favourite singers, got a pencil and paper and began to analyse the elements at my disposal.

That Euclid had never mentioned his relationship with Ángel's wife was, on the one hand, strange, but on the other logical. Let's suppose the following: Ángel takes his wife to the house of a friend; a house where Euclid also lives, a likeable father and great conversationalist who, between jokes, steals glances at the young woman. I know his behaviour well. Margarita is caught in his web and, little by little, begins to steal her own glances, which neither her husband nor Euclid's wife notice. One day, when the guys are doing something else, Euclid and Margarita arrange to meet, and that's the beginning of an affair Ángel will never know about.

Hypothesis one: when Euclid discovers that Ángel is the man I'm talking about, he feels embarrassed and even slightly ashamed. He opts not to tell me about Margarita and so avoid making Ángel look like a cuckold and simultaneously bringing shit down on his own head. And anyway, I knew nothing about the document at the time. There's a clear logic in that.

Hypothesis two: Euclid tells me about the document and says that the woman has given it – or sold it – to someone else. Ángel backs up this version when he says that Margarita no longer has the document, but she's left the country with no intention of returning, so she obviously must have sold it for the money, omitting to tell her husband, naturally. Why didn't she sell it to Euclid? Because Euclid's means were limited, of course. By this time, I'm aware of the existence of the document, Euclid knows about my relationship with Ángel but even so decides not to inform me that the owner of the document was Ángel's wife. Why? Because Ángel has nothing to add to our research; he'd been tricked and Euclid knows it.

Hypothesis three: Euclid and I want the document, but Ángel, still unaware of its scientific importance, also wants to get it back in order to give it to Margarita and so close the cycle. That might be a problem, although I don't think Ángel is really looking very hard for it; his thing is a romantic illusion and Euclid doesn't consider him an interesting element, preferring to explore other options: for example, Leonardo.

Hypothesis four: according to Ángel, Leonardo and Margarita were old friends. Leonardo is writing a novel about Meucci that will create waves because it is based on demonstrable historical events.

You're thinking what I'm thinking, aren't you? Leonardo might well have learned about the document through his friend Margarita, and may even be the one who bought it. Euclid doesn't know him personally, but I unwittingly confirmed that the author was a friend of Ángel's ex; this makes his initial suspicion more logical.

Conclusions: everything points to Leonardo. I therefore decided that if Euclid was unwilling to talk about Margarita, I wouldn't mention her either; maybe at a later date, but not for the moment because there was little point and I didn't want my friend to feel obliged to explain something I wasn't particularly interested in anyway. If Margarita had been two-timing Ángel, that was his problem and I wasn't going to be the one to dig up the past. Best to turn a blind eye, let sleeping dogs lie. In the meanwhile, given that I now knew who had the document in their possession, I'd be able to check tactfully if Ángel could add any further data and continue squeezing the Leonardo-lemon.

That same week, I turned up unannounced at the author's office. I told him that, as before, I was running an errand in the nearby ministry and thought I'd drop by to say hello. He didn't seem surprised by my visit, said he was delighted to see me and that I always arrived at the perfect moment. I asked if he'd won the Nobel Prize again, but he shook his head and told me it was something else and that if I wanted to hear about it, I could accompany him later to the house of another writer, where there was going to be a short series of readings. Barbara would be there as she was gathering information for her project on Cuban literature. Although I refrained from saying it, I was much less interested in sitting through another of those interminable readings than in talking to him, but luckily he added that he had something to do before the gathering. That would give me a little time alone with him. So, will you come along? he asked. And of course I replied in the affirmative. I'd find a way of escaping from the writers.

That was the evening Leonardo told me about his trip to Luanda. I remember it well. And the reason I remember it is that, after kilometres travelling in the hot sun – him pedalling, me on the back carrier – we arrived at our first port of call, which was the home of an acquaintance of his, an Argentinean woman who wrote for a theatre magazine back home, and to whom Leo, the bookworm, was bringing an article about Havana theatres taken from a 1933 yearbook that a close friend had borrowed from the National Library. Naturally, he didn't plan to offer the article to his acquaintance for free; he'd sell it for a modest sum in dollars. A man has to make a living one way or another. Right? Once that deal was done, we left her apartment and went to sit on the university steps, where Leo had arranged to meet Barbara. It was there he explained that the Argentinean woman's husband was a Cuban soldier he'd met in Angola. Leonardo had been a war correspondent. He didn't want to talk about it because the experience had been so awful, but even in the worst moments it was possible to see a glimmer of light. Then he started to describe the city, which he called Lovely-Luanda. Like I said, I adored listening to him, I thought he was a born novelist. Sometimes, when he was pedalling his Chinese bicycle and telling me some story, I'd find myself grinning behind him because it seemed so strange – sort of... the opposite of what you expect – that such a cultured, well-travelled person, a scholar with heaps of experiences, a man for whom the world was his oyster, should have no other mode of transport than a bicycle. But that's the way it is here. One day I shared this thought with him. And guess what he said: A bicycle is good for your leg muscles, everything else I keep inside myself. Leonardo had a great deal of positivity.

That afternoon, he spoke at length about his Lovely-Luanda and, as usual, I was enthralled by his narrative, until, when he ran out of stories and we started talking about travel in general, I seized the moment to ask if he'd ever visited Italy in his globetrotting days. That was the best way I could think of to lead up to Meucci, but unfortunately Leonardo said he hadn't. He knew a great deal about the country but had never been there. And talking of Italy: look who's here... He stood up just as I raised my eyes and saw Barbara coming up the steps, smiling as always, and, also as always, wearing a short, tight-fitting top that scarcely left her boobs room to breathe.

I liked Barbara. She was invariably pleased with the

world, as if life was marvellous and Havana smiled upon her at the break of each new day. But she's a foreigner, of course. She lived in a city ten centimetres removed from the one we inhabited because, although we occupied the same space, her Havana was different from ours. We were different species in the same zoo. Do you get me? She was an exotic species, the sort that visitors stop in front of; we were the everyday sort that no one bothers to look at, the sort that are given the skins of the bananas the exotic species eat. None of that was Barbara's fault, of course; she was likeable and did what she could for us. After her affectionate kisses, Leonardo said that he had some dollars from the sale of the article and wanted her help to buy one or two things in the store. Remember that it was still illegal to have dollars, so Cubans had no access to certain shops. Barbara gladly agreed, said she couldn't do enough for him, his son and everyone else on this marvellous island.

That night, the gathering took place in the home of another writer, a friend of Leonardo's. Now I come to think of it, it's funny that I decided to call him after Da Vinci, forgetting that there's a brilliant Cuban author whose name is Leonardo Padura, but that's beside the point. OK? I don't know Padura. Anyway, our host prepared tea from the lemongrass Leo had brought and we all sat out on the apartment's long balcony. When the readings began I, as always, used the time for introspection. After attending a huge number of such events over the years, I've come to understand that writers require undivided attention; they need you to be listening to them and praising them the whole time. They're just overgrown kids. No doubt we all require a certain amount of approval from others, but with authors the figure is multiplied, in some cases disproportionately. I've always noticed that writers and artists are seen as unique beings with exceptional lives, as if they spent their whole time entertaining great people and talking in capital letters about profound, elevated topics. That's OK by me, but I'm surprised that scientists aren't equally valued. Very few people think about scientists; yet behind everything we touch, however ordinary it might be, there are hundreds of brains who worked on its creation, because science is a collective endeavour: someone discovers something, then someone else improves it and another person improves the improvement, and so on. To give an example: now that smartphones are all the rage, does anyone know who Antonio Meucci was? Of course not. And, logically, I don't think that people should know the entire history of every inventor, but they could at least be generally recognised in the same way as artists and writers. Don't you agree?

Leonardo and his friends were a different kettle of fish, of course; they had what you could call author-essence but lacked everything else. What's more, in those days none of them were publishing because there was no paper, so they were completely convinced of the profundity of their texts and crying out for an audience, particularly if the participants included one of those exotic creatures who, to top it all, wanted to find authors for her research into Cuban literature.

I've no idea if Barbara had ever before felt so important, but that night she was queen of the ball. After the reading of each text, her every word was listened to with rapt attention, her every laugh provoked more laughter, when she crossed her legs every eye was on them, her questions received immediate responses and her thirst had the owner of the apartment going to his downstairs neighbours to buy homemade orange wine so Barbara could try local products. That was just after the readings had finished, and I was thinking of leaving, unaware that Leonardo had been waiting to announce his news. When our host returned, he poured everyone some wine, sat down and asked Leo to forget the mystery and tell us whatever it was he had to say. Leo took a piece of paper from his backpack, got to his feet, cleared his throat and began to read. '*Diario de La Habana*, December 16th 1844...'. It was a photocopy of an article about the gala event held in the Gran Teatro Tacón in honour of Meucci, whom the reporter praised and called an 'intelligent scene-shifter'. The article ended by saying something about how Havana theatregoers knew how to appreciate and honour worthy productions. When Leo had finished speaking, someone asked where he'd found the article and he proudly replied that it had cost him a bar of soap and a peck on the cheek for his friend who worked in the National Library. That was when the night started to get interesting.

According to Leo, his friend was an absolute gem because she'd even managed to lay her hands on one or two 'little books', although naturally she couldn't always help him. He'd consulted a great many newspapers in the library and had a list of all the photocopies he needed; now she just had to carry out the task and then wait for her well-earned gift. I used the pause to comment that it was brilliant that his novel would include the article and, as an apparent afterthought, asked if he'd come across any other documents about Meucci. He replied that he only had articles, but they were important because they gradually revealed the traces of Meucci in our city, and with that he stifled my attempt to find out more. Then, once he'd been assured of the others' interest in the inventor, he took centre stage.

I owe to Leonardo almost everything I know about Antonio Meucci's life and the fascination I felt for him: the truth is that Meucci was incredible. I imagine him as a hyperactive man, incapable of sitting still, curious and observant. If he lived in present-day Cuba, there's no doubt that he'd make a magnificent husband, the sort who, like my stepfather, fixes everything in the home that breaks down, with the difference that Antonio also had the urge to create new things; he was a born inventor. When he worked in the Teatro Tacón, for example, in addition to his normal duties as chief engineer, he used his inventiveness to improve the acoustics and created a water mirror in the cellar by diverting a subterranean river that passed nearby. This made his job more interesting, but it wouldn't have been enough for Antonio; he was a man who took note of absolutely everything around him. So, he developed a chemical process for mummifying corpses; it doesn't seem to have been completely successful, but did partly solve the problem of preserving dead bodies that had to be transported to Europe. A few years later, he made forays into the field of galvanism, which involved plating metal objects with gold or silver, a technique that was employed on weaponry to prevent rusting. Meucci succeeded in closing a four-year verbal contract with the governor of the island and started working on the army's swords and artillery; in order to do this, he set up a galvanising workshop, which was one of the first in the continent. Around the same time, the Teatro Tacón held the gala event mentioned in the article Leonardo read to us that night.

Then came the great hurricane of 1846, which left a wake of deaths, injuries and ruined buildings throughout Cuba. Many theatres were severely damaged, among them the Tacón, although it remained in a better state than the others. Once the initial repairs were underway, Meucci was put in charge of the restoration, and took advantage of that appointment to create a ventilation system in the theatre, and there's no doubt that, given our climate, his invention was appreciated. When the Teatro Tacón reopened, the technical and decorative changes had significantly improved the venue.

After that followed a period when things apparently didn't go so well and Pancho Marty, the owner of the theatre, decided to close it down again. Meucci had little work, his contract for the galvanisation of weapons had ended and he had to put his mind to new projects. That was when he started to experiment with electrotherapy. In those days, following theories of animal magnetism, it was fashionable to cure ailments by the administration of electric shocks. Antonio was no stranger to these studies and in his workshop in the theatre, he began to conduct experiments, first using other members of the staff and then actual patients as guinea pigs.

Then came the historic day in 1849 when, during one of those experiments, Antonio Meucci discovered that the human voice could be transmitted via an electrical signal. It seems that he was with a patient in the middle of administering the therapy; there were copper wires, batteries and electrodes, Meucci and the patient were in different rooms, the patient had a copper instrument in his mouth, Antonio was holding a similar instrument, and then, after the electrical discharge, he heard the patient cry out. But the cry hadn't come through the windows: it was a voice that had travelled through the wiring. Eureka! That was just the beginning.

Science is fascinating: while you're doing one thing, you discover something else. It's like the world opens up for you in a flash and you can see something that exists but is transparent. Like a spark that has to be produced before the eyes of someone capable of viewing it in order to be seen. I'll give you a second: click! If you can't see me, years and years might pass until someone manages to identify me. But Meucci did see it, and then he knew that the human voice could be transmitted electrically, and after that first flash of intuition he applied logical thought and all his previous knowledge of the subject in constructing his 'talking telegraph'.

The designs for those early experiments were recorded in the document Euclid and Ángel had seen, the document that Leonardo might be aware of, the document that had belonged to Margarita's ancestors. One of those ancestors may even have been present during the experiments that followed the first transmitted call and, who knows, could have placed the copper instrument in his or her mouth and shouted his or her name, aware that it marked the dawn of a new historical era, even if far too many years went by before that fact was recognised.

9

After the meeting with the writers, I attempted to call Euclid several times to tell him what I'd learned about Meucci and to inform him of my conviction that Leonardo was a lead worth following up, but the tone on the telephone at the Tech maintained the same constant, unvarying, infinitely prolonged note, no matter how often I dialled numbers. Don't laugh: it's true. The telephone was invented here in Havana, but in 1993 most were out of order half the time.

So I decided to go straight to his apartment. Although I'd earlier come to the conclusion that it would be best not to mention Margarita, the knowledge that Leonardo had photocopies of a number of articles opened up new possibilities because, even if the author denied having any other document, the following conclusions could be drawn:

First: what he said was untrue. That is, Leonardo had the document but, given its importance, was unwilling to admit that fact.

Second: what he said was true. That is, he wasn't in possession of the document, although this didn't exclude the possibility that he was aware of its existence.

What was absolutely clear to me was that the relationship between Leonardo and Margarita was extremely important, and when added to his interest in Meucci, he became a central, highly suspicious element. How could I ever explain these conclusions to Euclid without mentioning Margarita? The answer was, I couldn't. Do you see? My friend was a mathematician, accustomed to theorems and demonstrations, and I'd just realised that if he was interested in Leonardo, it was because he was already aware that Leonardo knew Margarita. She was the key variable I'd lacked at the beginning. If I turned up at his place stating that something or other was true just because I said so, Euclid wouldn't believe me, because the Holy Ghost doesn't exist in science. I therefore concluded that it would be better to have it out. There was no need to make a big deal of his affair with Margarita, it was just a matter of making it clear that she'd owned the document, and that was all that counted in relation to our objective.

But as it happened, when I arrived only his mother and Chichí were home. The frequent power cuts were destroying electrical equipment everywhere and his mum's fridge was on its last legs, so Euclid had had to go out in search of a necessary spare part. I waited for quite a long time. His mum talked non-stop about Blot who, having recovered from his experience in the streets, was now a beautiful white poodle and had been awarded the privilege of sleeping on the bed at her feet. Chichí, for his part, was plain comical; he decided to read his short stories to his grandmother, and she looked at me in astonishment, saying he was a genius, even if she didn't understand a word he'd written. Euclid didn't much like his son's stories, and to tell the truth, neither did I. Chichí was writing about the situation in the country, the growth in prostitution, bicycle theft, the boat people, the decaying society. Things we saw every day and that, quite honestly, I'd no desire to hear about, much less in a short story that would never be published. He was a bit like Leonardo's friends, just younger, more direct and much more practical: while dreaming of being a writer, he made a living selling contraband goods. That afternoon, I started listening to one story but the electricity cut out almost immediately and as Euclid was showing no sign of returning, I decided to go home.

I'm not sure how many days I was incommunicado due to the damned telephone in the Tech and then as soon as it started working again the director decided to limit its use. She said the phone was in her office, that it was essential for her work and, therefore, teachers were only allowed one short personal call apiece, two in cases of an emergency, and zero international. Stupid witch. I was forced to choose between phoning Euclid or Ángel and, naturally, I chose the latter because I wanted to see my angel. I could talk to Euclid during our regular Saturday meeting.

I think I arranged to see Ángel on the Thursday of that week. Yes, that's right, because something else happened on the Friday. So, it was Thursday when I went to his apartment and found him a little out of sorts because he had nothing to offer me for dinner and no money for food. The only good thing he had left was, he said, a little rum, but I wasn't interested in rum, and so announced that I'd take over the cooking that night. It was a simple menu of rice and cabbage fried with onions; healthy and nutritious, like the meal we'd had in the Japanese Gardens. You could say we were all getting thinner by the day, but 'more slender' sounds better.

That was the first time I cooked at home for Ángel and I have to say that, as experiences go, I liked it. I felt we were a real couple, me in the kitchen and him sitting in a chair with his feet on the table and a glass of rum in his hand. A normal couple talking about normal stuff: the dumb things my boss did, the crisis, Dayani. At some point I remembered Ángel's idea about renting a room to Barbara and asked him what had happened. He replied that he'd called to suggest it, but she hadn't wanted to leave her current place. She must be paying practically nothing, he said, because he'd offered a really low rent, for which she'd thanked him without accepting. I then commented that I'd seen her.

The fact is that I wanted to talk about Margarita, or rather the family legacy that included the document, and so I brought up the subject of Barbara in order to then mention Leonardo and get onto the subject of Meucci. It's funny, but every time Ángel talked about his ex, I felt slightly uncomfortable; yet I was the one who wanted to broach the subject that day. I wanted him to continue the story of the lost legacy in case any piece of information, however trivial, might turn out to be useful. There was nothing wrong in that, it was just a matter of accumulating data, squeezing lemons dry. Do you see?

While we were setting the table, I started talking about the readings at the home of Leonardo's friend. Ángel commented, a touch caustically, on my growing friendship with Leonardo and twisted his mouth in that way that made me stop the world, swallow and count to ten so as not to jump on him and tear off his clothes. Instead, I smiled, asked if he was jealous and he replied no. How was he going to be jealous of someone like Leonardo? We sat down to eat, poured a glass of water each and continued our conversation. According to Ángel, Leonardo wasn't worth anyone's jealousy; he was an inoffensive sort of guy, if a bit weird for his tastes at times. Then he launched into a wild, truly delirious monologue. He said Leonardo wasn't completely human, that he belonged to the race of the new centaurs. Haven't you noticed that instead of legs he has a pair of wheels? I burst out laughing. Ángel went on, claiming that Cuba had reached a high level of technological development and was experimenting with new creations, future beings. Among them, the latest were the new centaurs, who lived on diced soya and sugar water, perfect creatures that didn't need petrol for transportation and utilised the minimum of battery recharge to stop them falling to their knees. As far as Ángel was concerned, Leonardo was one of those creatures that wheeled rather than walked, pedalling smoothly along. Even when he was sitting on a sofa, you could see he wasn't comfortable because he didn't know what to do with his legs. They were like body parts that had evolved from a symbiotic fusion with the bicycle and now can't even remember their former function. There's no doubt about it, he said, the future Cuban will be legless; he'll have a tiny stomach and two wheels. What do you think? he asked before taking a mouthful of cabbage and chewing it savagely.

The ideas Ángel came up with! I pointed out that since *we* didn't have wheels, we were unfortunately on the road to extinction. He laughed aloud, saying that I shouldn't worry because Cuba was a country of mutants with a talent for survival: if we didn't develop wheels, we'd convert ourselves into something else to prevent our extinction. The weird thing is that he was right. After Year Zero, it's my belief that we did all become something else. Although we have difficulty admitting it, we've changed. There's a before and after. As I said, it's like war; and now the bombs are no longer falling, we're in a sort of post-war period that has unleashed each person's most basic instincts, the need to survive. And here we are, for better or worse, like cockroaches that, to avoid dying out, develop a resistance to poison, and are even able to devour it with relish.

Ángel continued talking about Leonardo in the same contemptuous tone, saying that he hadn't read anything he'd written and had no intention of doing so, that it wasn't for him to say who I should and shouldn't hang around with, but he'd always been suspicious of Leonardo's sudden friendliness to me, that invitation to the gathering in his home and to the readings. Julia, my dearest Julia, he said, I believe that what the guy really wants is to get close to me. I didn't understand what he meant and it must have shown on my face. Ángel smiled and stabbed his fork into the dish a few times without spearing any cabbage. Then he stated that Cuba was a small island, and Leonardo was aware that he didn't like him much but, for reasons of his own, he did all he could to get close to him. Ángel asked if I remembered the story of Margarita's family legacy, and I nodded. It turns out that as Margarita was a good friend, Leonardo was aware that the legacy contained a document written by that Italian telephone man and, naturally, wanted it for his little novel. The problem was, Leo believed that Ángel had it. At that point, it was as if a door, a window or something had suddenly been opened, letting in bright light: he'd just confirmed my intuition that the author did indeed know about the document. Do you see? I remained silent, but raised my eyebrows, pretending that I was interested in nothing more than the story, and Ángel continued. He said that Leonardo had given up on ringing to ask for the document, having received nothing but a polite refusal for his pains, and was evidently attempting to use me to get closer. But he was well and truly fucked because Ángel didn't have the document. He wasn't the one who'd appropriated something that didn't belong to him; that scrap of paper was part of a legacy that belonged to his ex-wife, and when he managed to recover it, he wouldn't be giving it to Leonardo; it would be sent to its rightful owner so as to close that chapter of his life once and for all. My angel sounded a little annoyed, and I could understand why, but there was no way I was going to waste this opportunity, so, adopting a neutral tone, I asked: Who does have it, then? His shoulders drooped. Your friend Euclid, he said, sinking his fork into the dish. And before he put that miserable cabbage in his mouth, he added: Margarita's father.

Fortunately, I had nothing in my mouth or I would have choked on it. Margarita's father. Euclid was Margarita's father. I can see you're thinking exactly what I was at that moment: Why the hell hadn't he told me? I was furious, not as furious as I would be later, but still furious because I couldn't believe my ears. Euclid in the role of Ángel's wife's lover made sense, but her father? What do you mean, her father? I asked, and he swallowed his cabbage before confirming that it was true: the father, the progenitor whose seed had spawned his ex was also the father of a friend he used to hang out with and through whom he met the sister, Margarita, who passed from being his friend's sister to his girlfriend and then his wife and ex-wife, so that his friend's dad became his father-in-law and then his ex-father-in-law. I didn't mention it before, he went on, because a few days after we all met in the street, Euclid phoned, asking him not to tell me about the situation, arguing his close friendship with me and saying there was no need to add his daughter to the mix since it was a painful subject. The thing was that, when Margarita settled in Brazil, she paid for her brother to come to join her, and that was a hard blow.

I still couldn't believe it, and Ángel must have noticed my confusion, because he took my hand and told me that it was the truth, and that Euclid must have had personal reasons for hiding it from me. Their relationship wasn't good, he explained; Margarita had stopped talking to her father long before leaving for Brazil. Ángel had been a witness to all those years of conflict; Margarita was very close to her mother, and the truth is that Euclid sometimes behaved very badly, cheating on his wife. His daughter wasn't going to stand for that. It seemed that Euclid was an attractive man and had a lot of success with women, particularly his students: both Ángel and Margarita had heard rumours of his many conquests at the university. I also knew about the conquests but, of course, held my tongue. Ángel was looking like someone who's just made a gaffe and is trying to justify it. He understood Euclid, he said, and to some extent he could understand his request not to mention Margarita, because she'd been the apple of his eye when she was younger. Take a look at this, he added, going to the bedroom and returning with a shoebox in which he kept things belonging to his ex. I saw a photo of Euclid standing beside three small children and another of him with the baby Margarita on his shoulders. Ángel was tactful enough to spare me the sight of the adult Margarita, although her image must surely have been in one of those packets of photos.

When they first met, he said, the relationship with her father was already going downhill. According to Ángel, Euclid was too involved in his own life, the university, his affairs, and didn't want to admit that his daughter was growing away from him until it became all too evident. She shunned him, gradually expelled him from her life. Ángel had witnessed it all: Margarita's concern for her mother, the outbursts against her father, the conversations with her brother. That, he said, was why such a strong bond had sprung up between Margarita and Dayani; it was as if they recognised each other, as though they saw themselves reflected in the other's eyes, the younger one seeing her future and the elder seeing her past, or perhaps they were imitating each other.

The last straw, by which I mean what finally prompted Margarita's mother to get a divorce, was the time she came home unexpectedly and found her husband in bed with a younger woman. That was the limit as far as she was concerned, and the same was true of Margarita, who decided never to speak to her father again. Naturally, Ángel continued, that event was added to Euclid's midlife crisis. A family friend had seen him in Las Cañitas, smooching with a young girl who was undoubtedly one of his students, one of those tarts that go around seducing their tutors to get better grades. That's exactly what he said, and I felt a stabbing pain in my guts, leaving me short of breath and only capable of mumbling: In Las Cañitas? Exactly, replied Ángel. When Margarita heard of it, she hit the roof, although she didn't have the courage to confront her father.

I swear I thought I was going to die, because the tart in Las Cañitas was me, but I had no need to try and inflate my grades since I'd managed good ones without anyone's help; I wasn't after anything, anything at all, I was simply the lover of a man who satisfied me and I was happy to be spending his fiftieth with him: it was his family life that was chaotic. So there I was, wishing the ground would open up and swallow me, and that Ángel would stop talking. But my angel continued his story.

That incident had caused a deep wound in the family, a wound that still hadn't healed the day my friend was found in the marriage bed with a girl. According to Margarita's mother, the bitch in her bedroom was the same one seen in Las Cañitas years before, but Margarita maintained that her actual identity was irrelevant. The problem wasn't the woman, it was Euclid. It was her father who was lying. I didn't know where to put myself, I was nodding, not knowing what to say about that whole scene Euclid had spared me, and I was feeling guilty. Even though, in the end, it wasn't my fault, I felt bad, very bad, and I had the urge to run out of the apartment and hug Euclid, tell him how beautiful it was that our friendship had survived in spite of everything. That's what I wanted to do, but Ángel went on speaking.

When he and Margarita decided to hitch up, she wasn't talking to her father, but as it was a wedding, she decided to visit him to give the news and smooth things over. It seems that after a long conversation, when it looked as if things might return to normal, Euclid asked about the family legacy. He was aware that his daughter would inherit it and that it included the document by the Italian telephone man. And the thing was that Euclid had also been interested in the document for quite some time, but Margarita's mother had never been willing to give it to him during their marriage. Can you guess what Euclid's idea was? Ángel asked. Well, he wanted Margarita to sell it to him. She was getting married, the money would come in handy and he'd just been paid for an article he'd published in a Colombian scientific journal. For Margarita, that was like a glass of cold water in the face at three in the morning in midwinter, so she told him to go to hell and stay there forever. Of course 'forever' was too long a time, because Margarita had a big heart and she did later attempt a reconciliation. She met him once, and he sometimes came to visit there in the apartment, and on one of those visits he managed to get his hands on the document. He stole it, Julia. He took her legacy without her knowledge. Do you see? That's what Margarita had tearfully told him in São Paulo, and that was why Ángel wanted to get it all back. To him it seemed unjust: no one had the right to steal another person's life. Take a look at this, he said, rummaging among the papers in the shoebox: it only contained a small part of her life, a few photos, school records. Look at this, he repeated, extracting a page torn from a magazine she'd kept as proof of the crime: it was the article Euclid had published in Colombia, for which he'd received the money he'd hoped to use to buy that damned Italian's document. I took the sheet of paper from him, looked at the colours, the title, my friend Euclid's name in large letters. Then, as I started to read, the world ground to a halt. I mean it: the Earth suddenly stopped turning and I felt as if a fire had been lit around my feet and was rising upwards, circling my body and burning me as I read the text at incredible speed, as if I didn't need my eyes, could easily have closed them and recited the article published under Euclid's name. And the reason was that what the article explained, what the distinguished Cuban professor demonstrated, what was original about his argument, the mathematical proofs, its small contribution to world science, the well-developed idea, had been written by me. You've got it: it was a summary of my university thesis, that paper which had cost me many sleepless nights and for which I'd received congratulations and a degree in mathematics but which had never been published anywhere; it was just a pile of paper I kept as a souvenir in a drawer of the family home. Euclid had stolen my brain. And my brain is my life.

Do you see what I'm saying? I think, therefore I am, and everything else can go to hell.

10

I'm certain I hardly slept that night. When I closed my eyes, sensing Ángel breathing beside me, images of Euclid floated before me. His expression as he listened to my explanations while I was writing my thesis, his smile in Las Cañitas, his hand taking mine to kiss it before he put his lips to mine, the look in his eyes, his praise of my intelligence, his questions, his naked body. Everything was Euclid, my greatly admired tutor, my good lover, my wonderful friend. Euclid, the liar who was sure to be sleeping peacefully as I tossed and turned, listening to the angels snore. Euclid, the thief, because that's what he was, a miserable thief, and at that moment I was completely indifferent to the soap-opera drama of the father-daughter relationship, the man who cheated on his wife, the children taking sides, the divorce, depression and tears: all that was a heap of shit in comparison with what he'd done to me, because he'd stolen my ideas, betrayed me by publishing something that didn't belong to him under his own name, earning money at my expense. Do you see? Just thinking about it still makes me furious. So there was no way I was going to sleep. I got up, poured myself a glass of water and went to stretch out on the balcony, from where I could see the street I loved so dearly. I needed to think things through.

There were a few details that remained unclear in Ángel's story, but I'd avoided asking about them since it would have been unwise at the time. Ángel was a nice guy who had fallen madly in love with a woman and clung to the idea that only by closing the cycle of that relationship would he be in any condition to start afresh with another story. The other story was me and, logically, I was deeply interested in the closure of that cycle. And for that closure to come about, it was imperative that my angel recover the family legacy, which included Meucci's damned document. Once he'd got it back, Ángel would be able to proceed to the final stage of his plan, send the whole thing to Margarita, feel that he'd cleaned the slate and then be able to dedicate himself to me. And there was no doubt in my mind that the first thing I'd do was to move permanently into the apartment in El Vedado with him and so inaugurate a new period in my life, a period that would be more interesting, with much better prospects than I had at present. Judging by what he'd said that evening, his greatest worry was that Euclid had managed to appropriate the legacy. He couldn't even imagine what use his former father-in-law had for the scribbled notes and sketches on yellowing paper, but he was sure that Euclid would never give the document up because he'd been on its trail for years. Which, therefore, made it very hard for Ángel to come up with a means of getting his hands on the legacy.

I didn't think it would be easy to get it back either. However, I hadn't the least difficulty in imagining the purpose Euclid wanted to put it to. There was no limit to what someone who is capable of stealing his student's ideas and publishing them under his own name – just to earn prestige and money – would be able to do with an original document about the invention of the telephone. You have to remember that Meucci was completely unknown at the time, except in Italy and among a few enthusiasts; even in his own day, some journalists had called him the 'crazy Italian' for trying to usurp an invention that clearly belonged to Alexander Graham Bell, as was proved by the legal documentation and the history books. There is no doubt that Bell invented the telephone, the only problem is that he did so a few years after Meucci. In 1876, to be precise, when he was granted the patent and pronounced what has gone down in history as the first telephonic communication: 'Mr Watson – come here – I want to see you.' But he should have called Meucci, not Watson, because long before, in 1849, the Italian had conducted his first experiment: the trouble was that, so far, there was no written evidence of this. The proof, as Euclid had said, was in that document that formed part of the legacy: those sketches Ángel referred to showed the design of his experiment and, as you know, in science you don't explain things in words, they are for art and philosophy. In science it's numbers that matter, formulae, diagrams and designs. Before speaking, a scientist grabs his pencil and draws things; doodles to the untrained eye, demonstrations for the initiated. If Euclid had been capable of stealing my work, imagine what he could do with the proof of the invention of the telephone. Or better still, what he could imagine doing with it. Okay, maybe the question of who invented that device isn't exactly of any great concern to the whole planet. Knowing the answer to that is nothing special. But don't forget Einstein: everything is relative. When you have nothing, a little bit can seem like a lot. It might even be everything. Here in Cuba in Year Zero, Euclid could become a celebrity and even achieve a level of renown in the international scientific community, travel to a congress, give lectures and remake himself overnight as what he'd always wanted to be – a distinguished scientist – rather than spending his time filling the storage drums in his home with buckets of water before the power cut out. At worst, he might earn enough money to eat a little better.

His objectives were clear, but there were a number of details that left me confused. According to Ángel, Margarita had told him that her father had the legacy. So, if Euclid did have the document, why had he ever spoken to me about it? If it were in his possession, the best course of action would have been to keep his mouth shut so that no one else knew anything about it. Aren't I right? Yet the minute I told him about my conversation with Leonardo and Barbara, he showed me the folder with the information about Meucci and came out with the story of the document. It was from him that I learned of its existence. And to me, that seemed odd. So where do we go from there?

Hypothesis one: Euclid wants to use the document to make a name for himself, but he doesn't have any important contacts outside Cuba. When I mention the author's interest, Euclid is worried because he's discovered that someone else is working on Meucci and, if that person hears of the existence of the document, he'll want to get hold of it. Euclid knows that the subject will fascinate me. He, therefore, decides to tell me about the document so I won't suspect he has it. And, in the meanwhile, he uses me to extract information from Leonardo and complete his Meucci folder, which will come in handy when he's finally able to use that document to make his name.

Hypothesis two: Euclid hasn't been able to do anything with the document because he lacks important contacts. His financial situation is so bad that his son, a black market trader, has to supply part of his daily diet. When I mention the author's interest in Meucci, Euclid suddenly sees a possible buyer for the document. He doesn't know Leonardo personally, but if he really is working on the topic of Meucci, he'll want the document, and the sale will solve Euclid's financial problems, at least in the short term. This supposing the author has the means to buy it, of course. Why did Euclid mention the document to me? Because I'd be hooked by the scientific interest of the topic, I knew the author and, in all innocence, could bring him and Euclid together.

But there was another important factor: Ángel. My angel had been married to Euclid's daughter, which meant my former tutor knew that Ángel had seen the legacy because his daughter had inherited it on her wedding day. Logically, the woman Euclid had spoken of, whom I'd imagined to be just another lover, was quite simply his wife. It follows that, during his marriage, he'd have done his utmost to get his hands on the document, but she'd resisted as it formed part of the legacy which would later pass to its legitimate heir, her daughter, Margarita. Euclid had then offered to buy the document from his daughter, but she too had refused to part with it. The first time we spoke about the manuscript, he'd stressed the importance of not mentioning the subject to anyone. Not even Ángel. Why? Well, that was logical: Euclid had the document and wanted to keep Ángel out of the picture, plus, more importantly, avoid stirring his interest in that paper. Euclid had no idea of my dearest's silly romantic notion, his high-flown ideal of closing cycles or his obsession about women with history. He knew nothing of all that. Consequently, he was completely uninterested in Ángel. The person who did interest him was the author, who had spent years collecting data and was aware of details that Euclid himself had only learned of thanks to my innocent intervention.

Whichever way you looked at it, I was the schmuck Euclid was using, just as he'd used me when I was researching my thesis. Talk about furious! Like I said, that night I hardly slept a wink; I went back to bed but didn't sleep. By half past six, I was up and dressed for work and making coffee in the kitchen when I suddenly felt a pair of arms encircling me from behind. I turned and hugged my sleepy-eyed, ruffle-haired angel. I was surprised that he was up so early, but he said that he'd felt alone, that the bed was too big without me, and asked me to hug him tighter than tight before I left. I did just that and then we had coffee together. I adored that newly woken Ángel; he was tender, slow and beautiful. I gave him one last hug and informed him that I wouldn't be able to come back that evening, so we should talk at the weekend.

My rage lasted throughout the whole day. As the students seemed even denser that usual, I set them a task they could work on individually and so learn to use their brains for once; I already knew how to use mine, and that day it was working overtime. In the afternoon, I left as soon as my classes were finished, walking at a terrifying speed. The intervening hours had only served to increase my edginess. Euclid was going to have to listen to everything I'd been bottling up.

When I arrived at the apartment, the door was open and his mother was fanning herself, sweating like a pig; there had been no power since noon, and so no possibility of turning on the overhead fan. Euclid had just gone to take Blot for a walk, but as I wasn't in any hurry, I told his mother I'd wait and we sat down to chat. Chichí turned up with some friends that afternoon, and the reason I remember is because the moment they were in the door

I heard a voice calling me 'Prof'. I looked around and saw a girl I honestly didn't recall ever having met. You know how it is: one teacher and thousands of students. But she insisted I'd taught her at the CUJAE, that she'd loved my course, and wanted to know how I was, if I was still at the university. I politely replied that I'd changed jobs, without going into detail, and she smiled and said she was working as an engineer but really wanted to be a writer. Chichí then introduced me to his friends, adding with pride that they were all future authors. I looked them over. The thin one with long hair, dressed in black, was a geography graduate. Another, also hairy and not unlike Conan the Barbarian, was a biologist. The thin-legged, curly-haired, blue-eyed young woman in short shorts who had spoken to me had graduated in electronic engineering. According to Chichí, they were rockers, avant-gardists and all wanted to write. In that case, why the hell had they studied sciences? In this country people graduate in one thing and then work in something completely different – except for me, of course – but... there would have been no point in mentioning that.

I listened to the young people's conversation about rock concerts in Patio de María and their literary projects until Blot appeared in the doorway, with Euclid behind him, smiling broadly at the sight of so many people in the apartment. I kissed his cheek, allowed him time to talk to his son, said goodbye to the visitors, waited for a lantern to be lit and only then told him that we needed to talk. He, no doubt, thought that I was bringing new information because he raised his eyebrows, lit a candle and invited me into his room.

You lied, Euclid, was all I said once he'd closed the door. He looked at me in surprise and, still holding the candle, moved closer to ask what the problem was. You lied, Euclid, I repeated, you lied to me. If at that moment it had occurred to him to ask forgiveness for having stolen my ideas in order to publish his article; if he'd begun to speak, apologise, attempt to clarify the situation; if he'd told me about Margarita, I don't know, if he'd given me the faintest sign, things might have been different, but he didn't; he merely begged me to calm down and again asked what was wrong: confirmation that there was more than one lie, and he wasn't going to make the mistake of condemning himself before hearing what he was accused of. Euclid was always very intelligent. I looked at him gravely, sighed, and said that he knew Ángel because he'd been his father-in-law, but that he'd apparently decided not to disclose that minor detail. My former tutor smiled reluctantly, sighed and, as he put the candle on a shelf, commented: Ah, so that's it. Then he added that I must have got that information from Ángel, that I shouldn't worry, he'd tell me everything; it was a sad story, but the time had come to put a name to that sadness, I was one of the people he loved most in the world and he'd never harm me, much less lie to me. In fact, he'd been wanting to tell me for ages.

My rage suddenly flared up again, a boundless rage, because I could still hear that phrase, 'Ah, so that's it'. They were words of relief, words of 'at least she doesn't know the rest', of 'what a fright you gave me just for the sake of it'. So why didn't you tell me? I asked. At that moment, the electricity unexpectedly returned, and with it the light, causing Euclid to smile at me before commenting: See? It's not so serious: let there be light. I ignored the smile and again asked, this time more loudly, why he'd lied to me. Euclid repeated his request for calm and opened the door to tell his mother that she could turn off the lantern and ask her not to bother us because we were working on a project. She called back that she'd knock on the door when the meal was ready. I asked for a third time why he'd lied to me. He didn't smile when he said that if I was so upset about nothing at all, it would be better not to let his mother and the neighbours know about it. Then he switched on the radio and tuned into CMBF, as he always did.

His version of the story was that he hadn't said anything because there was no need. Right from the start it had been clear that I was interested in Ángel, and telling me that my prospective lover had been married to his daughter would have made me unnecessarily curious and so obliged him to talk about Margarita. I was well aware – in fact I was the only person who knew – how deeply he'd been affected by the departure of Margarita and then Roberto. I was depressed, Julia. Don't you remember? And that depression had put an end to his university career and social life. The day we'd met Ángel in the street, he'd been tempted to tell me but later thought better of it, because my situation was independent of his. In fact, he added, he had to confess that he'd called the lad to ask him not to say anything either; it was a gentleman's agreement, but if my angel had broken it, that meant it was the right thing to do. Euclid only wanted what was best for me, and that's why he'd found the courage to make that call; the truth was, they didn't have much to do with one another. When Margarita was living with Ángel, she wasn't speaking to Euclid, so he'd been a phantom son-in-law. What use are ghosts, Julia? he asked.

He said that he preferred to think of Ángel as my man, someone new in his life rather than the son-in-law he'd never had, the husband of the daughter who wouldn't speak to him because she couldn't forgive him for being unfaithful. And it's true, I was often unfaithful, Julia, very often. I understood by this throw-away remark that he was letting me know I hadn't been the only one, although the clarification seemed unnecessary, as I'd never imagined I was; lovers are bodies that give themselves to each other for as long as the idyll lasts, and then comes the forgetting or complicity.

I'm certain there was a pause then. We were both silent. Euclid was speaking the truth. I was lost to the outside world, thinking about Las Cañitas, about what Ángel had told me, coming to the conclusion that Euclid's reasoning was logical, that he had no need to justify his affairs to me and there was no way he could know how much Ángel had learned from Margarita. And I was also thinking about all this and the other lie. I was deep in this series of thoughts when Euclid interrupted to say that those were the reasons for his actions; he hoped I understood them, and since I had all the details, there was something else he had to tell me. Now that we have light, let it be complete, he added.

I didn't reply; it was my turn to listen and I was definitely very anxious to hear what he had to say. His daughter was named after her mother, said Euclid. It was a family custom, nothing unusual. What was important, or at least what Euclid wanted to tell me since it affected us both, was that Margarita, his ex-wife, had owned Meucci's document: it was her he'd been talking about, and if he hadn't revealed her identity, it was because he didn't want to complicate my love life. But as I now knew, there was no reason to hide anything and I should hear the whole truth. I first saw the document at home, Julia, because it belonged to my wife, and that's why I'm absolutely certain of its existence: I held it in my hands, he announced. Things were getting interesting. I looked surprised and smiled before stating: So your ex-wife has it. But Euclid shook his head. For family reasons, sentimental reasons, that sort of thing, the mother had given it to her daughter. So then your daughter in Brazil has it, I confidently pronounced, but he shook his head again. The document was in Cuba; his daughter knew that he wanted it but, to make him suffer, she'd given it to someone else before her departure. In this very room, Julia, she told me about her decision to hand it to someone who, she said, would be able to put it to good use. The person who has it now is that writer you met, Julia. He was a friend of my daughter.

I had to laugh, couldn't stop myself. I swear he took me by surprise. I think I uttered a 'Euclid, please!' between guffaws, but he moved closer, looking at me with a strange expression and, almost shouting, asked if I thought he was lying. Margarita had said that she'd given it to the writer, and he solemnly swore that if he'd omitted to share that detail with me it was because of my relationship with Ángel and all the other things he'd explained. What's more, to clear everything up once and for all, since that meeting in the street, he'd been certain Ángel would be our connection to the writer Margarita had referred to. He himself didn't know him personally, but he was aware that he was working on Meucci, was a friend of his daughter and, consequently, a friend of Ángel. He couldn't tell me in the beginning because he didn't want to make things more complicated than necessary, but now everything was out. Euclid was euphoric. He took a deep breath to calm himself and, turning his back to me, said that Leonardo was still the best lead we had until it was proved otherwise – our only lead, if I still wanted to talk in terms of 'us'. Then he turned to face me and begged my forgiveness for his omissions, said that he'd behaved this way so that I wouldn't be hurt, but he wasn't lying. If anyone's doing that, it's them: my daughter, the writer, the history books. They're lying, Julia, not me.

With those words he brought his confession to an end that night. There was no mention of the ideas he'd stolen from me, no bright light, just a small bulb shining above Leonardo's head in an attempt to send me down some absurd path. I was in no doubt that Euclid had the document and wanted to use me to go on gathering information. Talk about fury! I was bursting to call him a thief and a liar, but I didn't. The moment wasn't right. His words had legitimised my anger and helped me to make a decision. Euclid most definitely didn't deserve Meucci's document. That piece of paper ought to be in other, cleaner, less sullied hands, hands belonging to someone who would put it to a better, more just use, but that was something I'd come to understand later. For now, I was simply determined to get the legacy from him. He'd been my tutor and I his best student; it was my duty to follow his teachings. Telling him that I knew what he'd done with my thesis would only put him on his guard and cause him to distrust me because he was aware that that I didn't trust him. No. My dear tutor had to continue to believe that I was his ally, never suspecting that the tables had just been turned.

I sighed and told him not to worry, we were still on board the same ship, he was my captain and Leonardo our best lead. Euclid breathed again and with a smile full of hope said: Let's keep going then, my darling Julia. I simply returned the gesture, not mentioning why I was smiling.

11

I didn't attend the following meeting of the science group because I quite honestly had no desire to see Euclid. I rang in the morning from the neighbour's apartment to say I had period pains, or some such thing, and was incapable of going out. I didn't care whether or not he believed me. While I was there, I called Ángel but there was no reply. I decided to try again later. Back at home, I think I might have done some laundry – I don't remember exactly – I just know I was feeling restless and the apartment was, as usual, crammed with people. It's always noisy, never peaceful for a moment. In this city, people talk as if we were all deaf; mothers shout to their children from balconies, music has to be played at top volume and secrets are never whispered behind closed doors. I lay the responsibility for this on the Caribbean, that warm, unsettled sea. What do you think? That's why when I'm feeling low, and not even touching my scar can help, I need the sea to calm me, to give me advice or at least to hear me out.

That afternoon I set out to walk along the shoreline. I had a lot of reasons for feeling down. First, what Euclid had done to me, which, naturally, I would never be able to get my head around. Then, because... How can I put it? It seemed like my life was only halfway to anywhere. You see, Euclid was my only true friend, but I'd just discovered a serious betrayal; it was probably a momentary weakness on his part, I had no doubt that he cared for me, yet it totally pissed me off that he was capable of doing such a thing but incapable of confessing it. So it turns out that my only friend wasn't my real friend. Do you get me? I've never gone in for close friendships – even as a child I was a loner – but you, or at least I, have to be whole; that's what I think. And then there was Ángel. What sort of a relationship did we have? We were lovers, nothing more. We weren't a couple, an item, a 'Can I introduce you to my partner?' No, we were lovers, and we were the only ones who knew it.

Around that time my brother had been getting my goat, always asking who I was sleeping with when I didn't return to Alamar at night. He'd tell me to be careful about going with foreigners, ask why I didn't bring the guy home. He's never known anything about my life, but he likes playing the macho-brother role. To be honest, I'd have liked to introduce Ángel to him, it was just that Ángel wasn't my boyfriend per se, it wasn't a complete relationship. Do you see? Somewhere between a lover and a friend, that was what I had. And the same went for my career, of course, because that rounded the whole thing off. A disaster area. Right?

I walked for quite a long time without finding a telephone so, when a *guagua* – that's our name for a bus – passed just as I reached the stop, I almost automatically got on board. I'd find a working phone at some point and, if it were possible to meet Ángel, I'd at least be on the right side of the bay. Dante Alighieri should have included a bus trip from Alamar to Havana among the punishments of his Inferno. On those buses, you feel truly close to your neighbour, so close that he's breathing straight into your face and your bodies are indistinguishable. You no longer know if that leg brushing yours belongs to you or the person next to you, if the hand reaching into your bag is yours or some other person's, if you like or feel uncomfortable about that thing pushing against your arse. You can't precisely define anything other than the bead of sweat trickling down your spine, at about the same rate as the bus moves in the tropical sun: slow and laboured.

I was incapable of bearing that torture for long, so as soon as I could, I got off and continued walking along the Malecón, beside the warm, unsettled sea. I really would have preferred to have been able to think of something else, but it was hard to take my mind off Meucci and the situation surrounding him – especially now that I'd decided to take the document from Euclid. I'd go on loving him in my own way, but he didn't deserve the document, there was no question about it. That afternoon, I began thinking through the options for getting my hands on the legacy, which he probably kept in his room. I could, for instance, hide somewhere near his house, wait for him to take Blot for a walk, then go in to tell his mother that I'd be in his room. Or I could be in there with him and wait for him to take a shower. Or pretend to be ill and persuade him to offer me his bed for the night. I could invent any number of ways that would, there's no doubt, make me a thief, but as the saying goes: it's no crime to steal from a thief. Aren't I right?

What seemed strangest was that, quite by chance, I'd reached the point they had all been circling around for ages. Yes, because we were all, for different reasons, after the same thing.

What was I hoping to achieve by securing the document? The truth is that my motives weren't particularly clear. It had started out as scientific curiosity and the desire to collaborate with a friend; now it was to punish that friend. I don't know. When I think about it, I believe I simply needed an objective, something to save me from the emptiness of that year. Ángel's interest in the affair was obvious: he wanted to recover Margarita's legacy, and that included the document. We've already mentioned Euclid's motives. As for Leonardo, it was clear that he wanted it as supporting evidence for the story he was working on. During one of our first conversations, he'd spoken of the need to demonstrate that his story wasn't fictional but unmitigated fact, History with a capital H, and, of course, he could only do that with Meucci's document. But let's recap: according to Ángel, Margarita had told him that Euclid had the paper. He was also sure that Leonardo thought he had it. That liar Euclid said that Margarita had told him Leonardo had the thing. And what did the author have to say? Zilch. So I decided to call him before trying to get in touch with Ángel.

I had to walk a long way before finding a functioning telephone. Leonardo answered in a friendly tone, happy to talk to me. He said that he'd be home all evening as his son was visiting, and if I had nothing better to do, I could call around. But I had to remember that having the child in the house was like the passage of a force five hurricane and his main task was to try to contain its fury. I told him to put the water on for the lemongrass tea because I'd be there shortly, and then hung up.

When I arrived I found the garage door open, the tea cold and Leonardo stretched out on the bed beside his son, showing him a world atlas. I immediately took to the boy. He was the image of his father: light brown complexion, glasses, a likeable face. The moment he saw me he sat up, responded to my greeting with a 'Hi' and, looking at his father, asked if I was his girlfriend. Leonardo got to his feet to welcome me in and explained that I was just a friend and, so that his friend didn't think they were a pair of hugger-muggers, maybe he should gather up the books on the bed and all the drawings and crayons on the floor. The boy made a face, pushed his glasses up his nose and set about following his father's advice. It really was lovely to see them together. While one picked up the paper littering the floor, the other heated the pan of tea, and it was as if they were the same person in two different sizes, except that, just then, the larger person was talking to me while the other furtively sneaked me suspicious-inspector looks. When everything had been tidied up, Leonardo suggested that his son should go to the main house for a while to see his grandparents. The kid didn't seem particularly pleased by that idea: he gave me a sideways glance and then asked his father why he wanted to be alone with me if I wasn't his girlfriend. His father made a face, pushed his glasses up his nose and pointed to the door. The child left, muttering complaints.

Just as soon as he was out of sight, Leonardo sighed and said that he was dying for a rum but didn't like his son to see him drinking. He took a bottle from the place behind the books where it was secreted and, pouring a generous tot into the lemongrass tea, told me that he'd donated blood that morning. This country, he asserted, has gone crazy. Since the situation had got so bad and people hardly had any food, very few were volunteering to give blood. No one had the energy. So what do you think they had thought up in his neighbourhood? They gave donors a bottle of rum. Madness! But the truth was that rum was expensive and he had an iron constitution, so he felt good about it: his blood might save someone's life and, in exchange, his body got a little of the drink it enjoyed so much. Do you want some? I decided to take my tea unlaced. Anyway, if I accepted his offer I was going to feel like a louse.

That evening I heard his favourite *trova* singer for the first time. I didn't know much about Frank Delgado back then, but I love him now; although, to tell the truth, that day he was just background music to Leo's words. The author was capable of making physical objects speak: each had its own story. I noticed that in the tin can where he kept his pens and pencils there was a Russian wooden spoon, one of the really pretty handpainted ones, and he told me about his brief stay in Moscow. He said it had been given to him on Arbat, an enchanting street full of cheap bookshops, craft outlets and record stores. He had little money, but he fell in love with the spoons and *matryoshka* dolls the middle-aged saleswoman had made and decorated herself. Leonardo greatly admired people capable of making something with their own hands, which may explain his own skill: he too was capable of making many things, although he never thought the results were anything special. That woman, however, was a magician, and he praised her work so roundly that she had no choice but to refuse payment for the spoon. And there it was, standing with the pens and pencils Leonardo was using to write his work.

His work was the novel about Antonio Meucci and there was by then no need for me think up ways of broaching the subject because it came up of its own volition. Leonardo was so immersed in the story that he couldn't help but mention it. He told me he'd just read some extremely interesting articles that cast light on the details of Meucci's first experiments. The distinguished Italian scholar and scientist Basilio Catania, who had written these articles, stated that although the telephones created in Havana were rudimentary, they involved the principle of variable resistance, which would be used by

Thomas Alva Edison in his carbon microphone. That's to say, Meucci's creation was already addressing certain issues that would later come to the fore. He was ahead of his time. While Leonardo was speaking, I had the pleasure of imagining Antonio during the period when the Teatro Tacón was closed, holed up in his study, working on designs, carrying out tests, making mistakes and starting over again, because that's what it's all about: trying hundreds of times until you get a satisfactory result.

After that first occasion, when his patient's cry marked a new path to be followed, Meucci resolved to continue his experiments. And since, logically, his intention was not to make his poor patients suffer by administering electric shocks that would cause anyone to yell out in pain, he designed an instrument that would reproduce the mechanism, but with the addition of a cardboard cone. So, on one end was the patient with his instrument, talking into the cone, and on the other was Meucci with a similar instrument, listening to what came through his cone. That small adaptation allowed him to utilize the acoustic potential of the cone to reduce the strength of the current and, above all, increase the quality of the sound transmission. I imagine that the scientist was hardly able to sleep from sheer joy.

1850 saw the reopening of the Teatro Tacón and the end of the Meuccis' contracts. Leonardo, however, was still unsure exactly why they left Cuba. It could have been the logical consequence of the termination of those contracts, but certain data in his possession suggested that other factors were involved. At that time, a number of voices in favour of independence from Spain were beginning to be raised on the island. Antonio was a personal friend of Garibaldi, had always sympathised with liberal movements and, in short, was on the side of revolution and independence, so – there's no smoke without fire – it should be no surprise that the flame took hold, and those sympathies may very well have annoyed more than one islander and thus caused Meucci difficulties. In addition, his scientific spirit had to be taken into account. Antonio needed to change jobs in order to concentrate on his 'speaking telegraph'. Of course he was well aware of the notion of 'being in the right place at the right time' and Havana at that time was the wrong place for developing his type of invention. Truth be told, there have been plenty of times when Havana was the wrong place for many things, but that wasn't Meucci's problem; what he needed was to set himself up in a place where he could continue his work. And that place, at that time, was the United States of America, which offered an increasingly favourable environment for inventors of any type. So, on April 23rd 1850, Ester and Antonio Meucci embarked on the yacht *Norma*, waved goodbye to the beautiful city of Havana and headed for the land of the future.

On arrival in New York, they decided to settle on Staten Island. Some months later Giuseppe Garibaldi came to the country seeking asylum and was received as a guest in their home, where he remained for four years. Nowadays that house is the home of the Garibaldi Meucci Museum. I don't know what funds the couple were able to draw on to establish themselves on Staten Island, but not long after their arrival, Meucci opened a candle factory, where he worked alongside Garibaldi and a number of other exiles. Can you imagine: Garibaldi a candle maker? According to Leonardo, Meucci also experimented with the use of different materials in the factory, including paraffin and stearin, neither of which had previously been employed in the manufacture of candles. There's no two ways about it: the guy had a fever for invention.

During his first years in the United States, Antonio divided his time between the candle factory and his experiments on voice transmission. And things seemed to be going quite well until a string of calamities occurred. In 1853, his wife developed a serious form of rheumatoid arthritis, which in the course of just a few months left her partially paralysed and condemned to passing the rest of her life as a bedbound invalid. In the same year, Garibaldi returned to Italy and, shortly afterwards, Antonio was forced to close the factory due to commercial and financial difficulties. So it was just one damn thing after another that year: he lost his business, lost his friend and his wife was ill. But Meucci wasn't the sort to be laid low by any problem. No way! He decided to perfect his communication system and install a telephone connection between Ester's bedroom on the third floor and his workshop, which was outside the main house, so that they could be in permanent contact. Brilliant!

Leonardo recounted everything he knew about the inventor's life and the things he was in the process of unearthing, which would eventually become part of his novel. He had a few fragments, some scenes, invented dialogues, things like that. But, he said, it was all subject to change because a book is a living organism that is constantly growing, breathing and demanding a space of its own. When I asked if he had any idea when his non-fiction novel might be finished, Leo grinned. He told me that he was still lacking one important detail, and when he had that, it would be a matter of writing-up and revising the text. It was a major work of literature, as revolutionary as the telephone itself, so it had to be perfect. I enquired how he could be sure of that perfection and Leo grinned again: because it would leave everyone open-mouthed, he said. I asked if the perfection depended on that very important detail he still lacked;

he agreed that it did, and I was about to ask another question... but you know how it is with kids: they have a gift for turning up at the wrong time. At that moment, the miniature Leo dashed into the remodelled garage and, on seeing me, stopped and blurted out: Gosh! Are you still here? His father reprimanded him but I said not to worry, I had to leave shortly. And that was true; I wanted to call Ángel again and I wasn't going to use the phone in the main house to do that. Father and son accompanied me to the closest traffic lights, where I could hitch a ride. I was angry about the conversation being cut short because, having got that far, I was convinced that the detail Leonardo was referring to was Meucci's document; although, naturally, he had no idea that I knew that part of the story. As we walked down the street, I attempted to pick up the thread of the conversation but with the little monster there, it just wasn't going to happen. I said goodbye from the window of the car that stopped to give me a lift and Leonardo blew me a kiss. Nice guy!

I liked Leonardo and I felt kind of sorry for him that day, because what he wanted was to write a great novel, but to do so he needed the document that Euclid had secreted somewhere. All that seemed so innocent now. Leonardo thought he'd revolutionise literature by narrating Meucci's real story and basing his book on a document that would certify its authenticity. I can hear you say that piece of paper wasn't any guarantee that the man could actually write a good novel. And you're right. But that brings us back to Einstein and his relativity. Like Euclid, Leonardo needed a dream he could believe in; that was what gave him the energy to keep pedalling each day in the hot sun. That was why he was obsessed by the idea of the book and why he needed the document.

He needed the document that I'd decided to find. I suddenly felt good, like a puppeteer or something. I could recover the document and give it to Leo so he in turn could use it in his book and become a famous author. Or I could hang onto it myself and become the reputable scientist who rescued Meucci from anonymity, the reputable scientist Euclid wanted to be. Or I could give it to Ángel so he could then return it to Margarita. No one was going to become famous that way, but there was no doubt that it would be a grand gesture, a just, tender gesture.

I arrived at El Vedado, found a telephone, dialled Ángel's number and almost jumped for joy when he answered. He said he'd been home all day, expecting me to call, without a sound from the damned instrument, and so it had been almost weird when it eventually did ring. Ángel, my angel. He told me he was waiting by candle-light as there was no electricity. Antonio, my Antonio, if your friend Garibaldi were to see us now with candles and no telephone...

That night, we sat on the balcony, waiting for the power to return because, what with the heat and the mosquitoes, staying indoors was torture. Ángel was very loving. We were sitting on the floor, him propped up against the wall and me leaning against him, feeling his body and hearing his voice softly crooning: 'A soul that gazes at me unspeaking, says everything with its eyes.' I was feeling sorry for Leonardo because his novel was never going to be perfect. Do you know what I've been thinking? I asked Ángel. And he said he hadn't a clue because there was no way of knowing what went on in my head. I've been thinking that I might be able to help you get the legacy back. Euclid is a friend of mine, so maybe I can do something. He turned me around to look into my eyes and asked if I really would do that for him. I nodded and we kissed, long and slow.

12

What followed were lovely, in some way really fun days. As I said, I was feeling like a puppeteer, up above, moving the strings without harming anyone, just deftly tweaking them to get the best out of each marionette. It's an odd but pleasant sensation. Don't you think so?

With Ángel, everything was going smoothly. That night on the balcony, we'd made a pact: I'd remove the legacy from Euclid's home and he'd return it to Margaritatheseaisbeautifulandthewind with a note saying 'goodbye'. He was so happy that he laughed aloud and embraced me, calling me a goddess, his dearest darling, a woman with a huge heart. He went on to say that he was well aware that what he wanted to do might seem a bit peculiar, he knew I thought it would be better to just tell all those ghosts to get lost, but he simply couldn't do that; he'd always been a mass of manias and weird rituals whose aim was to prevent life becoming a tangled mess. He wished he could be like me and exist in the perfect order of numbers, but he wasn't cut out for it. And he was right there: Ángel and I were very different. Maybe that's what attracted me; that and a warm feeling at the sight of his long, untidy hair, his smile and that look of a child who's just been given a huge sweet. It didn't occur to him to ask why I'd decided to help him instead of my friend, he was so happy that the question can't have passed through his mind, and I preferred not to mention the article published under Euclid's name that he'd shown me a few days before. What was the point? And neither was there any point in badmouthing my former tutor; the article was our own unsettled business. It had nothing to do with Ángel. He laughed, put his arms around me, and with all that fondling he soon began to undress me and we ended up making love. There's something wonderful about having sex on a balcony, at night, when the lights are out, there's no traffic passing along the avenue, no televisions or music blaring out and not the slightest breeze, just the mosquitoes and our naked bodies breaking all those silences.

That was the night Ángel shared one of his rituals with me. How could I forget it? After making love, we went inside on all fours, helpless with laughter, like children crawling around in nursery school, unworried by the idea of having no clothes on. We washed by candlelight, using up what little water was left in the drum. Then, after putting our clothes on, we returned to the balcony to contemplate the night sky and laugh at it until the power came back. My angel was in such a good mood that he looked into my eyes, said he wanted to show me something, took my hand, led me to the living room and asked me to sit on the sofa. I did as requested, and he went to the dresser. Then he said that I might think it odd, but he wanted to introduce me to his unknown favourite, the owner of the videotapes he'd found in the mistaken knapsack in São Paulo. I don't quite know why, but I was strangely happy. Talk about dumb, right? Ángel put one of the tapes into the video player and sat down next to me. There was nothing very interesting about the clips, in fact they were pretty boring. A little girl with a cone-shaped paper hat blowing out the candles on her birthday cake. The same child holding the cord of a piñata, surrounded by other boys and girls, also with paper cones on their heads and cords in their hands. All in black and white. No sound. Snatches of life, faces that must mean something to the owner of the video, but left me cold. Just blurry images that, with time, would disappear. What did have great significance was that Ángel was opening that door, allowing me to sit beside him and accompany him in the ritual. Do you see? I was entering an all-too-private place, a place no one else had access to, and that was a big deal. Too big a deal.

I think that, after that night, I was even more convinced of the justice of taking the legacy from Euclid and giving it to Ángel. So you can imagine, I was naturally very curious about the document; all the more so given the information I now had about Meucci. But whichever way things panned out, I'd get to see the paper because it was part of the legacy. It even occurred to me that, once we'd recovered that legacy, I might somehow be able to persuade Ángel of the scientific importance of the drawings and we could hang on to the manuscript. It was a thought. Whatever, that decision was further down the line right now the main thing was to recover the legacy intact. Ángel had last seen it in a wooden chest that had belonged to some member of the family. For a while we entertained ourselves inventing strategies I could implement in Euclid's apartment. Ángel had never been there, so I drew a ground plan and we added drawing pins to represent each of the people present: Euclid, his mother, Blot and I. He moved the drawing pins around like someone planning a bank robbery.

Things seemed to return to normal in my relationship with Euclid. He said he'd felt bad when I missed the meeting of our science group because he knew me too well to believe that story about period pains. Women, he claimed, always use the same excuses. I nodded. Yes, I'd missed the meeting because I was feeling bad too, but that was behind us now. From then onwards, I began to increase the frequency of my visits to his home and I believe that made all the difference: there was no way Euclid could be aware of the pact made behind his back, and so he firmly believed in my forgiveness and our continued alliance.

It was fun to be in his apartment because I again felt like Agent 007. I first decided to make a general inspection. As if my mind was on other things, I began to look carefully at each object. It wasn't my friend's home but his mother's, so the majority of the things in it were arranged to her taste and that was, to some extent, an advantage. Let me explain: in the living room/diner there were no large pieces of furniture where things could be stowed away, just a sideboard with a few drawers in which it seemed to me unlikely that Euclid would have been able to store anything. And neither did the other shared areas – the kitchen, bathroom and hall – appear to have any means of secreting something so precious. That left his mum's bedroom, to which I had no access, but then it didn't seem an ideal hiding place either; and, of course, there was Euclid's room, which I thought was my best bet. You could have hidden anything in there. There was a bookcase, a wardrobe, a bedside table and even a number of cardboard boxes under the bed. If I'm going to be honest, searching other people's rooms isn't exactly my favourite task in life. OK? But I had no choice. I knew that Euclid kept the folder with all his notes and newspaper cuttings about Meucci in the wardrobe because he'd openly taken it out to show me. Naturally, given the importance of the document and the rest of the legacy, it was no surprise that he wouldn't have it in full view where anyone could see it, and that's why I thought the boxes under the bed might be a good place to start. But exactly how was I going to get those boxes out from under my friend's bed? It even occurred to me to try to flood the apartment. That wasn't as crazy as it sounds. The water came on every other day, and then the storage drums had to be filled, so Euclid's mum used to put hosepipes inside them in the morning and leave the taps open, waiting for the moment when the water began to run through the pipes. It often happens here in Cuba that the water returns unexpectedly and if no one is home, the drums overflow. I thought up ways of distracting everyone: for example, persuading Euclid to take Blot out for a walk with me while his mother was doing the shopping, just at the moment when the water came back and so flooded Euclid's room. Then it would simply be a matter of returning to discover the disaster and volunteering to help clear up. And, of course, the first thing to do would be to salvage the boxes under the bed. Not such a bad plan, right? Nevertheless, I decided not to try it for the time being as it was too dependent on chance, and there was always the possibility that the water might damage the document. The last thing I wanted!

So I began by searching for the wooden chest in the most accessible areas of the room: the bookcase, the wardrobe and the bedside table. It wasn't in any of those places. I then moved to a smaller scale. For Euclid, the important part of the legacy was the document. Could he have thrown out the rest of it, only retaining that? I believed him capable of such an act, but it was also possible that he'd stored the other things separately. In that case, what I had to do was concentrate on the document: I could look for the family tree and all the other stuff later.

During those days, Meucci became almost our only topic of conversation. Anything else seemed to cause disagreements. Even the fractals that we'd been so enthusiastic about in the early days of the study group were a reason for disputes because Euclid had finished reading Mandelbrot's *The Fractal Geometry of Nature* and had a great many objections and reservations. So many that the moment he started out on them, I found ways to change the subject. Our only point of harmony was the invention of the telephone. And that was all I wanted to talk about.

Although Euclid continued to express his conviction that the author had the document, he didn't believe that Leonardo had sufficient scientific knowledge to interpret Meucci's diagrams. That was too big an ask. In his view, Leonardo only knew what he'd read in those famous articles he talked about, articles I had to get my hands on before he finished his blessed novel. Euclid was adamant that we not only needed the document but also all the other information in Leonardo's possession. And while I never said so, I understood perfectly how crucial my intervention was in obtaining the information he needed. That was when I became the puppeteer again. Just for the fun of it, I proposed attempting to find a way of getting Leo to show me the articles. Why not? I even said that, when the opportunity arose I'd search the author's desk and bookshelves. Euclid was surprised by that offer; he giggled and claimed it would be burglary, but considering the situation... He asked if I'd be really capable of doing that and I smiled, saying: And you wouldn't be capable of stealing something in the name of science? I know he didn't understand the reference, but that didn't matter; we agreed that any action was fair if it meant justice for Antonio Meucci. All in the name of science.

As for Leonardo, I continued to meet him. There was no longer any need to invent specious errands at the Ministry of Education as I believe we were beginning to enjoy each other's company. Naturally, Meucci was the main topic of conversation with him too. Leo used to say that I was becoming his notebook for the novel. To start with, I was a magnificent listener. What use is a story if there's no one to hear it? None at all. And I listened, but not merely that – I wasn't just a passive audience – I asked questions and always wanted to know more. Talking to me about Meucci, then, gave him space to think, to notice small details and organise his ideas. Speaking his ideas aloud, he told me, was like writing without the need to worry about the grammar. And I can tell you that I felt important, not merely an onlooker but a walking notebook. A nice thought, right?

Of course, anyone would have enjoyed listening to him. Meucci's life was the story of an unlucky genius. After the closure of the candle factory, thanks to the financial backing of a friend, Antonio was briefly able to earn a living manufacturing pianos and decorative objects; then he founded the Clifton Brewery, the first on Staten Island to produce lager. He was a gadfly, as they say, going from one thing to the next. But due to some shady business and a bad defence lawyer, in 1859 he had to resign the management of the brewery, which then passed into other hands, expanded and eventually became the great Bachman's Clifton Brewery. Meucci had a talent for invention but business wasn't his forte. In addition to losing the factory, his house ended up being auctioned, although the new owner did allow the couple to go on living there as tenants.

Another example of his bad luck and the ways other people took advantage of his misfortune had to do with the candles. Despite having patented a number of his inventions in that area, Meucci was forced to work like a mule for a miserable wage in a company owned by William E. Rider, to whom he'd ceded the patents.

Between 1860 and 1871, he was involved in a variety of different activities. He made improvements to the design of kerosene lamps, invented a special wick that produced a bright flame without black smoke, obtained patents for inventions related to paper production and manufactured hats and several forms of rope. Finally, he patented a way of treating petroleum and other oils to produce a new process for obtaining siccative oils for paint. Those oils were marketed and exported to Europe but, logically, not by Meucci. Who then? The Rider & Clark Company, created by someone called Clark and the same Rider involved in the candle patents.

Returning to the instrument we're interested in, he continued to perfect his design. During 1857 and 1858 he succeeded in producing a high-quality electromagnetic telephone that included almost all the characteristics of modern apparatuses, and even utilised two separate parts: one for speaking and the other for listening. A contemporary drawing made by the artist Nestore Corradi is still in existence. By 1860, the apparatus had been improved to the point where the sound transmission was perfect. Meucci then sought out possible investors in Italy, but that country was going through a pretty turbulent political period and no one was interested in the telephone. Never losing hope, Meucci continued to refine his invention.

But calamity had evidently taken a liking to him. On June 30th 1871, the boiler of the *Westfield*, one of the ferries that ran between Staten Island and Manhattan, exploded. Many people were killed or injured, among them Meucci, who almost died from his burns. The months of convalescence were hard for the couple, whose precarious financial situation was only worsened by the additional medical expenses. Fortunately, they had an employee who assisted Ester. The two women were forced to sell many belongings in order to survive, including Meucci's prototype for the telephone. It goes without saying that, after Antonio's recovery, he was never able to recover the things that had been sold. It's ironic that the telephone helped to save his life.

That same year, while still convalescing, Meucci joined three compatriots to co-found the Telettrofono Company, with the aim of continuing his experiments on the transmission of the human voice. He managed to acquire a patent caveat for a well-developed model of the telephone. The reason why he didn't apply for the full patent is simple: he couldn't afford the $250 fee. The temporary caveat had to be renewed annually and its only value was to prevent a full patent being granted to a similar invention during the period of its validity. That model had already resolved a number of the problems faced by earlier inventors: how to announce a call; using copper cable to increase the quality of transmission; the so-called 'local effect', which is the echo of one's own voice over that of the person on the other end of the line. He also proposed that the instrument should be used in a silent environment. Bell had to address all those issues too, but he didn't begin the task until 1877.

Meucci, as you well know, had genius on his side, but not good fortune. To continue the list of calamities, only a few months after forming the Telettrofono Company, one of his partners died. As a consequence, the two remaining partners decided to separate, one returning to Italy and the other moving to some other place. The company was dissolved and Meucci was again alone with his invention.

All that seems simply too unjust, don't you think? Here in Cuba, we'd say it was time for a ritual cleansing bath, but maybe it was right here that a lifelong curse was laid on him. I don't know. The only certainty is that nothing went right for the poor man, Leonardo said. That was why his novel was needed; so that Meucci would finally be recognised as a public figure and his genius never again trampled into the dirt by the shoes of the ignorant. I loved it when he said things like that. And I felt that the deeper I delved into Meucci's history, the longer I continued my task as the author's notebook, the more I came to identify with Meucci.

●

13

Haven't you ever considered killing someone? I mean, haven't you ever wanted to grab someone and wring their neck like a chicken. I've never done it, my stepfather took care of all that – with chickens, naturally. I think it's hideous; I mean, when you come down to it, what harm have chickens ever done me? None, but people, certain people, have. That's why I had the urge to kill. Just once. Of course I didn't. My limits don't tend towards infinity, they stop before reaching it, and in terms of committing murder, they get stuck on the mere formulation of a desire: I want to kill you.

The day I felt like killing was a Monday. I remember that clearly. I'd spent almost the whole of Saturday with Euclid, first at the group meeting and then at his place. Ángel was busy at his father's that weekend with family meals and the like, so I couldn't see him, which is why I decided to give Saturday over to my former tutor. We discussed fractals and chaos, walked Blot, listened to Chichi's stories, chatted to Euclid's mum and dined on a delicious meal of rice and split peas, accompanied by pseudo minced beef made from banana skins. Almost a miracle in those days. When the moment came to

135

retreat to his room and discuss our favourite subject, Euclid announced that he had a surprise; and boy did he surprise me. He told me that he'd made enquiries and now had the address of the Garibaldi Meucci Museum, which, according to him, was the house on Staten Island we should contact once we had the document. I was somewhere between astonished and disconcerted, but Euclid explained that, having given the matter serious thought, he'd come to the conclusion that the museum was the only place in the world where we'd find an audience who understood the importance of our discovery. It was Meucci's house, his museum. Anywhere else, we'd have to start by explaining who Meucci was and then put up with the laughter of people who would no doubt believe we were crazy. Just imagine the scene, he said, and I imagined it. I saw us at the entrance to the Academy of Sciences, telling the doorman we had proof that the telephone had been invented in Havana by an Italian man. After the titters would come the look of pity for those poor guys – us – who so much rice and split peas, so much sun and so much Special Period had sent mad. They would then politely invite us to leave and we'd end up sitting on a wall in the sunshine, gazing at the document, with no idea what to do with it. No way. Euclid wanted to save us that bitter pill and go straight to the place where we could be sure of receiving a hearing. Once we'd got hold of the document, we had to contact the museum, and that was when things would begin to move. Of course, he added, we wouldn't act like tame underdeveloped carrier pigeons, handing over our treasure to the first person who comes along. That wasn't going to happen. Contacting the museum was simply the initial step towards our future, because our future, he stressed, was to become the scientists who would ensure international recognition of Meucci's story.

Honestly, up to that point I hadn't been sure what should be done with the document. Both in the pact I'd made with Euclid and my current pact with Ángel, I'd never got past the recovery stage of that blessed scrap of paper. What came next was unknowable, and that was perhaps why I hadn't stopped to think about it. Nevertheless, Euclid seemed to have included everything in his calculations. And his plan was logical. The museum on Staten Island was definitely the best place to talk about the manuscript. That was elementary. What surprised me just then wasn't this line of reasoning, which I'd also have followed at a later stage, but that Euclid was sharing it with me, and even showing me the address of the museum, scribbled on a piece of paper that he'd already added to his Meucci folder. So, let's think it through. If Euclid was in possession of the document, why was he telling me all that? What did he want from me? He wanted me to get the information from Leonardo in order to complete his file. Agreed. Then I didn't understand why he'd show me the address of the museum. Of course, I didn't understand at that moment; but I soon would.

I spent Monday at work, longing to finish my classes so I could see Ángel. I told the director that my stepfather was ill, so I'd need to make calls every so often. She allowed me to use the phone in her office. During the morning, I attempted to call him hundreds of times, but all I got was a weird ringing tone: no answer. To hell with it! When I finished work I decided that, as had happened so often before, his telephone was out of order, but there was no way I was going to miss telling him the latest stuff about Euclid in person. I almost raced from the Tech straight to his building, ran up the stairs, knocked on the door and when it was opened... Wham! There was Barbara looking out at me.

I guess I must have looked like someone in a cinema watching a film, when suddenly the projectionist loads the wrong reel and, instead of continuing with the same plot, a scene from another movie appears, one you know nothing about. That kind of thing. Like when you're working on the computer, you haven't saved your document, there's a power cut and you're left staring at a blank screen, not yet able to grasp that all your work has gone down the drain. I stood there, frozen to the spot, but you should have seen how pleased Barbara was. She smiled, said how delighted she was and invited me in. I went in. She told me that Ángel had gone out to buy food because she was hungry; then she said that it was great to see me, asked if I wanted a coffee, told me she'd just made some, that she really liked Cuban coffee, and that we could have a cup while we waited for Ángel. All this was said as she moved around like a queen, while I followed her into the kitchen and watched her take down a couple of cups and pour out the liquid as if she were in her own home.

The coffee was good. It was the real thing. We drank it in the living room while she talked, because Barbara needed to talk, in that strange, comical accent that somehow felt familiar to me; I don't know... likeable. If she hadn't been such a chatterbox, we might have sat there like a couple of dummies who can't work out what the other is doing in the same room as her. But Barbara needed to talk, and then, when we'd run out of all the usual superficial topics, and given that Ángel had apparently gone to the other end of the planet for food and there was no coffee left, she enquired if she could ask me a question. I replied that of course she could, no problem. She gave a silly giggle and said she wanted to ask me something woman-to-woman. She actually said that, 'woman-to-woman', like in one of those crappy

cantina songs. She went on to say that she knew I was
Ángel's best friend and that was why she'd plucked up the
courage to ask me, because she had no one else to talk to
and she needed to unburden herself. Then she sighed and
confessed that she thought she'd fallen in love with Ángel,
that from the first time they'd gone out together, when
he'd taken her hand during the May Day march, she'd
been feeling something very different. And then... then
everything had been weird until the trip to Cienfuegos, a
really pretty city, with that lovely Prado and the beautiful
bay, the 'pearl of the south' he'd said they called it, and
everything went on being weird until, standing there by
the sea, he'd put his arms around her and crooned that
song by Benny Moré in her ear: 'How did it happen? I
can't tell you how it happened. I can't explain how it
happened, but I fell...' and then she couldn't bear it any
longer. No one knew that they were together; no one
besides me. And she needed to talk to someone. She was
confused, she'd heard plenty of stories about Cuban men
who had ulterior motives for falling in love with foreign
women, but she was feeling very strange things, not just
in her body. She asked if I *capichi-ed* her, and I nodded
robotically. Then she said that what she wanted to ask me
was if she could trust Ángel, and she begged me to tell
her the truth, told me that she trusted me.

Barbara trusted me and wanted to know if she could
trust Ángel. Funny ha-ha, right? I believe that it was there
and then that I got the urge to kill. Not Barbara, logically,
because that poor Italian woman was just looking at me,
waiting for an answer, the answer Ángel's best friend
could give her, woman-to-woman. I exhaled a long, slow
breath, then replied: He hasn't told me about you two,
but if you really want the truth... I know that he's in love
with someone else. Barbara pretended to smile, dipped
her head, bit her lip and swallowed; she raised her head

again, looked up at the ceiling, sighed, returned her head into a normal position and put two fingers to her eyes to stop the tears, which seemed to be ready to flow. Then she thanked me and got to her feet. I followed her to the balcony, where I saw her lean over to gaze down on the avenue I loved so well. From the door, I muttered a sorry and she replied that I wasn't to worry, it was always better to know the truth, even if it hurt. She turned around and, looking me in the eyes, told me how grateful she was. I asked what she intended to do, and she said that she didn't know, the thing was that she didn't live here, was just on holiday, and that it was probably no big deal, would soon pass. I nodded, repeated my apology and announced that I had to go. Of course I couldn't tell her, but I honestly had no desire to see Ángel in those circumstances. Barbara accompanied me to the door and put a hand on my shoulder, repeating her thanks and hoping she could go on being my friend; she needed a friend, and she knew from Ángel that I was a special person. She jotted down her phone number on a scrap of paper and asked me to do the same for her. But I had no telephone, so I promised to call her. Sometimes not having a telephone is like not existing.

That Monday, I made my way down Calle 23 with the very odd sensation that the city had turned black and white; in the blink of an eye, the colours had disappeared and I was walking through an old movie. Around me, people were strolling by and bicycles were moving along asphalt that was melting in the sun, but they all seemed weary, and the voices of people and the horns of the few cars blared with a slow echo. I had the sense that no one, including me, wanted to be there, that I was laboriously dragging myself along as if I were hunched over, carrying the huge weight of a steel sheet on my shoulders. And so I went on. If it had been a film, the background music wouldn't have been Ángel's 'Soul of Mine', but another song from the same album he used to listen to, the one that goes: 'Goodbye happiness, I hardly knew you, you passed by casually, not thinking of my suffering, all my efforts were in vain...' Maybe it had been my own efforts that had given colour to the city during that depressing year, and so that day everything returned to black and white. Walking, walking at a fast pace, I descended the avenue until I reached the Malecón. I wanted to see the sea, which always calmed me down, although I was unable to stop and sit on the wall because of my need for acceleration; my blouse was sticking to my back, but I needed to discharge all my pent-up energy. I continued walking. Walking and thinking. Sometimes thinking is a way of maintaining the acceleration.

Ángel, my angel, was a sonofabitch, a shit-faced bastard, an arsehole. He was the biggest sonofabitch I'd ever known. I mean, you had to have seen Barbara's face as she told me how she'd felt when he took her hand during the May Day march. The film could be called *Proletarian Love*, or *How a Daughter of Capitalism Achieves Class Consciousness Amidst the Patriotic Fervour of the People.* The final scene would be sublime: an aerial shot of Plaza de la Revolución showing the parade and, in the crowd, the big strong hand of the young proletarian clasping the dainty hand of the youthful capitalist, while flags wave victoriously all around them. Everything perfect, marvellous, except that the young proletarian had had the balls to tell me that on May Day he was at his father's house, dealing with his sister's trauma. And while I was imagining him busy with all that, he was playing the tourist guide, showing a foreigner the exotic spectacle of a revolutionary march on the workers' very own day. I could almost see him holding a small Cuban flag. I was well acquainted with the flag Ángel had offered

141

Barbara. The sonofabitch. And then there was the trip to Cienfuegos. That was the last straw. I'd heard the version of the considerate brother comforting the poor little traumatised girl and, yes, he was comforting someone: he was a tropical comforter of Italian women. I could have diced him into little pieces! I swear I went from astonishment to fury at the speed of light.

I walked practically the whole way to Alamar that day. I was hyper, but the worst of it was that my fury gradually degenerated into sadness. I arrived home when the telenovela was on and found Mum and my stepfather on the sofa; his arm was around her shoulder and she was resting against him. My brother was sitting in a chair on the other side of the room with my sister-in-law behind him, shaving his head while he watched TV. It was a lovely scene of family harmony, everyone gathered together in the place where I slept. They greeted me and Mum said that dinner was in the pot. I didn't feel like eating so went to the kitchen for a glass of water and drank it on the balcony. At that hour no one's in sight, not even looking out of windows or standing on balconies, because they're all watching the telenovela. My rage-cum-sadness and I were alone. Suddenly I wanted to cry. That's right, I really did want to cry an ocean, to flood my neighbourhood, the whole city, until my tears merged into the sea. What I hate about that kind of situation isn't the desire to cry, or even doing it, because crying is good, it's healthy, and if you don't cry you explode, and it must be horrible to explode and cover the walls with the remains of your lunch. No, what I hate about those situations is not having a place to cry. I had nowhere to shed all those tears. If I went to my mother's bedroom, she and my stepfather might come in, Mum would be concerned and ask what was wrong, and the truth is that I honestly didn't feel like telling her that I'd fallen in love with such a prize specimen. If I opted for my brother's room, he or my sister-in-law might turn up and then – just like when we were kids and I used to sob during a film – he'd start calling me a sniveller, say that he didn't know what my problem was but I should take my snotty nose out of his bedroom. There was always the option of locking myself in the bathroom and muffling the sound of my tears with the noise of the shower, but the water was off. It was Sod's Law. And that's why my fury-cum-sadness, which had become sadness-cum-desire-to-cry, was already turning into desire-to-cry-cum-fury. Back to the point of departure: fury.

I hardly slept that night, as always happens when I've got something on my mind. That's the way I am; there are people who, even when they have problems, fall exhausted into bed, but not me. I have a brain that doesn't seem to have been designed for rest, because it takes the slightest worry as a justification for working all night long.

Hours before dawn, I'd already decided to take the day off work. My students could go fuck themselves. It's not as though they would miss my maths course. Just after eight, I rang the director to say that my stepfather was still in a bad way and I needed to take him to see a doctor. When I returned home, everyone else had gone to their respective jobs and I had the apartment to myself. I undressed, put on a dressing gown, slipped a Roberto Carlos cassette into the tape deck and sat on the sofa to finally cry. I bawled my eyes out, using all my strength and every nerve in my body, every muscle and bone, digging my nails into the palms of my hands, slapping my legs, stamping my feet, shouting the name Ángel all around the apartment, asking the walls why. I cried until I couldn't go on, until the well of my tears ran dry, the snot stopped running and my nose was sore.

There was something ridiculous about the whole story Barbara had told me. Somehow it felt grotesque to imagine Ángel creeping up slowly behind her, like a tiger after its prey or the worst sort of Latin lover, to sing 'How did it happen?' I mean, how dumb! Apparently the courtship rituals of the higher species have no limits; anything goes so long as the prey surrenders, and then days later she's still asking herself how it happened. He hadn't needed to sing a bolero to me, much less take me to Plaza de la Revolución; those were tactics employed when the prey wasn't a national product. But his relationship with me had been stuck on amber for centuries. I mean, days and days, rains and rains, had gone by before we first slept together, even though I fell for him just about the minute we met: oh, that angelic face, that long, fair hair, and that innocent little boy air, I think even Mother Teresa of Calcutta would have fallen for him. Yet it was my fate to have to wait for him to make the decision. How long had Barbara waited? Not long at all, practically no time.

Up until then, I'd thought our relationship was special because it had developed slowly but deeply. Little by little, I'd entered his life, come to know intimate family details, the story of Margarita, even the stranger's videos. At great personal expense, and very gradually, Ángel had allowed me into almost every area of his life, and that's why I found it hard to believe that someone so cautious would, at the drop of a hat – or the wave of a flag – get involved with another woman. Of course, it was Barbara who had said they were an item, that's to say sleeping together, but sleeping together didn't mean having a window open into Ángel's inner life. Yet for me, simply getting as far as his bed had been hard going. For me, everything was complicated, while for her it was all so simple. It was like a cruel joke. Do you get me?

When I don't understand something, I mean when things don't seem logical, I get jittery. Every problem has a solution, and if I can't find the definitive solution, I at least have to discover a path to follow, something, a halfway solution, because otherwise this brain of mine goes crazy. I must admit that the worst of it was that if I didn't understand then, it was because at heart I was refusing to see the obvious. There was a small difference between Barbara and I that set us poles apart: she wasn't Cuban.

In those years an Unidentified Foreign Object was an obscure object of collective desire and, despite the pain it caused me, I finally had to consider the possibility that Ángel wasn't what I had imagined, was merely one more of the many Cuban men who sought out foreign women for a basic exchange of goods. I imagined him offering his tropical flesh for the price of a delicious meal, clothes, presents, anything; maybe if the bottles of rum that appeared in the apartment or some of our meals had been paid for by that Italian woman. Shit!

The problem was that I loved him. Do you see? I liked him too much, plus I was determined to leave Alamar behind and live with him in El Vedado. It was that simple. The whole thing with Barbara would ruin all my plans and dreams, and I wasn't going to tolerate that. It had cost me too much effort to get where I was just for that woman to come along with her boobs hanging out and destroy my equilibrium. By that moment, the fury, the sadness, the urge to cry had all been completely overcome by shock. I loved Ángel. I loved him, it was almost an obsession and there was no way I could bear the idea of losing him, particularly not to some dumb tourist. Forget it!

It was then that what I imagined to be a brilliant plan occurred to me. If Ángel had betrayed me by sleeping with Barbara, well, he'd get his comeuppance at some point. She'd have to find herself another native specimen to liven up her holiday; there would be no lack of applicants. And in the meanwhile, I'd continue working on my objectives. Naturally, to achieve all that I needed a little collaboration, and only one person could help me, someone who, given the right incentive, would lend me a hand. I had the incentive, so, without giving it a second thought, I began to dress to pay Leonardo a visit.

14

When I told him that we needed to discuss something important, Leonardo smiled and peered at me over his glasses. He asked what the mystery was and I replied that there wasn't one, but that I'd prefer not to talk in his office, with so many people coming in and out. Walls have ears, I added. At which he smiled again. It was almost time for him to leave, the only problem was that he had to get his skates – or rather wheels – on because he'd arranged to pick up a cake for his son's birthday before six o'clock, and the place was near his home. He suggested that I come with him and then he'd treat me to a glass of lemongrass tea and we could talk. Wonderful idea.

We made the trip in record time thanks to Leo's urgent errand, plus the fact that the clouds were black and there was thunder in the air. I believe a tropical storm had been forecast; not quite a hurricane, but with a lot of rain, and pedalling in a downpour is no joke. At the house where they sold cake, we had to wait a while for an obese woman to come out with our order. The first drops began to fall when we were just a few metres from his door.

I know Leonardo was curious about the very important matter I wanted to discuss with him, but the fact is that I had no idea where to start, so we were silent for a while. He put the cake in a cupboard and pottered around, positioning a cloth under the door to stop the water coming in, then heating the lemongrass tea and lighting a cigarette. It was only then that he sat down opposite me, commenting that he was all ears. I still wasn't sure where to start. I asked if he was a friend of Barbara, and he said he was, then I confessed that I was in love with Ángel, that we had a relationship, still not well defined, but one that had been going on for some time, and that I wanted to continue. Really wanted to continue, I stressed. Leonardo received this news with an amused half-smile and when I finished speaking asked: So? I told him that I'd just discovered Ángel was sleeping with Barbara. His amused smile disappeared. He wanted to know who'd told me and, without going in details, I replied that it had been Barbara herself during her woman-to-woman confession. Evidently that news was unwelcome, because he stood up, saying they were a pair of shits, that he hadn't expected something like that from Barbara. For a moment I thought the poor man was in the same situation as me: he'd got together with the Italian and, cool as a cucumber, she was two-timing him. But Leonardo replied that they were just friends, although he'd thought it was a true friendship and friends confide in one another. What's more, he was a clown because he did like her a little – that was understandable – but it hadn't gone anywhere and he was the one who'd intro-duced her to Ángel.

Leo poured two glasses of lemongrass tea for us and when he returned to his chair added that, in any case, it didn't matter so much to him: it was me he felt sorry for. He wanted to know how deeply I felt about Ángel and I said that I loved him and had no intention of losing him to a tourist. When I get a notion into my head, I don't rest until I've carried it through, I pronounced, and I loved Ángel for better or worse, which was why I'd come to talk to Leo, so he could get Barbara out of the running. Since they were friends, he could help me ensure that she gave up on Ángel and found some other tropical male ready to offer his services. There was no lack of them in Cuba. I clarified that Leo wasn't included in those 'tropical males', and he understood what I was saying. In exchange for his help, I'd offer mine. Leonardo looked at me over his glasses, affirming that he was more than willing to lend me a hand, but he didn't see what I could do for him. I can help make your novel perfect, I replied. And he seemed to catch my meaning. I stood up, suddenly feeling important, and reminded him that for his novel to be so perfect that it left everyone open-mouthed, he still lacked one thing. He was clearly curious and nodded his approval of my words. I rested my hands on the back of the chair, looked at him like someone about to drop a bombshell, and said: You need the document Antonio Meucci wrote while he was working in the Teatro Tacón, the document that now belonged to Margarita. Leonardo was even more astounded than I'd been on hearing Barbara's confession. He really hadn't been expecting that. After a few moments of staring into space, he reacted by saying it was what might be called a total surprise. He got to his feet, grabbed a bucket, went to the door, and while he was wringing out the soaked cloth, announced that, given my prologue, our conversation was going to be longer and more interesting than he'd expected. I'd warned him.

When he sat down again, I told him that I might be able to access the document and, this being the case, I proposed a pact: I'd get hold of the paper and hand it over to him; in return, he'd find a way of removing Barbara from Ángel's life. It was a fair deal. My idea was that Euclid would lose the legacy as punishment for what he'd done to me; Ángel would only receive a partial legacy as a punishment for Barbara; Leonardo would end up with a document he was capable of putting to good use and I'd end up with Ángel. What could be more just? At least that's what I thought. The author sighed, saying that it seemed like a good plan; the only problem was that there was something I clearly wasn't aware of: Barbara was on the trail of the document too. Wham! The bomb had dropped on me. So that likeable Barbara – that woman who wore bras two sizes too small and always seemed so cheerful – also knew of the existence of the document and wanted it for herself. By that stage, I swear I was even beginning to suspect the director of the Tech.

Apparently Leo was amused by my surprise, because he said, 'Touché'. Then he sat back, adding that things were more complicated than I'd imagined, so it was up to us to unravel them.

How did you find out about the document? he asked. I responded that it was through the person who now had it, although I didn't name names because it was essential that I maintained exclusive access to Euclid. I wasn't going to go around revealing to all and sundry the identity of the person who was in possession of what we all wanted. Right? Leonardo didn't bat an eyelid. Ángel told you, he stated. I shook my head and said that it was the person who now had the document, but he just looked at me in surprise and reiterated that Ángel had it. And then we flipped the tortillas over and over: me denying it, him saying it was true, until he asked if I'd actually seen the manuscript. Of course I hadn't. Without mentioning Euclid, I explained that someone had told me of its existence and then Ángel had said that a certain

150

person had it. Leonardo laughed. If I'd never set eyes on it, and Ángel – he said Angelito – had told me that someone else had it, then that was all clear as daylight. I'm sorry to have to tell you, Julia, but there are times when Ángel can be a shit, he concluded before beginning his story.

Leonardo and Margarita were very close friends, and years ago she'd shown him the document that formed part of the family legacy. In fact, that was when he'd had the idea of writing the novel and had begun to gather information. Margarita knew this, encouraged him and promised that, when the moment was right, they would do something with that old piece of paper. Her decision to leave Cuba was taken when his novel was still in its infancy, but before her departure, she'd concluded that, given the importance of his work, it would be best to leave the document in his custody because he was the only person who would be able to make good use of it. What happened was that she walked out on Ángel a little earlier than anticipated. Leo had known about everything: the contract in Brazil, her intention not to come back and the decision to break up with Ángel. But Margarita hadn't made up her mind to talk to her husband until that night when, in the heat of the argument, it all came out. She left, never to return, and in her haste, forgot to pack the legacy. You can imagine how bad the fight must have been for her to do that. When she rang to reclaim it, Ángel announced that if she wanted it so much, she'd have to come back to him, something that Margarita, of course, never did. Conclusion: Ángel had the legacy containing Meucci's document, and it was never going to fall into the hands of its legitimate owner: that's to say, him, Leonardo.

As you'll understand, his story surprised me. Ángel had told me that Leo thought he had the document, but there was a certain logic in the author's story. Two issues particularly worried me. First, according to Euclid, his daughter claimed that Leo had the document, and, according to Leo, she'd intended to give it to him. That sent big red lights flashing. Two arrows pointed to Leonardo as Margarita's designated heir, yet it might also be true that someone – by which I mean the spiteful, abandoned husband – had intervened. The second was that if Ángel had the document, why had he invented the story about recovering the legacy, and why had he put the blame on Euclid? What was the sense in that?

Leonardo noticed my doubt and, with a smile, assured me that it was natural for me to believe Ángel; I was in love with him and he'd told me a different story. People sometimes tell lies, Julia, he said before reminding me that my angel had slept with Barbara. He was right, people didn't always tell the truth or, like Ángel, were simply economical with it. If he'd failed to mention his relationship with the Italian woman, why shouldn't he also lie about the document? Leo told me that he'd spent years searching for that blessed scrap of paper, initially to recover it, as Margarita would have wanted, and then to buy it, since money spoke louder than words. Ángel had strung him along, made promises and cracked jokes about Leo's work-in-progress, but appeared to have no intention of letting the document out of his hands, at least not to give it to Leo. And he was convinced that Ángel didn't like him much; yes, he tolerated him but didn't like him, so it wasn't going to be easy to persuade him to part with it. I was aware of that animosity towards Leo and, although I never mentioned it, I wanted to know the cause, but Leo wasn't sure. There are men who can't stand their wife's best male friends. Perhaps that was it, he didn't know. Whatever the case, he was certain that Ángel would never give him the document. It was just a matter of spite. But my presence in the affair changed things, and that's why our pact seemed the most just course of action: I'd take responsibility for the paper and he'd get Barbara out of the picture. There was nothing to worry about because, he stressed, all she wanted was Meucci's manuscript.

Barbara's side of the story also astonished me. It appeared that in 1990, approximately a year after Margarita's departure, Leonardo had met an Italian freelance journalist who was interested in the changes occurring in Cuba. They became good friends and Leo ended up acting as his guide to Havana. During one of those nights on the town, the author mentioned his novel and the other's face lit up. He said that he was interested in Meucci too, that a book had recently been published in Italy about the inventor's life, and that same year a well-known scientist had been appointed to get to the bottom of the matter, searching through the archives and visiting the places where Meucci had lived. In fact, not long before their conversation, the scientist had spent some time in Havana. Leonardo thought it was a pity he hadn't come across the researcher, because he would almost certainly have been a good source of information. But it wasn't so very serious because he intended to get the jump on them all by demonstrating what no one else had been able to prove. Having said that, and after another rum, Leo declared that the irrefutable proof of Meucci's invention of the telephone existed in Havana, and he mentioned the document. At that, the journalist's face lit up so brightly that night could have been mistaken for day. They were already friends, but from then on they were brothers, partners in the same project: writing the book. The freelancer promised to send him all the information he had on his return to Italy. So the day came in 1993 when Leonardo received a phone call from an Italian woman who had recently landed in Cuba and was bringing news. Barbara, the likeable Italian, told him that his friend, whose articles tended to be very critical of the Cuban government, had been refused a visa, so she was taking his place. She'd brought the articles Leo had already mentioned to me, written by Basilio Catania, the scientist undertaking the research; she also had a letter from his friend, some money and a staunch determination to buy the document. That seemed absolutely fine to Leo for a number of reasons. First, the awful situation in the country that year would help persuade Ángel to sell the paper without him having to get on his knees and beg. There was ready money for the purchase, and money wasn't something that he abounded in. And finally, the feminine factor always softened men's hearts. Barbara and Leo had made a deal: she'd coax Ángel into selling the document; Leonardo would write the book, but would give her and the freelancer exclusive rights to reveal the discovery in the press, and they would receive a percentage of the copyright. Do you remember that party at the artisan's house? I said that of course I did, it was where I'd met Barbara. Leonardo continued his story and I learned that he'd invited Ángel along that night for the express purpose of introducing him to Barbara so that she could start out on her mission. From that came the meal at the *paladar*, when she and Leo had spoken about Meucci until Ángel changed the subject. In Leo's opinion, this was because a) he didn't want the topic mentioned in public and b) he wasn't yet aware that Barbara was interested in the document.

Just think of it! That was the first time I heard the name Meucci, while the others had already been on his trail for ages. Leo put his explanation on pause and told me that I'd have to forgive him but, at first, they hadn't known just what kind of relationship Ángel and I had, and that was important because Barbara had to employ her charms on him. While he was about it, he took advantage of the situation to tell me that he'd invited me to that *tertulia* at his place because he liked me and it was only later that he discovered Barbara had invited Ángel. He'd thought it was a mistake, but then it occurred to him that it was an opportunity to check if we really were together. And he'd come to the conclusion that we weren't, of course, because I'd spent the whole night playing dominos with him while Ángel was talking to Barbara, who, as far as I was concerned, seemed more and more like a bitch. I'm not kidding; I was beginning to feel like a complete imbecile. You know, like a knight on a chessboard that believes it can gallop freely through the fields and has no idea that someone is moving it; that's how I felt, like a puppet that had dreamed of being the puppeteer.

Barbara had spoken with Ángel about the document and she and Leo had thought that he was stringing things out so as to raise the price. They had foreseen that. What hadn't been included in the picture was for her to end up sleeping with Ángel and not even tell him. Which showed that Barbara was playing a game of her own behind his back, he said with evident annoyance. I used the pause as he stood up to comment that they had got together in Cienfuegos; he smiled and said he knew Barbara had hired a car to take Ángel and his sister there, but when she got back the piece of shit hadn't said a word about romance. It was clear that she was plotting something; or worse, that she and Ángel were plotting something together. They might even have reached an agreement to exclude him from the whole business. Leonardo wrung out the soaked cloth under the door and as I watched the movements of his hands, it made me laugh to think that what he saw them wringing wasn't the fabric but that Italian woman's neck. Just like I really wanted to wring

Ángel's. The discovery that the trip to Cienfuegos had in fact been a sibling thing – although with a key role for Barbara – was to some extent a relief, but only to some extent, because I was still annoyed. Very annoyed.

Leo sat down again and, taking my hands, said that we had to act promptly. He'd take care of scaring off Barbara. If she'd gone back on their deal, well fuck her; we were free agents. Once he had the document, he'd finish his novel and the plaudits would be all his; he promised to include me in the acknowledgements and give me part of the money from the sale of rights. That was the least he could do, he added. But first the document had to be extracted from Ángel, and that was my task.

There was just one problem: I was still unconvinced that Ángel actually had it. According to Leo, Margarita had said he was in possession of the legacy, but Ángel claimed she'd told him that someone else had it. True, somebody had committed robbery, but somebody had also lied. When I communicated this thought to Leo, his reaction was close to despair. Why would Margarita lie to him? And who was going to rob her in her husband's home? Her father, I finally replied. He looked at me in surprise. The professor? He didn't believe it. Leo had never actually met him, but he was aware that Margarita had stopped speaking to him long before she left for Brazil. Ángel really knew how to tell them, he commented. I smiled. He might be right, but I still didn't understand why Ángel said that Euclid had the legacy. Why would he do that? I asked. Leo pushed his glasses up before expounding his simple but incisive line of reasoning: to protect himself. He lied to protect himself. From his point of view, Ángel was sleeping with Barbara to help the deal along and because she was a foreigner. I knew how it was; decent beer, food and cigarettes. He was with her for what he could get, but there was no doubt that he liked me and didn't want to lose me. What would happen if I found out about their relationship? One: I'd want to leave Ángel, in which case he'd do his utmost to win me back. Two: I'd want to harm him in some way to get my revenge, and the worst I could do would be to steal the document, the most precious thing he possessed. That was why he'd decided to try to patch things up by telling me that someone else had it. Take it from me, Julia. I'm a man and a writer, I know the psychology of certain characters, Leonardo concluded.

Suddenly, I could see it all clearly. For one thing, the theory of patching things up before I could harm him made perfect sense, considering that Ángel had come out with the story of the legacy after his return from Cienfuegos; that's to say, when he was already with Barbara. I had to admit that my angel had a lot of imagination. And then, Euclid was loudly proclaiming his innocence. He was the first person to mention Meucci to me and to show me his data and articles; he maintained that Margarita had given the document to the author; he'd just shown me the address of the Garibaldi Meucci Museum and was planning our next move. Euclid definitely didn't have anything. Yes, he'd stolen my thesis, but he wasn't a complete bastard. The real bastard was that louse Ángel, who was sleeping with the Italian woman and inventing intricate stories to make a fool of me. That was the man I loved. Do you get it? Why can't love be more rational?

Leonardo continued gazing at me, waiting for some comment. I agreed, it was just as he said, and maybe 'Angelito' was right: there were two options. Breaking up with him – which I had no intention of doing – or getting my revenge, which had justice on its side; get my revenge by extracting the document from his apartment and giving it to the person who most deserved it. The author smiled, clasping my hands. I could see his eyes

157

behind his glasses and asked if he really did believe that Ángel was sleeping with that other woman just for the sake of the document and a few beers. He nodded. I commented that I'd definitely fallen in love with a piece of shit, but Leo kneeled before me. Ángel isn't so bad, he asserted. According to Margarita, the greatest defect of Cuban men was their weakness for the sins of the flesh. Ángel liked women too much, but otherwise he was a good sort. He really loved Margarita, but then he'd also been unfaithful. I shouldn't take it to heart; it was a national defect. Aren't I right? Leo made me laugh. I put my head close to his and murmured that his novel was going to be perfect. He promised that Ángel would be mine and stroked my cheek with the back of his hand. With a smile, I closed my eyes, thinking about my angel and his naked body, about Barbara's expression when she uttered the word Cienfuegos, about the first time I met Leonardo. What did you say the national defect was? I asked. And in reply, his tongue entered my mouth. The rain didn't stop during the whole night.

15

Yes, I slept with Leonardo. I hope you're not getting the wrong idea about me, because it had nothing to do with love. Love and sex are different things that can be enjoyed in their own ways, and the truth is that we both needed it just then. Do you see? The two of us had been betrayed. That Italian woman had used Leonardo: she'd led him on with promises, possible translations of his work, little gifts of a few dollars, all just to get at the document. Once she'd achieved her objective, she'd had absolutely no scruples about breaking off her deal with him, and heaven knows what she was plotting behind his back. And then there was my darling Ángel, who, as Leo said, was sleeping with Barbara for the proceeds of the sale of the document and a few beers. That sort of behaviour made him a rat; an untrustworthy person with his own interests at heart. But since I knew what he was like, I had only two choices: accept him as he was or not accept him. That was my problem, as it must surely have been Margarita's, who, it would seem, had put up with her husband's infidelities for a long time. After having listened to Ángel's idyllic version of his marriage and his inability to understand why she'd left him, it was a surprise to learn that he'd cheated on her. But Leonardo had known them back then, and if it was true, as Ángel claimed, that Leo had also been interested in Margarita, he'd naturally have been irritated by the situation and that was why he was so willing to tell me. To sum up: Ángel had been in the habit of two-timing his ex-wife, was selfish and, above all, had got his hands on the Meucci document. A real beauty, right?

That night, Leo and I talked long and hard. Making love, or whatever else you want to call it, was a relief, something like loosening a belt that's too tight or taking your head out of the water after you've been snorkelling for a long time. I felt really relaxed, clean, I don't know what... Lying naked in Leonardo's bed seemed natural, the right thing, the next step. We'd already spent so much time in conversation that, to tell the truth, the only difference that night was the lack of clothes. I believe that, if it hadn't been for Ángel, I could have fallen in love with Leo, although I didn't tell him that, merely commented that I'd never been indifferent, and that was the truth. Leonardo's words and manner were a source of fascination for me; what's more, I just couldn't help it: I've always found mixed-race Cuban men attractive. Even before I became aware of their hidden qualities, because after that night... Now that we're on friendly terms, I can tell you: Leo was the Battleship Potemkin. Hell, if our literary output depended on him, I'd bet my life it would be in wonderful shape. My obsession is a curse. From quite an early age, my scientific spirit led me to explore the whole gamut of masculinity: male bodies, male habits and manias. At university, I even used to amuse myself classifying them; so just as numbers can be categorised as natural, rational, whole and real, for me men also needed some form of classification. The only thing they really have in common is that they are all – every single one of them – naked under their clothes, and based on that I began my search for the properties that grouped them into the same sets. Penises were a key element. There are penises for every taste: they come as big as the Empire State Building or as small as a Disney elephant's trunk; there are the ones that rise up like hooks, looking up to the sky or down to the earth, others that are always staring aggressively straight ahead, ones with different political leanings, some tending to the left, some to the right; some are as plump as Sancho Panza and others as skinny as Quijote; there are lazy, hyperactive, explorative, conventional penises, some that are as fast as Speedy Gonzalez or as slow as the wise tortoise. And then come all the possible combinations: quixotic Pisas, hooked tortoises, hyperactive lefties, lazy right-wingers, conventional Speedies, Disney-Sancho explorers. Something for every taste and distaste, and I had a great time classifying them. It's a professional tic; don't worry, we mathematicians are like that. And while I'm on the subject, do you know why there isn't a Nobel Prize for mathematics? Well, malicious gossip has it that Alfred Nobel was so busy inventing dynamite, his wife found a mathematician who made her 'explode' in bed; the offended husband never forgave them and that's why we have no prize. So, if that mathematician had resisted the temptation to jump into someone else's bed, there would be a Nobel for us too. If I'd resisted the temptation, I'd have saved myself other problems, but it was too late by then.

I know we slept very little that night, that the rain never stopped and Leo had to get up several times to wring out the cloth under the door. Leo had convinced me that Ángel had the document, and that his only aim in putting the blame on Euclid was to dispel any doubts about his innocence. But I honestly found it hard to understand why he'd invented that whole tale about giving the legacy back to Margarita. Yes, it was a beautiful, tender, romantic tale, and I like a romantic tale, which is why that whole muddle had seemed logical in someone as apparently fragile as he was. I told Leonardo the story, without mentioning my pact with Ángel or that I'd been ready to get the document from Euclid to give to him. If I mentioned all that, I'd have run the risk of losing the author's trust in me. Do you see? I merely remarked that, according to Ángel, his aim had been to return the legacy to Margarita, but then Euclid had stolen it. In Leonardo's opinion, the possible restitution of the legacy was just something Ángel had dreamed up to escape suspicion and play the hero of the movie before me. He wanted to kill two birds with one stone, and there was no better way of doing that than by telling a story so logical it left no room for doubt. Ángel definitely didn't want to hurt me, Leo stressed; he was simply trying to shift my attention from the document onto himself because he needed to be important to me, needed my admiration, to be my knight in shining armour, that sort of stuff. My knight in shining armour. Can you imagine? That brought a smile to my face. Leo burst out laughing and then said that men required admiration. Ángel wasn't a bad sort, but since the Brazilians had kicked him out of the company, he'd had no job, no money, not even a short-term future. His greatest merit was living alone in an apartment. But we men are like kids being constantly put to the test, we crave applause, Leo said, and I was an intelligent woman who, like Margarita, would end up getting bored if Ángel didn't do something to prevent it. And given that Ángel was also intelligent, his idea was to win my admiration, to invent cunning ways to become, once and for all, my knight in shining armour.

His words gave me an amazingly warm feeling. I didn't even want to ask too many questions because I'd just learned that Ángel hadn't quit his job; he'd been sacked. Poor guy, I almost pitied him, inventing stuff like crazy just to get my attention. Luckily the author's feet brushed against mine and I came back to the real world. If I was lying naked in that bed, it was because my knight in shining armour was sleeping with someone else. OK? In any case, Leonardo had been right in what he'd said. He'd definitely been right, although I never had the chance to tell him.

That night, it occurred to him that we could utilize Ángel's lie to distract Barbara. Since a complete, totally coherent version of events was in existence, there was no necessity to invent another. That week, he'd get in touch with her to say he'd contacted the original owner of the document, who had, to his surprise, told him that Ángel didn't have it; her father did. And what's more, he could tell her that he had a means of getting at that man. I thought his idea was brilliant, particularly because there was a role for me in it; Leonardo didn't know Euclid, but he could tell Barbara he had a connection, and that connection was me, the professor's close friend, a fundamental piece in the jigsaw. During our woman-to-woman conversation, she'd mentioned that she wanted us to be friends.

Well, I'd promised to call, but would wait until Leonardo had had a chance to inform her of my importance in the business. And we could be sure that, having got that far, Barbara would forget about friendship and want to be my sister. Then, with the addition of the spell cast by the author's words, she'd gradually begin to leave Ángel behind and move closer to me. And I – the pied piper of Hamelin – would slowly lead her towards my former tutor.

It was undoubtedly a magnificent plan, one that might turn out to be fun. The hard part was that, while all that was going on, I'd have to search for the Meucci document in Ángel's apartment. I initially thought it would be a complicated operation because, while in Euclid's case the sphere of action was limited to his room, the new scene was a whole apartment, and a large one at that. But, even so, there existed the advantages that my darling lived alone, was not the world's most organised person and, if the worst came to the worst, I could offer to help him spring clean the place. Obviously, before getting to that point, I'd have to sort out another small detail.

I was − or rather, we were − almost certain that Barbara had mentioned my visit to Ángel; she thought he and I were friends, so there was no reason to hide the information. We didn't know if she'd told him about the woman-to-woman confession, but in fact that was unimportant. How can I put it? Ángel knew that I'd discovered Barbara in his apartment and that I'd left before he returned, so he must suspect that I'd found the situation odd and hadn't liked it. Are you with me so far? And given that he knew he was guilty, he'd be worried about what I might think. That would be enough to create conflict between us, a minor problem. My stance, therefore, had to be that of the offended lover, without giving details of the cause of the offence. And when we next saw each other, I should just maintain the pose of the outraged woman and listen to his explanations to see exactly how far he was capable of going. If he didn't confess to his fall from grace, my anger would be justified by jealousy of Barbara. If, on the other hand, he did confess, that in itself would be the cause. Whatever the case, I'd end up forgiving him. There was no other way: first, because I wanted to continue being with him, and then because I needed to get back into his apartment to search for the document. Elementary, my dear Watson. Elementary.

We enjoyed that night of making plans. For Leonardo, I reasoned like a novelist; for me, however, my reasoning was mathematical. We burst out laughing and agreed that they were two sides of the same coin. In early human history, art and science were a single entity, and it was only later that they branched out into separate specialities, but they had a common origin. In Leo's view, I did with numbers what he did with words. Numbers are mental constructions that mathematicians use in an attempt to define the properties of and relationships between everything in the universe. Authors did something similar, but with words. Reality is all around us, it exists, even though it can't always be touched; a mathematician has intuitions about its nature, observes it and then proceeds to describe or codify it. And that's also what an author does: transform our attitudes and feelings into a common code, so that, for instance, the word 'love', which is basically just four letters, carries a wealth of meanings. Leo and I were doing the same thing, the only difference was that our languages used different symbols: mine was made up of numbers, his of words.

I'm not sure if it was due to the physical activity or the rain, but that night sleep evaded us, and I suddenly realised that we were sitting up in bed absorbed in a litero-mathematical or mathemo-literary conversation. Whenever I had the chance to talk to Leo, I learned so much. For example, that Lewis Carroll was the pseudonym of a maths lecturer who, long before the publication of *Alice's Adventures in Wonderland*, had written widely on his chosen profession. The Argentinean writer Ernesto Sábato had graduated in physics and mathematics and had continued his scientific career until he decided to resign his university post to write. And there were many more like them, such as the British philosopher and mathematician Bertrand Russell, who was awarded the

Nobel Prize in Literature. And to top it all, there was the Oulipo group, founded in the 1960s by Raymond Queneau and François Le Lionnais, which brought together mathematicians who loved literature and writers like Italo Calvino who were attracted by mathematical ideas. Wow! All of a sudden, I felt enormous pride in my profession. I had no intention of embarking on a literary career, of course, but it was good to know that world literature was being nourished by people like me. Leonardo told me that the members of the Oulipo group used to define themselves as 'rats who build the labyrinth from which they plan to escape'. I said that it was more or less what he was doing, building the labyrinth of his novel and then, on his own, finding a way out, and he smiled and assured me that the labyrinth was already built; all that was needed now was a helping hand from me to keep it standing. And that hand reached out to pull him close and kiss him, after which I leaned back and demanded more stories. I was definitely becoming addicted to Leonardo's words.

The author rose to his feet, saying that it was going to be hard to get any work done the next day, but the damage was already done. What with the rain and the good company, there was no point in trying to sleep. All that was lacking was a bottle of red wine and an attic, nothing more, as long as they were both in Paris. But since we had only lemongrass tea and a garage, we'd have to settle for Havana. He added that he had no complaints about the company, quite the reverse. He'd been to Paris, it was beautiful, but he could tell me about it another time; that night his interests lay elsewhere.

Leonardo wrung out the cloth yet again; it was so thoroughly soaked that a puddle of water was forming under the door. Then he put water on for another round of tea and went to the bathroom. When he returned, he extracted a book from beneath a pile of papers on the table, pressed the play button on the tape deck and sat down at my side. Frank Delgado began to sing very quietly. Leo opened the book, took out a sheet of paper and showed it to me, asking if I'd ever seen Antonio Meucci's face. I straightened up. Before my eyes was a monochrome photo of a man with a thick white beard and moustache. He was wearing a dark suit and looking gravely to his left. What could Antonio have been gazing at? Impossible to say, but it seemed extraordinary that I was able to see him. Leo grinned at my surprise; his Italian friend had sent him that copy, he said, and he was obsessed with it. He felt that Meucci might turn his head to greet him if he looked at the photo long enough. When we get the document, I'm going to need one more little bit of help from you, he added.

Leo had seen the paper and explained that it consisted of three diagrams. One was a floor plan of the Meuccis' suite in the Teatro Tacón. In it were two small figures: a man in the laboratory and another in one of the rooms, connected by a cable that ran through the whole suite. It was like a snapshot-for-dummies of the moment when the experiment had been carried out. The problem was that the other two diagrams explained the technical details of the connection; that is to say, designs of the electrical circuitry, something, Leonardo confessed, he knew little about. As I was a scientific woman, I'd surely be able to interpret them, and that was the favour he had to ask: to decode the diagrams into simple language that he could understand and then recode into literary language. Euclid's suspicions had been right: the author had no idea what the designs represented; he only understood their significance. I agreed to undertake that task, although I had to stress that electrical circuitry wasn't my speciality and, as I hadn't seen the document,

I didn't know what they might contain. He shouldn't get his hopes up. Leonardo smiled, said I had all the signs of being a Grade A student, and he was sure those designs wouldn't present any problems for me. Leonardo certainly knew how to praise intelligence. And I liked that. Not that I needed praise to feel good about myself. No. It was merely part of a game that he played well. We were quits, that's all.

Accompanied by the chill of the rainy night and the warmth of the lemongrass tea, the author continued the story of Meucci's life. We'd got as far as the closure of the Telettrofono Company, right? Well, in the following years, our tireless inventor continued to address a variety of problems. During his months of convalescence following the ferry accident, he'd faithfully stuck to the diet ordered by the doctors, which included a great deal of fruit and plenty of liquids. And since he had an inherently restless mind, he began experimenting on a fruit-based fizzy drink, which he eventually patented. There was also a 'sauce for food', domestic utensils like coffee and tea filters and even an instrument for testing the purity of milk. In addition, he began to analyse the possibility of creating a special steam-powered boat for navigating canals, and designed a prototype telephone with a waterproof capsule that could be used underwater for communication between divers and a ship. What a genius that man was!

In terms of his pet project, 1876 must have been a tough year, because various factors came into play. Four years earlier, Meucci had shown his telephone design to a certain Edward B. Grant, vice-president of the American District Telegraph Company of New York, in the hope of persuading him to test the prototype on the company's lines. Mr Grant promised to help him but, after two years of excuses, he eventually confessed that all the papers

Meucci had handed over to him had gone missing, so that there would be no tests. Leo didn't want to make rash judgements, but in Mr Grant's supposed loss of the documentation there was a small, dark cloud that floated back into the picture years afterwards. We'll get to that later, he promised. Antonio had also been turned down by Western Union Telegraph, whose directors were all so busy that they couldn't find time to witness the demonstration of his 'speaking telegraph'. The last straw was that the provisional patent, or caveat, for the telephone that he'd obtained in 1871 had to be renewed annually, and in 1874 he didn't have the funds for that, so the caveat expired. It was only a question of ten dollars, but that was ten dollars more than he possessed.

And that was how matters stood when, one fine day in 1876, Antonio woke to the news that someone had succeeded in patenting the telephone. The situation was strange because on the same day (February 14th), two different requests for the patent of the invention were submitted in separate patent offices. One of the applicants was Alexander Graham Bell, a Scot, and the other, a few hours later, was an American called Elisha Gray. This forced the patent office to study both applications until it was decided to award the patent to Bell. As you might expect, Gray wasn't happy about this and filed a lawsuit that ended in confirmation of Bell's precedence, thus making him the official inventor of the telephone.

Poor Antonio. As soon as he heard the news, he set about regaining authorship of the invention. Since he could no longer base his claim on the provisional patent, which of course had expired by then, he was forced to plead that his invention had been in the public domain. That was when his torments really began: the race to achieve recognition and, I imagine, the despair of knowing that he'd got there long before the others and with a more advanced product. Poor Antonio. I was the last person to join the hunt for his document, and there I was in mid-torment, trying to do something – maybe to rearrange the variables one more time, clear away a few unknowns – already fairly desperate, although, unlike Antonio, as yet with no success.

16

Just as we'd suspected, Barbara had told Ángel about my visit. So the day after my adventure with the author, I found him waiting for me outside the Tech. I was dead beat, but I swear that seeing Ángel was like the sun coming out... I don't know, as if the colours had returned to the black and white city. And what's more, I remember that he was looking lovely: he was wearing sandals, jeans and a white shirt with the top buttons undone, leaving a view of his scant chest hair crowned by the choker he often wore.

The moment he spotted me, he began to walk in my direction. If I hadn't slept with Leonardo, I think I'd have burst into tears there and then; you have to believe me, I can be quite the drama queen. Thankfully, my literary escapade gave me strength, so I stopped, took a deep breath and waited for him to reach me. He said hello, and I helloed him back, feeling the full heat of his gaze on mine. He commented that he'd come to meet me the day before, but I hadn't been at work. I nodded. Then he added that we had to talk and, you know, at that moment I had a very strange feeling. The words 'We have to talk' have always terrified me; they sound like 'I don't know how to tell you' or 'maybe you should sit down first'. They are words that nearly always precede bad news, break-ups, employment contracts ending; in short, problems, and in that nanosecond before I replied, my body went into petrified mode. In all my conversations with Leonardo, we'd taken it for granted that Ángel had feelings for me, yet in that short time the possibility passed through my mind that he'd decided to break things off in order to dedicate himself to that Italian woman. It was like the pavement under my feet turned to jelly. You can't imagine how bad I felt, and the only response that came into my head was: Let's go to the park. I needed to be in a public place, a neutral territory where the presence of others would force me not to create a scene. Believe me, I really can be a drama queen. Moreover, I needed Ángel to be outside his home turf so that he wouldn't feel too comfortable. Plus I didn't want to go to his apartment because I could still picture Barbara moving around there like she owned the place. In addition to being a bitch, she had a lot of nerve.

Ángel said that we could talk wherever I wanted, and we set off without exchanging another word. He looked pretty edgy and glanced at me from time to time, like someone waiting for a word from me to start the conversation, but I couldn't give that word; it was up to him. In the park, out of sheer spite, I chose a bench right opposite the artisan's building, where the infamous party had been held. I asked him if the place was all right, and he said it was my decision. So we sat down next to each other, me looking straight ahead, again feeling the heat of his gaze. I was frozen with fear until my angel said that he loved me; that's right, he said that he loved me very deeply, like he hadn't loved anyone for a long time, and that I was right to be angry with him, but he could explain, and I had to understand because, Julia, I really do love you like crazy. I looked at him and couldn't help myself; tears welled up in my eyes, more or less the way they had welled up in Barbara's when I told her Ángel was in love with someone else. Thank goodness we were in the park, with other people around; that prevented me from making a fool of myself. I sighed and gazed straight ahead again. Ángel also heaved a sigh and said it must be hard for me to believe him after finding Barbara in his apartment. Just the sound of her name was like a knife turning in my guts. I closed my eyes but was unable to stop a tear trickling disobediently down my cheek. He kneeled at my feet, asking forgiveness, he'd been going to tell me everything, lord only knows what she'd said, but I had to listen to him because things weren't as simple as they seemed. You lied, Ángel. You lied to me... I hissed, with a fury that had its source in the same place I'd felt the knife turning. Then I opened my eyes and saw the look of desperation on his face, his eyes as damp as mine. In a barely audible voice, he begged me to listen. Ángel was in a park, on his knees at the feet of a woman, close to tears. Can you visualise it? He apparently wasn't worried what anyone else thought, but it occurred to me that if any of my students happened to pass, I wouldn't want them to witness the scene. Best to keep calm, I said, so I could hear him out. He nodded, sat down on the bench and began.

After their first meeting, Barbara had started calling him all the time. She phoned to say hello, to ask silly questions, and had even invited him to that *tertulia* at the author's place. He hadn't intended to go; however, when he heard that the author had invited me, he decided that his presence was required but, much to his disappointment, I'd spent the night playing dominoes while he had to put up with Barbara droning on. Poor him. Right? It felt like I was pushing him into her arms. That was when it had occurred to him that he could earn a little money by renting her a room, but when he'd proposed it, she'd turned him down. And I knew how short of money he and his sister were. I'd have preferred not to have to interrupt him, but Leo's *tertulia* had happened after May Day, so I reminded him that he'd already had a date with Barbara by then. He didn't seem surprised by my remark, it was as if he'd seen it coming and had an answer ready to hand, or as if he wasn't trying to predict anything and was just telling the truth. He agreed that he'd gone to the parade with her on May 1st. What happened was that, as I knew, Dayani had been staying with him that week, having her crisis, and he'd decided to take her back to discuss things with their father. The trouble was that their dad never got home until late in the evening. Dayani had spent the whole day in her room and, despite Ángel's insistence, wouldn't even come out for lunch. When his tolerance was wearing thin, Barbara called to say she'd never seen a May Day parade and really wanted to go. Would he accompany her? If he wanted, they could have a beer together afterwards. Since he was expecting a fairly unpleasant evening thanks to his sister's messed-up life, a refreshing beer didn't seem so bad an idea, even if it did mean joining the parade in the heat of the day, and, to make matters worse, having to act as a tourist guide. He said he didn't know why he hadn't told me about it before, he'd been so immersed in his own family problems that it had initially slipped his mind and then there was no point: it was a trivial detail. He'd just forgotten, that was all, because he wasn't the least interested in Barbara. There were other reasons, he said, for what happened later.

Ángel had already decided to take Dayani to Cienfuegos, and when he mentioned this to his father, he offered to arrange the journey. As you know, travelling around here has always been a little complicated, you have to queue for days to buy tickets, but in 1993 going anywhere was like journeying to the centre of the earth or undertaking an odyssey. A horror story. What people usually did was to go to the highway and wait for a truck to take you somewhere. Like I used to do to get home to Alamar; only Cienfuegos was just over two hundred kilometres away. With his father's help, Ángel would be able to avoid those inconveniences. But he wasn't keen on letting Daddy solve all his problems; he wanted to play the older brother to Dayani, give her confidence and show her that they could make lives for themselves without anyone's help. Do you see? That's why he decided to find another way to take his sister to Cienfuegos, even if he had to carry her on his back. He'd been thinking about how to achieve that aim when the telephone rang: it was Barbara again. Ángel was clearly at the end of his tether with all the complications of the trip and when he told her about it she, kind soul, suggested the following: as she hadn't been to Cienfuegos yet, and since foreigners could hire cars – something that was in those days prohibited to the indigenous population of this land – she'd take care of the rental and drive Ángel and Dayani there if he'd show her around the city in exchange. What you might call the perfect solution. Ángel accepted the offer without hesitation. But he made one mistake, he said. He knew now that he should have told me it was Barbara who had taken them, but at the time it had suddenly occurred to him that I might not have liked the idea. He couldn't quite say why, but he'd had a kind of premonition. I made no response because he was right: Barbara's presence would have seemed odd to me, although I couldn't quite explain why either.

So he made it to Cienfuegos. The visit had been, in many senses, very difficult. His paternal grandmother had always had a soft spot for Dayani, and while he was used to that, going back to her house was like returning to his childhood in a family where he wasn't really wanted, a situation that made him remember his other grand-mother, who had been an emotional support for him. And then there were the conversations with Dayani that turned his stomach because, in his attempts to help his sister recover her strength, he discovered that he was feeling increasingly fragile, that his life had no meaning, Cuba was a disaster, he had nothing and wasn't even capable of taking his sister on a trip without help.

Ángel spoke with deep sadness, and I can tell you that I really wanted to hug him, right there, in front of everyone, but that wasn't possible. I had to go on listening because we still hadn't got to the crux of the matter. Ángel was feeling bad about it all, and that was when he found out what Barbara was really interested in and so understood her behaviour. The thing was that, as promised, he'd taken her for a walk through the city and they had chatted about this and that until Barbara said she'd been wanting to tell him something for a while but hadn't had the courage, and given that they were kind of friendly by then, she thought the time had come to speak. So she explained that she was very interested in Meucci; she knew of the existence of a document related to his experiments, written by the inventor here in Havana, and was ready to pay for it. What's more, she knew that Ángel had something to do with that document. He was dumbstruck, he said, because that Italian woman was referring to Margarita's legacy. Do you see, Julia? he asked in astonishment. And I replicated his surprise. Naturally, he quickly realised that her information must have come from her friend Leonardo. Who else could it have been? And maybe it was Leonardo himself who had set her on his trail, since the writer believed that he had the blessed scrap of paper and had asked him for it hundreds of times for his pathetic novel.

At first Ángel had been very annoyed because, as he told me, no one had a right to touch anything belonging to Margarita, much less an Italian woman who'd turned up out of the blue, but then, alone that night in the silence of his grandmother's patio, he'd begun to think that the whole situation – every single part of it – was a huge heap of shit. Euclid had stolen the document from his daughter, Leonardo was trying to use it to write a novel, Barbara intended to buy it, while he wanted to send it to Margarita. And why the hell do I have to send anything to Margarita? he'd asked himself. No reason at all, he'd answered. Absolutely no reason, he repeated. So that night, sitting in the patio, he'd come to the conclusion that if Barbara wanted the document to give to that writer or whatever, he couldn't care less. Margarita could go to hell, we could recover the document and sell it to Barbara. Life is short and things are tough.

We. Ángel said 'we', but then I had to interrupt again, because we is plural and, in that case, included me; except that I hadn't been informed of his plans. As far as I was concerned, it was still the romantic story of returning the legacy, the letter sent to Brazil with the word 'goodbye', and that whole rigmarole. Ángel smiled and, ducking his head, said that I was right, he hadn't told me anything, but this time it wasn't a matter of forgetting or a presentiment, but his own decision. He hadn't wanted to tell me anything because he was trying to repair the damage, which luckily hadn't got as far as damage, but even so he believed that it had to be repaired. Because there's something else you need to know, Julia. A shiver ran down my spine.

When Ángel went to São Paulo, his idea had been to win Margarita back and stay there with her. But, as you already know, she had other plans. Margarita was very upset about some of the things that had happened, silly couple stuff, according to him, and that led to another argument during which the subject of the legacy arose. Logically, Ángel knew about the legacy, but he hadn't realised how valuable the document was until he read an article in *Granma* about Meucci's invention. He remembered his wife's manuscript and had the brilliant idea of suggesting that they sell it. Of the whole legacy, that piece of paper was the only thing that wasn't really part of the family history. Why not make some money from it? Margarita had taken his suggestion as an insult and from then on constantly accused him of wanting to sell her legacy. That was why, when the topic came up in São Paulo, she repeated her accusation and told him that her father, a man who was just as contemptible and selfish as Ángel, had stolen the legacy. Then Ángel, who was more concerned with demonstrating that he wasn't some form of monster than with the few pesos they could make from the document, said that he'd get the legacy back and send it to her. Naturally, Margarita hadn't believed him, but he returned to Havana with that aim in mind. Of course, once he was here, he had no way of getting to Euclid, since they scarcely knew each other, so time went by and one day... One fine day he met me by chance and then saw me again in the street with Euclid, and it occurred to him that I might be the connection he needed. That's why he'd come to see me at the Tech that first time, why it had all started. And that's why I also felt pretty confused at that moment; grey, uneasy, back in black and white, back in a movie, with the plot changing before my eyes, and once again with the urge to wring his neck, although I didn't actually do it. I closed my eyes without turning to look at him and sensed his breathing and his faltering voice saying it was thanks to that initial impulse of his that we'd come to know each other. But later, everything was completely different because, without quite realising it, I went from being the connection he needed to achieve his aim to the aim itself. He loved me and was feeling ashamed that his first contact with me had been out of self-interest. The damage, even if it hadn't really caused any harm in the long run, had to be repaired, and that was why he hadn't told me about his relationship with Margarita and sell the document to Barbara. Deep down, he added, it pained him that his relationship to Margarita hadn't ended as he'd have liked, with the return of the legacy to its owner and the closing of a cycle. It pained him that she'd had to leave the country because of the economic catastrophe, it pained him that his mother had left because she found the political situation asphyxi-ating, it pained him that his sister now wanted to leave too, it pained him that a piece of paper which had been carefully preserved for so many years would go from having sentimental to financial value; but that's how it had to be, because we were in the Havana of 1993 and he needed to turn his life around, he needed to be able to offer me something, because he didn't want to lose me. You're not going anywhere, Julia, he said, looking at me, his eyes again shining with tears. I swallowed, attempted to speak, but he asked me to let him finish. That night in his grandmother's patio, he'd decided that with my help he could recover the document, sell it to Barbara, give part of the money to Dayani, and then the rest would be for us; I'd move in with him – if that's what I wanted, of course – and he'd hang on to the idea that the legacy had actually been returned to Margarita. That was the plan. But then came the major error.

When he told Barbara he was willing to get hold of the document and sell it to her, she was so pleased that she proposed sealing the pact with a celebration.

There was rum, a lot of rum, an awful lot of rum, way too much rum, and they ended up in bed. That was an error, he repeated, because from then on things moved into another dimension. Barbara wasn't only interested in the document and he was afraid that an abrupt brush-off on his part might make her change her mind about the future purchase. It was an error, he knew, but he had no idea how to get out of the mess, only the sale of the document could resolve the conflict of interests. Only that wretched scrap of paper could get his life back on track, because he loved me, he swore on all he held dear that he loved me heart and soul, he didn't know what Barbara had told me, but I had to believe him, not her. I'm telling you the truth, Julia. If someone's lying, it's the others: that Italian woman, the government, they're all lying, he said with a feverish look in his eyes, his hand on my arm.

Can you imagine how I felt? In the course of a few moments, Ángel had told me that he'd used me to get to Euclid, that he wanted me to move in with him and, what's more, that he'd slept with that Barbara woman because he had no idea how to avoid it. Do you see? I didn't know whether to shower him with kisses or beat him to a pulp. Ángel always disconcerted me. Right from the start, he always managed to disconcert me. I often asked myself whether my obsession with him was real or I was falling into the trap of this country, the trap of the single man, the apartment in El Vedado, my frustrations, of searching for something I could hold on to. No. In the end the answer was always no, because my feelings for him bore no resemblance to anything I'd ever experienced. How can I put it? There are people who have a strange effect on others at deep, natural, instinctive levels. It sometimes happened when I was watching him talk, and would hardly be able to follow his words: I wasn't listening, I was simply looking at him, watching the movement of his lips, his facial expressions, his hair, the look in his eyes, and then I'd discover that I hadn't the least idea of what he was talking about, and it wasn't that I had no interest in his words; it was just that looking at him was like escaping to somewhere else, as if the sound had suddenly been cut in a film and you sit there watching the lead character's lips moving, as if everyone had disappeared from the cinema and you and the hero were alone, with you looking at him. Moreover, Ángel had that damn habit of touching me, simply putting his hand on my shoulder, my arm, my forearm or my hand, like someone trying to stress what he's saying, but my whole body would start to vibrate; it was a chain reaction originating in the patch of skin he was touching that spread through the rest of my body, and I'd even begin to sweat, feel my heart beating fast, my skin would rise in goose pimples and shivers would course through my body, plus dampness, I also felt dampness, something I couldn't quite define, but at the mere touch of his skin my flesh triggered a furious, animal revolution. It was as though his body were emitting a wave on a frequency in tune with mine. Do you see what I mean? When the resonance frequencies of a system match, it can cause destruction, and that's how I felt when I was with him: overwhelmed, smashed to pieces.

And that's exactly how I was feeling when he finished his speech that afternoon. I know I sighed deeply and avoided looking at him: anything might happen if I did. All the strength I thought I possessed due to my horizontal encounter with Leo had either melted or was racing away through the park, far from me. I remember that I heaved another sigh, this time to stop another disobedient tear trickling from my eyes. Ángel was looking at me, waiting for some reaction, a word, a slap, an embrace, a yell, something to show that I was still alive, but I was too confused to speak coherently. Albert Einstein is credited with saying something I really like: 'If you want different results, don't repeat the same things'. In my case, that would mean the two of us trying to reason things out together, asking questions, understanding, but none of that made sense then. I sighed a third time and got to my feet, saying the best thing would be to meet up some other time, he was not to worry, but I needed to walk for a while. I'd call him later, of course I would, but first I needed some air. I needed to be alone. Ángel rose and stood before me. I saw his face. His eyes were still shining and his expression was downcast. I love you, Julia, he repeated. I love you too, I said as I walked away from him.

17

I know very little about classical music; there are melodies that sound familiar, but I don't know where they come from. I can only identify the most popular ones, Beethoven's Fifth, things like that. Yet there's one that I'm never going to forget because it's linked to my childhood, and to the childhoods of so many other people on the island: Rachmaninov's Piano Concerto No. 2, which was the background music of one of the Russian cartoons we used to watch when we were young, the story of the greedy piggybank that bursts from trying to swallow a coin bigger than itself, while the cartoon characters gaze at a rainbow with Rachmaninov's piano in the background. It's a really lovely concerto. Do you know it? That was what CMBF was playing when I arrived, downhearted, at Euclid's apartment the day after my conversation with Ángel.

Euclid was in his room, repairing a fan with the radio on, and as soon as he saw my face he wanted to know what had happened, but I wasn't in any mood to talk. The truth is that I was feeling too dispirited and the music seemed so marvellous that I said I'd prefer to lie down for a while. I was tired. He thought that odd, but nodded, so

I stretched out on his bed with my eyes closed to listen to Rachmaninov.

Ángel had, quite literally, done for me. I'd had a plan, a project, but Barbara's appearance in the plot had triggered a series of minor repercussions that, in a matter of hours, had turned my world upside down. I'm aware that mixing emotions and concrete objectives can lead straight to chaos, but I'm also aware that sometimes it's inevitable. What was I going to do? I had a whole heap of cards on the table that had to be organised, but some of the elements were contradictory. In fact, many of them were. By that time I'd obtained information from Euclid, Leonardo and Ángel. They all coincided in the story of the legacy; the problem lay in which of them had the document. The author had managed to convince me that it wasn't Euclid, but after discovering that Ángel's initial approach to me had been motivated by his desire to gain access to my friend, I was back where I'd started: not understanding anything. If Ángel had the document, if he did in fact love me, if, as he said, his relationship with Barbara was based on his intention to sell her the document, then why insist that Euclid had it? I already knew the worst: he'd slept with that Italian woman. So what was the point of keeping up the farce? What did it achieve?

Everything was a mess of random and premeditated events. My meeting with Euclid and Ángel in the street, Ángel's desire to get to know me better, Barbara's appearance, Leonardo's invitation to his party. By that point I was incapable of identifying which had happened by chance and which were planned. What's more, there was one point that greatly worried me in the three men's confessions: Margarita, who was like a hand moving things around beneath the Ouija board. According to Euclid, she'd said that Leonardo had the document; according to Leo, Ángel had it; and according to Ángel, it was in Euclid's possession. A perfect closed circle. In the case that they were all telling the truth, Margarita – despite being physically distant, thousands of kilometres away – was the demiurge who had constructed the labyrinth in which we found ourselves. I could no longer find reasonable explanations for anything, and you know how mortifying that is for me. Losing the thread drives me crazy because I know there's a logic behind everything, even if I don't know what it is. There's always a theory to explain things, even those that are unpredictable.

In the view of determinists, everything in the universe is governed by natural laws and a chain of cause and effect. Everything, including human thought and actions. Therefore, chance doesn't exist. This implies that, being aware of situation A, and given the laws that govern the process that leads from A to B, then situation B is predictable. If we can't predict something, it is simply because we don't know the laws governing the process. It's ignorance, not chance, that makes certain situations unpredictable. That's what determinists say.

From the viewpoint of chaos theory, however, the universe is governed by a mixture of order and disorder; in other words, it doesn't always follow a determined, predictable model. Some systems, like the orbit of the Earth around the Sun, display fairly predictable behaviour, and so are termed 'stable'. But these are in the minority because, in fact, there are a whole host of unstable systems in the natural world whose behaviour can be chaotic, which often means that they begin to manifest disorder for no known cause. Take the weather, for instance; it's practically impossible to accurately predict it over a matter of days. These completely unpredictable instabilities aren't determined by knowledge of the laws that originate them, it isn't the observer's ignorance that prompts us to call what we don't under-stand 'disorder'; disorder exists and manifests itself in this way, without further ado, when we're least expecting it. Why? Well, because it depends on a great many uncertain circumstances that determine whether a small variation at any point on the planet generates substantial effects on the opposite side of the world. That's what is called 'the butterfly effect'; the fluttering of a butterfly's wings in some distant place is later capable of producing a hurricane somewhere else.

Something like that was at play here: Margarita was the butterfly who had fluttered her wings years before to produce the hurricane we were experiencing. Margaritatheseaisbeautifulandthewind, Margaritabutterfly, Margaritapieceofshit.

Why fall prey to the Margarita effect? It was suddenly as if my thinking had blossomed. Like I said, there's always a theory to explain things, even unpredictable things, and I swear, it's not that I need two and two to make four. For heaven's sake, there's nothing more inexact than the exact sciences, you can take it from me. Bertrand Russell defined mathematics as 'the subject in which we never know what we are talking about, nor whether what we are saying is true', so figure it out for yourself. I don't need — and I didn't need then — the accounts to be completely clear, it was simply a matter of not losing the thread, of finding a system that would in some way allow me to explain what was happening. Chaos theory was also perfect for that because, in addition — as I realised that afternoon — it was the only one capable of interpreting what was going on around us. Why Ángel had slept with Barbara, why I'd slept with Leonardo, why Euclid was lying, why Dayani wanted to leave the country, why I had to sleep in the living room, why Margarita was toying with us remotely and why we were all collectively obsessed by Meucci. All those situations were nothing more than manifestations of chaos. Margarita was just one more butterfly who had fluttered her tiny wings, another disorder in a system that was already behaving chaotically. Because it was the whole country that was going through a chaotic moment. A butterfly had fluttered its wings on the other side of the Atlantic, bringing down a wall in the beautiful city of Berlin, and the effect of this gradually materialised on this side of the world, on this island, in this unstable system. Do you get it?

I'll try to explain it more clearly. According to chaos theory, the universe is governed by cycles, with an orderly one being followed by a disorderly one, and so on. For change to occur, a certain amount of instability is necessary, so it's in the disordered or chaotic periods that alterations in the system take place. Are you following me? Now, chaos tends to be progressive, by which I mean it gradually increases. Sometimes small events occur that have no apparent meaning – we hardly notice them – and yet later on their effect continues to expand and become more visible. This type of evolving chaotic system is increasingly susceptible to the influence of the surrounding environment, which means anything that happens outside the system is capable of influencing its behaviour. The fact that the Berlin Wall fell and Cuba went into a state of crisis shows that Cuba was an unstable country, which isn't at all difficult to demonstrate in the light of our economic development.

So far, what we have is that, on the one hand, the chaos is progressive, and on the other, external influences accentuate it. Then, of course, comes the culminating moment when the glass is full and we reach what is known as the point of bifurcation. Boom, bang, whoooosh, whaaaaam. That's where the system, whatever its name, has to change, eee-volve. After that point there are two possible consequences. One: return to the point of equilibrium that preceded the mess, attenuating or correcting the changes produced en route. Two: allow oneself to be carried along by the chaos until it begins to self-regulate and change the situation, building a new structure, an evolution, which, if I may say so, doesn't necessarily mean reaching a more favourable state; it's merely that the system, whatever its name, reconfigures into a new structure that is different to the previous one. Do you get it?

Taking everything into consideration, I came to the conclusion that, in its recent history, Cuba had passed through two points of bifurcation. The first was in 1959, when the chaos into which the country had sunk sparked the revolution that overthrew the ruling regime. Gradually, over two decades, through readjustments, purges, laws and alterations of social consciousness, a new system was established and, with it, a new society with totally different values to the previous one. That was the society I grew up in. The second point of bifurcation was in 1989, with the beginning of the end of the socialist system, and that again changed our society. The government made an attempt to return the country to its pre-'89 equilibrium, but it was impossible. A butterfly had fluttered its wings in Berlin and the ensuing hurricane was inevitable. The chaos continued to progress slowly, enveloping us, changing our values, unsettling points of equilibrium. How can I explain it? In 1987, an egg was the most common thing in the world, but in 1993 we were only allowed four eggs a month. If before '89 it was a source of pride and a point in your favour to be a lawyer or engineer, after '93, that changed to being an assistant in a dollar shop or petrol station. And if before '89 Euclid had got into trouble with his wife for taking me out to Las Cañitas in the Hotel Habana Libre, in '93 nothing would have gone wrong because Euclid, I and every other person born on this noble island was prohibited from setting foot in the hotels. Do you see what I'm getting at? The point of bifurcation in 1989 produced a new society with new values that had nothing to do with the ones we knew. The construction of that society began in the nineties, and the work is still in progress. Fortunately, in some areas, chaos has given rise to a form of order: nowadays we can enter hotels and we eat better than we did in the early nineties. But in terms of everything else, we continue to float in a sort of limbo, a never-ending state of transition. The only thing that's clear, at least to me, is that we changed our values and other values came into force. Remember that cartoon I used to watch as a child? The story of the greedy piggybank that burst when it tried to eat a coin bigger than itself, while the other characters gaze at the rainbow, and Rachmaninov's piano concerto is playing in the background. Well, if that story were being told now, the piggybank would have worked out a way to swallow the coin, and the other characters would ignore the rainbow and try to sell someone the piano belonging to Rachmaninov, who, naturally, would have left the country years before. It's that simple: new society, new values. What do you think?

Don't get the idea that coming to those conclusions helped me to solve anything; it just relieved my confusion, because everything, absolutely everything, took on a coherence I'd been unable to see before. If you think about it, the obsession with Meucci also started in '89, on the hundredth anniversary of his death, when *Granma* published the article Euclid had first spoken of and now Ángel had mentioned too. I hadn't even felt the need to ask Leonardo about it because, given the amount of documentation he'd amassed, there was no way he could have missed it. He later confirmed this assumption, and I learned that it was also the *Granma* article that had prompted Margarita to mention Meucci's manuscript to him. In other words, at the point of bifurcation in 1989, Leonardo set out to write a novel about Meucci's life with the silly illusion that the addition of his friend's original document would make it a masterpiece. As for Ángel, imagining the future financial benefits, he got the idea of suggesting to his wife that they should sell the document. In the meantime, Euclid, who already had an eye on his daughter's inheritance, began to worry that the document might attract the attention of others. That situation was the start of an evolutionary process that led to the point at which we found ourselves.

That evening, I didn't even notice when Rachmaninov stopped playing, but I do know that at some moment I opened my eyes and discovered that I was alone in the silent room. I'd evidently dozed off, which was no surprise, as I'd spent the night before pacing back and forth in the living room of our apartment – I'm incapable of sleep when I'm fretting about something – and between the piano and my thoughts I hadn't been aware of Euclid leaving the room. I remember that I sat up on the bed and looked around me. I didn't know how long I'd been asleep, but my friend had gone out, and I was alone. Days before, when I still believed he had the legacy, this would have been a golden opportunity, but now the idea made me laugh. Why would Euclid have it? Well, if my poor tutor had been capable of publishing my damned thesis just to gain a little weight, what wouldn't he have done to get his hands on that blessed original document about the invention of the telephone? He'd already have been famous. Right? We'd have been calling him sir.

What the hell! My former tutor definitely didn't have it. Ángel's version was looking increasingly thin, it was as if a flower were wilting and each fallen petal became a vote against him. I'd never before seen matter being so effectively transformed. Ángel didn't care about Meucci, so the manuscript in itself had little value for him. His final objective wasn't possession of the document; that was just a step along the road to obtaining something he needed more. The fallen petals of his version were becoming votes against him because they gradually revealed the veracity of what Leo had said: Ángel had the document. It was highly probable that he'd kept the paper at first, thinking that Margarita would return to claim it, but as that didn't happen, he must have put it back in the place where she'd stored it. He'd become the custodian of Margarita's legacy, just as he was the custodian of the life of the unknown person in the videos. Ángel and his stories. What was indeed clear was that, despite Leo's insistence, he hadn't initially thought of selling it. Ángel himself had commented that, even if he'd had it, he'd never have given it to the author. No, he wanted to preserve the legacy.

I know it might seem a bit silly to you but, even with the knowledge that Ángel had slept with Barbara, I believed what he'd told me in the park, believed that he loved me. I really did. If he didn't love me, things would have been simple for him; he could couple up with Barbara, sell her the document and to fuck with everything else. He had no reason to justify his actions to me. Yet, as Leo pointed out, Ángel didn't want to lose me. Fact. That's why I believed him and also believed the rest: his desire to win Margarita back, the delightful story of returning the legacy so she would think well of him, his love for me and his decision to sell the document when Barbara appeared on the scene wanting to buy it.

I believed it all. I also believed that his reasons for not confessing to possession of the document were to protect himself and gain my admiration; to become my knight in shining armour, as Leo had said.

Shall I tell you what my problem is? Because I have this big problem that, like everything else, depends on how you look at it. There's a line from a sci-fi story I read years ago that goes something like this: When you're on the bank, the boat moves, and when you're in the boat it's the banks that change. Everything is relative, right? Good old Einstein again. My problem is that I have no family traumas. I had a happy childhood, no one abandoned me or stopped loving me, I have a mother, a father, a stepmother and a stepfather, all happily mixed up together. They all love me and love one another. They love my brother and me and they love my stepmother's children. Believe me, it's disgusting. Pure harmony. And what's more, I obviously grew up without any major difficulties because when people love one another, they can put up with all the other stuff: lack of water, power cuts, cockroaches, getting upset for no good reason... What does it matter? When people love one another, things just flow along sweetly. I swear, it's incredible how my parents fucked me up. You might think otherwise, but growing up in that sort of environment causes real problems because it makes you too structured. How can I put it? It makes you very sensitive to the feelings of those around you, but you also have a great sense of justice. Other people's pain wrings my heart. The emotional neglect Ángel experienced in his childhood wrings my heart, because you have to remember that he'd already been abandoned twice and was frightened that his sister would leave the island. So that's also why I believed him and understood why he'd keep all that stuff about the document from me. In fact, the document was his only lie. And then, what did I actually want? To be with him, live with him. And that was what he'd just proposed. What else could I ask for?

Nothing. I wasn't going to ask for anything. I understood my angel and was unwilling to lose him, although understanding didn't necessarily mean forgiving. Understanding: that Italian woman wasn't going to stay in Cuba forever, so I decided to give my angel a break, tell him that I could see what a fix he'd been in, and that I'd stick with him. Forgiving: continuing to carry out Leonardo's plan of steering Barbara in the direction of Euclid and getting the document from Ángel to give to him. That was justice, aren't I right?

Don't look at me like that. Sharing Ángel with Barbara had really pissed me off, but I didn't want to lose him and he had to pay for his lapse. Like I said, I'm both sensitive to the feelings of those around me and have a great sense of justice. You can't hurt people if that's the way you are. I've never been able to do that. For instance, a while ago I told you that I decided to leave the CUJAE when two of my students came into the toilets saying that I was grouchy because I was starved of it. Remember? Those words wounded me to the core. And you think I just sat there and took it? Of course I didn't. There would have been no justice in that. Those two girls didn't pass a single exam in that course. They weren't particularly intelligent, so that helped; let's say they played their part and the rest was due to mathematical inaccuracy. Both of them ended up in the August crammers, poor things, studying while everyone else was on holiday. One of them passed the following year and the other had to drop out of university, but I know they learned a lesson, because I taught it to them. When they came to the department before the crammer, I recommended that they work hard instead of making stupid comments about their teachers' sex lives. Maybe it doesn't seem that way to you, but it's called justice, and the same goes for Ángel. I understood him, but I wasn't going to sit there with my arms folded. I had to do something. We were living in chaos. Right? Barbara was an external element that had affected Ángel's behaviour and I wanted to be the butterfly that would bring about a new hurricane.

When Euclid returned to the room, he was carrying a small lamp and announced that the power had gone off a while before, but that his mother was cooking on the kerosene stove if I wanted to stay for dinner. I accepted the invitation and then he moved closer to ask what was wrong. I remember that his face was illuminated in the semi-darkness and I felt a great warmth for him, but there was justice – a great deal of justice – in the fact that he didn't have the document. Euclid had also lied to me and he had to pay for that. Right? If anyone deserved that piece of paper, it was Leonardo, because his novel would justly restore Meucci's reputation: Margarita and I coincided in that belief. There was no going back by then, the chaos had to continue its evolution. I asked Euclid to show me a picture of his daughter and he gave me a very strange look. It was the first time I'd seen Margarita's face. A princess as fair, as exquisite as you, Margarita.

18

Events began to speed up after that. I think it was the very next day that Leonardo phoned me at work to say he'd spoken to Barbara. As we'd agreed, he'd told her that Ángel didn't have the document and, since stories were his line, claimed that he'd received a call from Margarita in Brazil; the poor woman had been drinking, was feeling homesick, as happens to almost everyone who leaves, and so had picked up the telephone to ring her old friend Leonardo, and during their conversation it emerged that it was her father who had the Meucci document, not Ángel. According to Leo, Barbara had no reason to distrust him; after all, if she'd believed the story about Ángel, why not this one about Euclid? In fact, she swallowed it hook, line and sinker and then expressed her concern that neither she nor Leonardo knew that Margarita woman's father. Then came the masterstroke: Leo told her that I was the person closest to Euclid, so they had to do whatever they could to make use of that connection. Leo went on to say that Barbara had been silent for a few minutes, thinking this over, and he'd thought that she was going to tell him about her relationship with Ángel, but no, she was keeping that secret to herself, and finally said that if this was the case, Ángel was no longer so important and I, Julia, had moved to the top of the list. Touché, Leo yelled so loudly that I was afraid the director would hear him and remove my right to use Meucci's invention. Luckily, she not only didn't hear but, when I'd hung up, surprised me by asking if I'd mind looking after the office for a moment as she had a fitting with a dressmaker who lived nearby. Having time alone with the telephone was exactly what I needed right then, so I gladly agreed to her request.

Leo and I arranged that I would go to his place on Sunday to update our plan. We both felt that it was necessary to act as soon as possible. If Ángel hadn't yet shown Barbara the document, it must be part of an attempt to raise the price; however, each day was one less of her remaining time in Cuba and he was obviously not going to let her get away before the sale went through. So, we needed to get our skates on. I imagined the director of the Tech arriving at the dressmaker's door and dialled Barbara's number.

She was delighted to hear from me. I asked how she was, how things were with Ángel and, although I moved the handset away from my ear because I wasn't interested in her response, I did hear her little voice saying that she was going to do everything she could to win his affection, but she was worried because he'd be at home with his sister that weekend, which meant they wouldn't be able to meet. Do you think he's telling the truth, Julia? I felt the urge to put my hand through one of the tiny holes in the handset as far as the other end of the line, take that hand out and, using my thumb to propel my middle finger, rap her on the nose. Instead, I said that it might be true, that his sister did stay with him at times, so best not to worry too much, and why didn't she tell me how other things – like, for example, her project on

Cuban literature – were going. Naturally, I couldn't care less about her project, but it was a good opening because, after she'd gone on for a while, I proceeded to inform her that I knew a young writer whom she might want to meet: the son of my best friend Euclid. Barbara only hesitated a second before responding: Ah. Then she asked if the young writer had published anything and I replied that I didn't honestly think so, he was still only about twenty. Well, yes, that generation does interest me, she responded with completely believable earnestness, while I smiled to myself because the magic word 'Euclid' had done the trick. I told her that I'd be seeing my friend on Saturday, mentioning his name again, of course, and said that if she wanted, we could meet beforehand and go to his place together; his son visited regularly and sometimes even brought a few other young writers with him. I can tell you, it was as though Barbara saw herself as the Columbus of the nineties literary generation, as if the door to the most select group of the hidden Havana literary world had opened for her. I, however, was aware of her real intentions. And my own, naturally. We arranged to meet at the Coppelia ice cream parlour – I'd be there with Euclid after our study group meeting – and then we'd all go to his apartment. I added that my friend was delightful and she said she was sure he must be.

My director must have still been trying on clothes, so I passed the time cleaning the telephone. It was one of those classic black models that gathered dust under the rotary dial, sounded lovely and were so solid you could crack someone's head open with one. With that thought in mind, I dialled the number I knew best and Ángel answered: Hello. What can I say? Nothing. I'm not going to bore you any further with my ridiculous love and how beautiful it was to hear his voice. I said hi, he called me his darling Julia and told me how much he was longing to see me, but that he couldn't talk for long right then. Dayani was with him. Why didn't I come around after work? I agreed that I would and hung up. I've no idea how well the director's new clothes suited her, but she seemed very pleased with herself when she got back.

Dayani opened the door to me that evening. She looked exactly the same as the first time I'd seen her, dressed in black and with a tragic expression on her face. Although I have to admit that she was quite friendly. She invited me in, announcing that her brother was taking a shower. We sat together on the sofa. When she put her feet up on the coffee table to go on watching a music video, I noticed that, just as on our first meeting, she was wearing military boots. At the opening bars of the next song, she informed me that it was her favourite band, *Extreme*, her favourite song, 'More Than Words' and her favourite man, Nuno Bettencourt. What a pity there are no men like him in Cuba, she sighed: that was why she had to get away from the place. To tell the truth, I had no idea how to respond. And, anyway, she wasn't even looking at me. I moved my eyes to the screen and saw two men with long hair: that Nuno guy was in fact good-looking, and the song was pretty too. I did know men like him, though: Ángel, for instance, with his flowing locks and his angel's smile. It remained to be seen if the two men in the video would be capable of doing what her brother did, but there was no reason to say that to Dayani. She just went on gazing at the screen and singing along quietly. This idyll was interrupted by Ángel's voice saying: Fuck it, Da, get your feet off the table. Dayani sulkily removed the offending items and I stood up so that Ángel could see me. He smiled. I gave a half-smile. Dayani sang along with the men on the screen: I love youuuuuuu.

Ángel told his sister that we were going out and instructed her to unplug the fridge if there was a power cut and take her boots off if she wanted to put her feet up. He wouldn't be gone long. I waved goodbye to Dayani and hurried out. We needed to talk and that was exactly what we did: talk, scarcely even touching, as we walked along. He told me that Dayani was staying for the weekend, that he'd been waiting for me to call and was generally in despair about the whole situation because he loved me and so on and so forth. He said a great many things, but I'd already taken a decision, so at some point I interrupted him, asking when he thought he'd be able to sell the document to Barbara and get her out of the picture. He looked at me in surprise and said that it was up to me; I was the one who had to find the scrap of paper. Yes, but when is Barbara leaving? I asked. And he replied that he wasn't exactly sure, it had to be fairly soon, so the faster we got things done, the sooner we'd be free. I remember that we'd reached Quijote Park, and as the pavement was crowded, as usual, I turned aside to sit on the low wall near the statue. How am I supposed to believe you, Ángel? He took my hands, looked into my eyes and those lips that melted my heart asked: Will you marry me?

You heard me right: he was asking me to marry him. There, in the middle of all those people waiting for the *guagua*, just a step away from the guy selling peanuts and in the shadow of that naive nobleman, Ángel asked if I'd marry him. As I was clearly frozen to the spot, unable to speak a word, he added that it was the only way he could think of to convince me of his love, that his fling with the Italian woman was just a product of the circumstances, an opportunity fate had laid before us, one we ought not to let pass; the blessed scrap of paper could change our lives, change Dayani's too; if we were resolute and acted with intelligence, that moment would be behind us, and then we'd laugh ourselves silly because the two of us would be together. Because I love you, he concluded in a louder voice. I looked around and saw the guy selling peanuts observing us with a foolish grin, he made a gesture like a toast with one of his paper cones, accompanied by the chant of: *getyerpeanutshere*. I turned back to Ángel. We gazed at one another. I thought he looked downright crazy but also wonderfully handsome.

No one had ever proposed to me before, not that it bothered me; the fact is that people don't get married so much here, you pair off with someone and what the hell... It's simpler that way, although tying the knot has the advantage that you're allowed to buy cases of beer at a reasonable price, and in those days that was a luxury; and getting divorced isn't complicated; you go to an office, sign something and then you can marry someone else the next day. It's that easy. But to be honest, hearing the words 'marry me' churned up so many emotions. I don't know... it was as if my romantic spirit had reared its head with a Roberto Carlos song playing in the background. And the weird thing was that I suddenly saw myself wearing a long veil and heard the people at the bus stop cheering, 'Long live the happy couple'; Don Quijote was declaring us 'man and wife' and the guy selling peanuts was throwing his goods into the air. Ángel must definitely have been mad, but I was too. And for that reason I smiled broadly and said: Okay. Okay what? he asked. Okay, let's get married. If he really did want to do it, then it was fine by me. Ángel flung his arms around me, hugging me tightly, whispering in my ear that he loved me and, I swear to you, I experienced a moment of pure, unadulterated joy. It might seem stupid, but my mind went blank. For a second I forgot all my plans for securing the Meucci document from him and his lies about not having it. I forgot Barbara and her intention of seducing Ángel. I forgot Leonardo and his novel. I forgot all that, because nothing else existed besides Ángel and his embrace at the foot of the statue of Don Quijote de la Mancha.

We continued to walk for a while longer, but he had to go back home and take care of his depressive sister. As we wouldn't see each other during the whole weekend, we agreed that I'd call him on Monday, as soon as he'd freed himself from Dayani, and we'd begin to plan our wedding. I arrived home gleefully full of my news. Perhaps it was a bit premature on my part, but to be honest I was bursting with joy and needed to share it. I remember Mum coming out of the kitchen, asking what all the fuss was about, and me, like Jack Lemmon in *Some Like It Hot*, repeating: I'm engaged, I'm engaged, while dancing a tango. My brother and stepfather moved closer together as if impelled by some strange force, and my brother asked to whom, while my stepfather said that whoever he was, he had to meet the family first. For her part, my sister-in-law smiled and commented that I'd kept it very quiet. I went on dancing and informing anyone who'd listen that I was going to marry an angel and live with him in El Vedado. The reaction to this second piece of news was different. Mum was incredulous. My sister-in-law shouted: El Vedado? No way! My brother frowned and said he hoped I wasn't mixed up with some foreigner. My stepfather repeated that I had to introduce them to the man as soon as possible. And I *was* going to introduce him, but in my own time, when it was necessary, not when all I was capable of doing was dancing with a joy so boundless that it was spinning my body around. Why bother with so many words? My happiness had, quite simply, a limit approaching infinity. It was an explosion.

I didn't give any further thought to the problems until the next day, when I'd arranged to meet Barbara:

she was a bone stuck in my throat. I honestly wanted to throw it in her face that Ángel and I were in love, were going to be married and live together, and she had no place in that story, she was an extra piece that needed to be multiplied by zero. I wanted to tell her all that, but it wasn't really appropriate: best to talk it over with Ángel first. On the day of his proposal, we naturally hadn't even mentioned her, but we did need to discuss the situation calmly. My task was to continue to draw her away from Ángel and deposit her into Euclid's arms, far from us, until she left the country. Ángel had the document and would hang onto it, because Barbara wasn't meant to inherit it. No way was that going to happen. So, I decided that I wouldn't tell Euclid about the wedding for the moment to avoid it cropping up in conversation because, given that he knew nothing about Barbara, he might well mention my news in her presence, thus provoking an awkward, inappropriate situation.

As we'd agreed, after the group meeting Euclid and I walked to the ice cream parlour to meet Barbara. On our way, I briefly told him about her: she was an Italian journalist, working on Cuban literature, whom I'd met through Leonardo. The moment I uttered that name, my friend's eyebrows shot up. I attempted to calm him, told him not to worry, said that the world was full of Italian women and authors, what had brought Leo and Barbara together was undoubtedly literature, and that was exactly why we were going to meet her: she wanted to get to know Chichí. Since the crisis had reduced publications to the absolute minimum, it was impossible to discover new writers through their books, so Barbara had set out to meet them in person. She could explain her project better than me, but I thought it would be interesting for Chichí to be in contact with her and... who knows... it might even lead to a publication in Italy. Euclid nodded at that. And in any case, he'd prefer his son to earn money from an honourable profession rather than by selling food on the black market.

Barbara was waiting for us outside Coppelia and – why change the habit of a lifetime? – the moment she spotted us her whole body broke into a smile, she kissed me on both cheeks, pointed a finger at my friend, saying Euclid, and moved closer to kiss his cheeks too. My friend received this welcome with pleasure, and I couldn't help but notice that his eyes rather obviously lingered for a few seconds on her cleavage.

I know I had ulterior motives in bringing about this meeting, but I also know that there are meetings and meetings; for Euclid, that one was like a ray of sunshine entering the boring routine of his life. That's why I'm certain I did the right thing, and that knowledge was a comfort.

Euclid's mum made coffee for us and we sat chatting for a good while, waiting for Chichí's arrival. Barbara explained her project, said she had contacts in a number of publishing houses in Italy that were interested in Cuban literature. European publishers, she added, were well aware that this island had its own cultural life, and they were curious to get to know the post-'59 gener-ations, particularly those who were writing during the difficult period we were going through. And that was why it would be a good moment to open the market to Cuban authors. Euclid evidently wasn't so keen on her way of presenting things, because he commented that there had always been people who saw the suffering of others as a way to line their pockets. But Barbara didn't take the hint and, leaning towards my friend, said it was quid pro quo; the authors she'd spoken to were crazy to get their work published, whatever the country, and she was merely an intermediary, the woman who, on discovering them, could offer that possibility. With a broad smile, she rounded her speech off: I'm Columbus, not the Kingdom of Spain. Euclid returned her smile, I'm not sure if that was because, as she bent over, he had a perfect view of her cleavage or because he was admitting the validity of her point. Whatever, the two of them did a lot of smiling that evening, and when – without Chichí having made an appearance – we decided it was time to leave, Barbara announced that she would call by to visit Euclid another day. Magnificent. The occasion had exceeded all my expectations, everything was moving along at full sail, just like Columbus's ships.

When we'd left, Barbara said that if I had no other plans, she'd like to invite me to dinner in a *paladar*. I accepted: as if I'd do otherwise! I remember thinking that she must have got to know the city well because she took me to a very good place, and after the first beer I almost got a fit of the giggles: imagine, there I was, sitting across a table from the woman who'd been sleeping with the man I loved. Crazy, right? But, well, it was necessary. I was ensuring that Ángel was at home with Dayani, that Barbara wasn't going to turn up there and, to top it all, I was nourishing my body with delicious food.

Our conversation in the *paladar* was like an unexpected gift because, among other things, I learned the date of her departure: a very important piece of information in relation to the plan Leo and I had hatched. Barbara had little time left on the island, and don't get the idea that I wasn't thinking what you're thinking right now. The simplest thing would have been to come to an agreement with Ángel, allow him a few days with her so he could sell her the document, and then afterwards live together on the proceeds of the sale. Aren't I right? That would, perhaps, have been the most logical course of action, but it would have involved breaking my pact with Leonardo, allowing Ángel to go unpunished and, above all, would have been a betrayal of Antonio Meucci. Look, if I broke all those pacts – first with Euclid and then with Ángel – it was because they forced me into it. I'm loyal, but they had lied and so they deserved a dose of their own medicine. Don't you agree? Selling the document to that Italian woman would have been a mistake because it wasn't really the money that mattered to me – even though I did need it – but getting justice for a scientist whom history had forgotten. And the only person who could do that was the author. No one but him could bring that genius to life and ensure that Meucci's discovery wouldn't be lost in the mists of oblivion, certainly not a bunch of opportunistic journalists who'd just squeeze all they could out of the news for a few days until the tide of current events carried Meucci and his manuscript back to where they had lain unacknowledged.

To my surprise, we hardly mentioned Ángel. Maybe the conversation with Euclid had given her food for thought, but what happened was that Barbara took the reins and began talking about Cuba. She told me that what she liked about the country was that things smelled differently: smelled of earth, rain or something she couldn't put her finger on, something that definitely wasn't to be found in Europe. Even the bad smells were unique. I was somewhere between laughing and throwing up, thinking of the open sewers flowing through certain neighbourhoods, the *guaguas* crammed with passengers sweating in the Caribbean heat, our shortage of cleaning products, but Barbara just went on and on about the smells being unique. Armpits, for instance, were pure stink and not a disgusting mix of body odour and perfume; even libido had its own smell, and no one tried to hide it. People here, she said, touch each other, look each other in the eyes, tell you their life stories the first time you meet and aren't ashamed to laugh or cry. All that was getting so much harder in Europe; there were too many artificial smells to hide behind, too many creams and clothes. Too much makeup. How curious that Barbara had too much of exactly what I lacked, but no doubt she lacked the only thing I could have: human warmth. I became aware of that because she went on talking, praising our ability to survive on so little, admiring things I detested, musing on laughter and physical contact until she became slightly maudlin. I placed my hand on hers and asked her not to be so stupid: if she had too much perfume, she could give me a bottle or two, plus a jar of face cream and another beer. Why not? She burst out laughing and to my mind, at that moment, we unconsciously started to become friends. I know you think it's weird, but that's how it was. I still knew very little about her besides the fact that she'd been sleeping with my angel, and what I did know made me want to wring her Italian neck. Yet that night I felt sorry for her; somehow, for a moment, the image she'd initially projected of a strong, decisive woman slipped to reveal a person filled with uncertainties who said that Cuba was turning everything, all her certainties, upside down. This country is turning us all upside down; take my word for it, I told her. And she smiled and said: But there are people who'll never get back on their feet. It wasn't until later that I understood what she meant by that.

19

I went back to Leonardo's on Sunday afternoon. He opened the door with his habitual smile, bent and kissed me on the lips. All I could think to say was: Ángel and I are engaged. He raised his eyebrows. Tell me all, he said. And to my surprise, he kissed me on the lips again before adding: Here's to the happy couple. Leo was incorrigible, but one thing I can tell you is that he had really soft lips. After I'd told him all, he took out a bottle and said we ought to celebrate; but since the alcohol he drank was crap, I decided to wait for a lemongrass tea.

Leo thought it wonderful that Barbara was already in touch with Euclid. That Italian woman certainly knew what she wanted and she wasn't the sort to overthink things, she went straight for her objective, and there was no doubt that she was going to throw herself at my professor friend and forget about my husband-to-be, he said, before we made the toast: I with tea and he with his homebrew. Then he gazed at me seriously over his glasses. Now that everything was sorted for me, he asked, now Ángel wanted to get married and Barbara had met Euclid, did we still have a pact? I grinned, kissed his lips the way he'd done mine on my arrival and said exactly what I've just told you: All I want is justice for Meucci. So our deal was still on, with the only modification that I'd shortly be moving in with Ángel, which would make everything much simpler. Leonardo smiled, pushed his glasses up his nose with one finger and told me that he had fresh news about our friend Meucci.

In the Museo de la Ciudad, Leo had met the young man who had assisted the Italian researcher Basilio Catania during his visit to Cuba and, among other things, he'd photocopied an article by José Martí for him. I have a friend who says that Cubans are a 'martyred race' because, whatever the subject, Martí's written an article about it; joking aside, though, he really did write about everything. In the text Leo showed me, published in 1886, Martí claimed that there were good reasons to believe that Bell's patent had been fraudulently obtained; this being the case, the United States government was under an obligation to investigate the matter.

In 1886, José Martí was thirty-three and Antonio Meucci seventy-eight. They were both living in New York. Leonardo wondered if the young journalist's curiosity had ever taken him to the house on Staten Island to meet the inventor friend of Garibaldi, whom Martí also greatly admired. This possible encounter was a mystery that he hoped to unravel in the future. But in any case, he did know of one slender thread linking Martí and Meucci: Margarita. One of her ancestors had worked in the Teatro Tacón, and that was the same person who ultimately came into possession of his designs. But that gentleman, together with his wife and daughter, had had their first family photograph taken in Esteban Mestre's studio, where the boy Martí later had his portrait taken. Things are often connected in strange ways, aren't they? History with a capital H is always overtaking us, it's always there, brushing up against us, only sometimes we can't see it.

That day, Leonardo and I turned this idea over and over, fascinated to think that our national hero had written about the patent for the telephone. At that point, as you know, we still lacked many details; Leo had only a vague notion of some of the story, so it wasn't easy to get a clear idea of the events and exactly what Martí was referring to. It was Basilio Catana's thorough research in the nineties that brought the mislaid details of the story to light, and that's how we learned more about Meucci's calamitous life, which is close to being a soap opera. I'll make it short.

When Bell was granted the patent in 1876, he decided to set up his own company. He had a major clash with Western Union Telegraph, which owned the greater part of the telegraph network in the United States and had founded a subsidiary to deal with telephony. There was a court case, which Western Union lost, but a compromise was reached in which they agreed to share the market: the telephone went to American Bell Telephone and the telegraph to Western Union. Not so bad, right? Just one thing: there are suspicions that Western Union was already aware of Meucci's work thanks to Mr Grant. Remember him? The guy Antonio had provided with the paperwork for the 'speaking telegraph' years before, and who claimed to have lost it. That's the black cloud that was floating over our man.

In time, complaints began to be made about the poor quality of American Bell's service and other companies, such as Globe Telephone in New York, sprang up in an attempt to market alternative telephone systems.

Meucci knew perfectly well that it would be no easy task to demonstrate that his invention had preceded Bell's. And, in fact, it took him several years to gather the proof of his precedence and borrow money to reconstruct several of the prototype telephones his wife had been forced to sell. He took all that documentation to the firm of Lemmi & Bertolini and signed a power of attorney, designating them as protectors of his rights. Things began to get more heated after Lemmi & Bertolini published a letter in which Meucci announced that he was the one true inventor of the telephone. They received a number of proposals and Meucci finally ceded his rights to Globe Telephone, who appointed him as their technical manager. On the one hand, he was happy because the articles written about him in the press had gained him a certain amount of public attention. On the other, he was in low spirits because just when things were beginning to improve, his wife Ester died.

The chaos reached its bifurcation point in 1885. A number of companies began to make strategic moves to involve the government in their battle against the Bell monopoly. And the Department of the Interior eventually decided to investigate the claims of fraud in relation to the award of the telephone patent and the rumours of Meucci's priority.

The Bell Company clearly wasn't going to take that lying down. It had already begun to prepare for the imminent attack and had even hired a detective agency to gather information on Meucci and Globe Telephone, accusing them of patent infringement. Attack is the best form of defence, right? But as this was going on, the government filed a suit against the Bell, with the aim of annulling its patent. It was around that time when José Martí wrote his article.

Legal processes are inevitably complex affairs and Bell's lawyers were so skilled that they succeeded in delaying the opening of the government case while working simultaneously to strengthen their own. In the latter, the judge refused to admit a large part of the evidence submitted by Meucci and, what's more, the technical testimony was given by a physics professor who was a friend of Bell. So, on July 19th 1887, the judge pronounced against Globe Telephone, stating that Meucci's transmission of the human voice had been produced by mechanical rather than electrical means. The Bell Company had won, the case was closed, a report was published and that is the documentation that went down in history.

But there were two lawsuits. Remember? The government still hadn't managed to open its case. Notwithstanding, Meucci and the Globe were so sure of victory that they didn't appeal against the verdict of the case they had just lost. Major mistake. As Pablo Milanés puts it in his song, 'Time passes and we're getting older.' On October 18th 1889, Antonio Meucci died in Clifton, Staten Island, at the age of eighty-one.

All that remains is the froth.

That same year, the government's case finally came to court. The Bell Company's patent expired in 1893 and they suggested that the case should be closed, but Whitman, the government representative, refused, claiming that a clear verdict was an important point of reference for the country. When Whitman died, the then Attorney General proposed discontinuing the proceedings to avoid further costs, and on November 30th 1893 his recommendation was implemented, leaving neither winners nor losers. And since nobody won and nobody lost, the report and the evidence that would have been presented were never published. Without the relevant paperwork, there's no history. It's shrouded in dust. And for over a century, Meucci was covered in that dust, until a new bifurcation point brought about a change in history.

Whenever I think about all this, it saddens me. And when I think about us, I feel a sort of mix of mirth and tenderness. We had the dumb idea that the document Margarita's family had guarded so carefully would be capable of changing history and making 1993 a bifurcation point in the story of Meucci's life, and in ours. We were deluded.

That night, Leonardo was so excited about Martí's article and his conversation with the guy from the museum that he decided to read me parts of his novel. He put on music and sat on the floor, while I sipped my lemongrass tea on the bed. It's strange the way we have of creating rituals; in his house, I drank lemongrass tea and listened to *trova* musicians: Frank Delgado, Santiago Feliú, Gerardo Alfonso, Carlos Varela and so many others. Believe me, I hadn't intended to stay over, but he started reading and talking and it got very late. I also hadn't intended to repeat our night of sex, but his words spun a web around me and by the time I became aware of what was happening, we were once again tangled up together. I know you must think it odd that a person who's in love and planning to get married would fall into someone else's arms for a second time, and you'd be right because it is odd. And what's more, the following day I'd arranged to see Ángel, and I make it a rule never to go to bed with two men on the same day. Unless it's at the same time, but that's another matter. The thing is that I hadn't planned for the night to end that way. It's infuriating.

I remember that I woke the next morning feeling a little uneasy and I mentioned this to Leo, but he joined his hands before his face and solemnly promised not to touch me again; although, he added, if I got the urge to touch him, I shouldn't repress it. I burst out laughing, and it was probably thanks to his promise that I didn't think about him at all during my working day.

In the afternoon, I went to Ángel's apartment and found him exhausted but incredibly affectionate, as he always was after spending time with Dayani. That weekend she'd turned up bathed in tears. The cause wasn't her father – they scarcely spoke – but a bust-up with her new boyfriend, who, luckily, had then arrived on Sunday to ask forgiveness. Ángel had gone out to give them some time alone and, when he came back, Dayani jubilantly informed him that the boyfriend – the son of diplomats – had promised that, just as soon as his parents had finished their holiday and returned to the country where they were stationed, she could move in with him. As you can imagine, that was wonderful news for Ángel: for as long as Dayani and the boyfriend were together, she'd be living away from her father, and he'd have a breathing space to find the money for a future rental. In addition, the idea of leaving the country was on hold for the moment. I thought it was tremendous that the girl's problems would be solved, and that, thanks to the boyfriend, Ángel would be rid of her for a while. The only difficulty, he said, was that he'd prefer me not to move in with him until Dayani was installed in the boyfriend's house because, given that she didn't want to go back to her father, she'd still be a bind. Which is to say that, in order to live with Ángel, I had to wait for the diplomats to depart and pray that his sister didn't have another row with their son. I was, to be honest, beginning to feel a level of dislike for Dayani, but I said nothing because Ángel embraced me, saying that he was just dying to wake up every day with me beside him. He'd already told Dayani that we were going to be married. What did she say? I asked. Congratulations, he replied with a grin. Dayani had said congratulations, nothing more.

When the 'dear little sister' argument had fizzled out, it was my turn to tell him about the events of the weekend, and I announced that he was going to find it weird, but I'd had dinner with Barbara on Saturday. Ángel did indeed find it weird. I explained her interest in getting to know young writers, which had led us to Euclid's place so she could meet his son. So she met Euclid, said Ángel, and I nodded. There was no point in trying to hide that fact from him: I was afraid that if I didn't tell him, she would. Ángel frowned before responding that, knowing Barbara wanted Meucci's document, I'd taken her to the home of the person who had it. Was I mad, or what? And then he went on about how that scrap of paper could change our lives, but if Barbara discovered that Euclid had it and Euclid found out that she wanted it, then they could pull off the big deal, and we'd be left high and dry because that woman was something else. I was angry. I didn't like his tone and so reacted by saying that she was so something else that he'd been forced to sleep with her. Ángel attempted to soothe me, saying he'd already explained what had happened. I knew why he'd done it, but I was still annoyed and warned him that if we were going to get married, I wanted him to stop seeing Barbara because I found it hurtful. We were sitting on the sofa in the living room and Ángel started stroking my hair, as he always did when he was trying to convince me of something. He said that I was his one and only love, that he perfectly understood my irritation, but Barbara could change our lives and that was why it was important to keep her on our side, and if we didn't succeed in selling her the document before she left the island, he'd have to remain in contact with her so that, just as soon as we got our hands on that paper, our buyer would be there, waiting for it, cash in hand. And we really needed that money, we couldn't pass up the chance. So what he was saying was that they would still be in touch after she left the country. I can tell you, I was so absolutely furious that, from the depths of my soul, came a cry of 'enough is enough', he should tell me the truth. If he wanted to use her as a means of getting out of Cuba, he should say it straight out. Naturally, he denied my allegation, wondered how I'd thought that one up and returned to the document, the sale, our future. The truth is, I'd exploded like a pressure cooker, and I started shouting again, but this time what I said was that I was fed up of lies, that I knew he had the document.

Ángel was suddenly lost for words, he gave me a really weird look, as if I'd spoken to him in a language he didn't understand, and asked me what I was talking about, where that idea had come from. Having calmed down a little, I replied that the document belonged to his wife and was in his apartment. He gave me that same weird look. I was right, he said, it had been there but Euclid had stolen it, and that information had come straight from Margarita. Then he smiled, shook his head and added that if he had the manuscript, he'd already have sold it to Barbara and we'd be feasting on lobster instead of arguing. Just where had I got that story? Leonardo told me.

My reply lit a fuse. Ángel was beginning to get so angry that I could almost see the sparks flying from his eyes. He asked where the hell Leonardo had got that story from and, in a very quiet, calm voice, I told him that Margarita had told Leo. Ángel punched the sofa and stood up, commenting that it was interesting to learn that the writer and I talked about him, Margarita, the legacy and the document.

And just when did my wife tell her dear friend all that? he asked with a grimace before adding that it must have been when they were in bed together, after a fuck, because that sonofabitch Leonardo had slept with Margarita before she left and, as if that wasn't bad enough, was now making stuff up; first he'd set Margarita against him and now he wanted to do the same with me. And you believe him, Julia, you believe him... His eyes were sad, his expression confused, but I was bit confused too. I said that I knew nothing about the thing between Leonardo and Margarita, and Ángel heaved what seemed like a long-suffering sigh. He wasn't surprised that Leonardo hadn't mentioned that detail; he'd also spared me the knowledge, but in his case it was because of the pain it caused him. Right from the start, he said, he'd tried to warn me about Leo. There had always been a degree of rivalry between them, they used to buzz around the same flowers and had both settled on many of them. Ordinary, everyday male competiveness. But it was different with Margarita, because Leo really did like her, so he'd never been able to accept that she married Ángel, and he was always tempting her to see if she'd relent, and finally the imbecile had fallen into his trap and gone to bed with him. Leonardo now realised what he was missing and was coming out with the tale that he, Ángel, had the legacy. What that guy wanted was to set me against him so he could sleep with me, it was part of the old rivalry; he'd already won with Margarita but that wasn't going to happen again. Not with you, Julia. Ángel was silent. He rested an arm on the door to the balcony and stood there with his back to me, looking out.

You've no idea just how shitty I felt at that moment. I'd fallen into the trap too, although, logically, there was no way I could let that show. I took a deep breath, moved across to him and put a hand on the shoulder of my fallen angel, asking him to forgive me. He turned around. As he had no way of sounding the exact depth of my apology, he cupped my face in his hands and repeated that if he'd had the document, the whole business would be over by now, because all he wanted was for us and his sister to be happy. Then he embraced me, saying that he loved me, and I kissed him, murmuring that I adored him, and there we were on the sofa again, making love.

Making love is gorgeous. Particularly when the whole situation is confusing and you really don't want to think about it. That's how I felt; I was confused and had no desire to think, much less about how, that very morning, I'd woken up in Leonardo's bed. No, better not to think, better to allow my body to block out my understanding or even increase it. Who knows? The body is wise. When my body and Ángel's were done, we continued to lie on the sofa, hugging one another, without saying a word. I don't know what was going through his mind, I simply didn't want to think. At least not about what was happening to me. My one wish was to stop Ángel getting the wrong idea, stop him believing that there was something between Leonardo and me that exceeded our own bond, and so repent having opened the door to his innermost feelings to me. And that was why I put my lips to his ear and asked him once more to forgive me, not to believe that I made a habit of talking about Margarita with Leo. Ángel gave a shiver at the sensation of my breath on his ear and suggested that we forget that idiot, but I insisted that Margarita's name had been mentioned in the course of a simple comment about his novel, and that, in fact, all Leonardo ever spoke about was that novel and his travels.

Travels? What travels? he asked. And I, with a sudden sense of reticence, replied that I was talking about his trips abroad. Ángel sat looking at me with a grin on his face before stating that they couldn't be Leonardo's trips because the man had never been outside Cuba. At that moment, the author would have said 'touché', but I made no reply because I was the one who'd been touchéd: twice in one day. So, making a great effort not to look ridiculous, I adopted an absentminded expression and got to my feet, saying oh, of course, he'd been talking about a friend's trips, but I couldn't remember just what his name was: the author was a great talker. Ángel agreed, he did talk a lot, and someone who talks too much ends by talking bullshit. He kissed my forehead and also rose, announcing that he needed a piss. As he walked away, he began to laugh, saying that the furthest Leonardo had ever got was Pinar del Río, and that was when he was serving his time in the Countryside School. And another of the things Leo was never going to forgive Ángel for was having left Cuba on one single occasion. His voice faded as he walked down the hall to the bathroom. He thought that, during the Angolan war, Leo had been called up for military service or something like that, but he'd got sick and hadn't even been able to board the plane. I heard him laugh before shouting: That guy's a real wimp! Then came the distant sound of a stream of urine. Then silence. Then I wished the ground would open up and swallow me. Then silence.

I stayed over that night, although, naturally, I couldn't sleep. After dinner, Ángel had said that we needed to finish our conversation about Barbara. If it hurt me so deeply, he said, there was no problem, he'd just stop seeing her. It was no hardship for him. All he wanted was to sell her the document, but if that was going to make things difficult between us, to hell with it, we'd think up another way of making money. Our relationship was more important than anything else. Can you imagine? The worse I felt, the more divinely he behaved. Unbelievable. I spent the whole evening holding back my tears until we went to bed and, the moment I heard his breathing slow, I carefully sat up. He was sleeping peacefully. Naked. His hair falling onto his face. Like a lovely child. Ángel asleep is one of the most beautiful images I've ever seen. In general, I like contemplating men while they are sleeping, when everything is in repose, they have nothing to prove, are vulnerable, sometimes snoring slightly, at others breathing rhythmically, but always lightly, unworried, as if nothing were happening. I think that there are only two occasions when we humans are completely equal: when we're asleep and when we're dead. Age, language, gender, religion, political beliefs, financial status, none of that matters; in sleep and death, we are equals. A sleeping man, whether he's the president of a country or some poverty-stricken wretch, is simply a sleeping man. Someone who dreams. And does no harm.

I took Ángel's Walkman out onto the balcony, inserted a cassette poor Leo had given me and put on the headphones. I was nude and Havana was empty. I gazed down over my beloved street. Everyone was sleeping: Ángel, Leonardo, the entire city. But I was awake with a Polito Ibáñez song sounding in my ears: *And with apparent love in our eyes / without signals or witnesses / we offered up our bodies until the morning / when we learned of the mistake.* Mistake? What mistake? When did the mistake begin? Who knew about it? In such cases, the best thing to do is to make love, not think, offer up the body, the body, the body, the body, to the point of exhaustion, until you reach your limits, have nothing more to give, and the next day another body, and not thinking, not thinking, not thinking. Finally, rain began to fall. And only Havana and I were aware of that rain, the rest of the world was asleep, and Havana and I started to cry, naked, in the night, where no one could see us.

20

The next day, when Ángel asked me to come back to the apartment after work, I told him that I had to return to Alamar to pick up some papers. Naturally, I couldn't explain that I hadn't been home for two days. Or that I was feeling alone, mired in an enormous mass of confusion and that he couldn't help me. Who had Meucci's document? By that stage, I had no idea, but the worst was that I was beginning to suspect Euclid had been right when he'd said, some time before, that it was Leonardo.

I went through the day on automatic pilot, putting up with my students. There's a mathematical rule: your students' stupidity is directly proportional to your mood; the worse you feel, the denser they become. I called Leonardo a couple of times, but his work number was evidently out of order. Another mathematical rule: your need is inversely proportional to the probability of satisfying it; the more urgently you need to communicate, the fewer telephones are working.

After my classes, I went to Euclid's; I had to talk to him. He was the only one I could have a conversation with and, while logically I wasn't going to go into detail about the reasons for my mood, we could at least discuss other things; things like geometry, fractals, chaos, anything that would in some small way alleviate my despair. But, of course, mathematical rules apply: Euclid wasn't home. His mum said that someone had called to pick him up. Guess who? That Italian woman I'd introduced him to a few days before. His mum was sure they would be back soon. The only reason I didn't burst out laughing was that the old lady wouldn't have understood. Instead, I accepted a cup of coffee and played with Blot while I waited.

How long did I wait? I don't know, everything seemed incredibly absurd that day. When Chichí appeared, telling his grandmother that he'd brought some stories for his father's Italian friend and she told him they'd gone off somewhere together, I really did think I was going to have a giggling fit, but I managed to control myself. Blot was by then drowsing so I switched my attentions to the chatter of the young writer, who was very excited about meeting the future publisher his father had spoken of. He was carrying a folder of stories written by him and all his friends. It was, he said, the opportunity they had all been hoping for, a door opening to the international market. His naivety was heart-warming. He thanked me profusely because he was aware that I was the go-between, and he hoped that I wouldn't be offended if he offered me a carton of eggs as a token of his gratitude. Good intentions, he said, should be rewarded. At that moment, if I'd been able to choose, I'd have liked to be in Blot's skin. No kidding. But I wasn't being asked to choose anything. Blot was sleeping peacefully and I went on feeling like a veritable piece of shit. It was getting late. Chichí had to go to the hospital to see someone or other. He left. Euclid and Barbara were notable by their absence. And then the electricity went off. Euclid's mother began to fret about her son being away from home during a power cut. It got later. I decided to leave. I gave the old lady a kiss and stroked the dog. Definitely a day multiplied by zero, I thought as I waited for a car to take me to Alamar.

I think I must have been very hyper around that time because everything happened so quickly. The following day, I tried to get hold of Leonardo again, but with no success. Fortunately, I did mange to see Euclid, who greeted me with one of his mysterious looks and, after I'd done the usual hello-how-are-you, led me to his room and switched on the radio.

He'd heard from his mother that I'd waited for him the night before. I already knew, also from his mother, that he'd gone somewhere with Barbara. So he told me the rest of the story. He began by commenting on how likeable she was. After her first visit to the house, she'd called him once or twice. They had finally decided to have a beer together and one became two or three. Euclid hadn't drunk beer for a while. He'd almost forgotten what it tasted like, he added with a smile. They were getting along so well that she suggested they have dinner in a *paladar*. It was the first time my friend had been in one and he thought it was great, plus his kindly companion had even ordered a dish to take home to his mum. As Euclid spoke, there was a kind of glint in his eyes. I looked scornfully at him. So you like the likeable little Italian woman, I commented. Grinning, he replied that he was past all that, but what wasn't there to like about her? It was a shame he was an old rooster and, even more, that she was looking for something else.

I'm very worried for you, Julia. Worried for us, he added, his grin vanishing. Barbara had spent a long time talking about her literary project, but that wasn't the only thing that had brought her to Havana. She was also here to find Antonio Meucci's original document, the one written in the Teatro Tacón, which she needed for some research she was doing on the inventor. When he'd heard that, he almost choked on his beer, although he did manage to disguise his consternation. I wasn't drinking anything when Euclid told me this, but if I had been, I'd have choked on it too because Leo was right; Barbara was the sort of person who came straight to the point, she wasn't going to waste her time beating about any bush. Euclid had expressed his interest and willingness to hear more, and I did just the same for him, even though I already knew most of the story. Barbara then told him that she wanted to buy the document, but didn't know who had it. Euclid opened his eyes wide in desperation. Barbara knows Leonardo, he said, and if she finds out that he's in possession of the document, our project will go down the drain, because there's no doubt that he'll sell it to her. We have to save the document, Julia. He was almost shouting.

Suddenly the whole situation seemed unclear once more. Euclid was convinced that Leonardo had the paper because that's what Margarita had told him. Margarita had been angry with both Euclid and Ángel and knew that each of them wanted the document. It was perfectly logical that she would pass it on to her author friend just to give the finger to the others. And then, I was the one who'd told Leonardo that Barbara was sleeping with Ángel. There was a longstanding rivalry between Ángel and Leonardo. So it was perfectly logical that Leo would try to get her away from his rival and me into his bed, just for the sake of it. Thanks to me and my idiotic weakness, Leonardo was succeeding in both objectives: keeping Barbara away from Ángel and sleeping with me. If he really did have the document, he could sell it to the likeable little Italian whenever he pleased; I'd already witnessed him selling an article to that Argentinean woman who wrote for a theatre magazine, which went to show that he was used to doing such things. Moreover, Barbara might be useful in helping him to get out of the country or something like that. What a sonofabitch he was! Everything he'd said about Ángel was perfectly applicable to himself.

That whole line of thought developed very quickly; I was still sitting across from Euclid, who was waiting for me to respond. I finally said that he was right, the situation was dangerous. I wasn't sure how close the friendship between Barbara and Leonardo was, but I did know that she would soon be leaving Cuba, so we had to act immediately. Euclid would take charge of entertaining her, which would be a pleasure for him. I, for my part, would focus on the author. My friend thought it was a good plan and even suggested that he could scatter a few red herrings in Barbara's path. It was all a matter of timing, he said. Once she'd boarded her plane, we could continue with our own project. We shook on it to seal the pact, exchanging victorious smiles. Then Euclid sighed, took my hands in his and, serious once more, said that there was another important issue. Barbara knew the document had originally belonged to the ex-wife of her Cuban boyfriend, and when Euclid had casually enquired who that boyfriend was, she'd described him before mentioning his name: Ángel.

I pushed his hands aside and stood up. As Ángel had said, Barbara was something else. Do you see? She didn't go in for mystery; she was as obvious as her bra size. I was surprised that she'd have told Euclid that and, naturally, annoyed, but before I could find the appropriate words, my friend also got to his feet, saying that it wasn't his intention to hurt my feelings, but he felt I ought to be told. He'd never had much of a chance to get to know

Ángel, but Margarita's mother had informed him of a few things, such as that he was sometimes unfaithful to their daughter, and that those infidelities had finally led to their divorce. Euclid hadn't mentioned it before because, as the song goes, every story is a different story, but when he'd heard Barbara saying that Ángel was her boyfriend, he'd really felt like boxing that guy's ears: for his daughter and for me. You know, his words moved me. They seemed like a huge expression of affection and friendship, because he wanted to protect me. Lovely, right? I'd have been capable of telling him everything, but then I'd have had to tell him absolutely everything, and I wasn't going to do that. There was no way I was going to let Euclid realise that Barbara's presence in his home was planned by the author and me, so I had to give a modified version of the facts. I turned around and announced that I already knew. Yes, Ángel and Barbara had had a fling before we got together, but she still hadn't given up on it and kept ringing him, despite the fact that he wasn't interested. Of course, she didn't know Ángel and I were an item, but the thing is that, on the one hand, he could hardly even bear to talk to her on the phone, and on the other, she was no friend of mine. Our visit to Euclid's home had been for purely professional reasons. Euclid nodded, but without making any comment. I went on to say that I also knew Ángel had two-timed Margarita; he was very sorry for what he'd done but, as Euclid had said, every story is a different story. I kissed my friend's cheek and thanked him for telling me, reassured him that there was no need to worry, that everything was under control. He smiled in relief. You know, I said, Ángel wanted to box your ears too when he saw Margarita crying because you were cheating on her mum, and that ended in divorce as well, right? He burst out laughing and replied that he hoped everything really was under control and that I'd be very happy. That seemed the right moment to tell him about the engagement: there hadn't been time before. Euclid was incredulous, he'd never in his life imagined me married, but he thought it was great news. We agreed that he shouldn't mention it to Barbara, as it was my affair and so up to me to tell her. That evening, Euclid gave me a bear hug, wishing me all the very best and uttered a phrase I loved. It was something like: When the city and everything around you is a shambles, the best course of action is to build something, however small, something that will bring back the taste of the word *future* to your mouth. Beautiful, don't you think?

Speaking of the future, my conversation with Leonardo was still outstanding. His phone continued out of order the next day, but I'd had enough of waiting, my patience had run out, so the minute I finished work I was off like a shot to his place, ready to wait as long as it took to see him. That wait took place outside his garage-den, and it was a miracle that I didn't wear a furrow in the ground from so much pacing back and forth before I spotted his bicycle in the distance and stopped. The author's figure grew larger until he was there before me with a huge smile and sweat running down his face. He started to say what a surprise it was, but I interrupted to tell him that we had to talk. He dismounted, opened the door, wheeled the bike inside; I followed behind like a hyper madwoman and went straight to his desk. Where is it, where have you hidden it? I yelled as I rifled through all his photocopies, typed pages, children's drawings, handwritten notes and bills. Leonardo approached, asking what was going on, and then I informed him that I was looking for the Meucci document, that I'd had enough and he should tell me where he'd put it. He seemed to be astonished by my words, my attitude, but for me it was as if I'd lived that scene before. I mean, they were all astonished all the time. I'd had it up to the back teeth. He began to reorder the papers I was scattering around and asked if I was crazy: Why on earth did I think he had the document? I continued to rummage through the desk until Leo shouted: For fuck's sake! Then I stopped. He took the papers I was holding and re-organised them, asking me not to mix up his son's drawings with his writing. What was bugging me? Then I was doing the shouting: You lied, Leonardo! You lied to me! He had Meucci's document and he was just using me, because it was Barbara he was really interested in, but he couldn't bear the idea of her sleeping with Ángel, and that's why he was using me to lure her away from his rival. Leonardo watched me, his eyebrows rising higher and higher, as I went on to say that there was no point continuing to lie because I knew everything: he'd told me that Ángel had the document to throw me off the scent, to toy with me. Leo suddenly reacted, saying that I was off my head, that if he'd had the document, he'd have finished his novel long ago, that I should calm down and tell him why I'd invented this rigmarole. I haven't invented anything, I countered, and continued with the same arguments. He attempted to defend himself, to deny my accusations, but I was drowning him out because, like I said, I was so hyper that I couldn't stop. And that's why I said: Because you, Leo, slept with Margarita.

Leonardo only hesitated for an instant before commenting that Ángel had apparently been filling my head with a pack of lies. But it was true that he'd slept with Margarita, and so what? He loved her, and he'd loved her before Ángel appeared on the scene with his oh-so-charming smile, and then she went off with him, only to have to tolerate all his two-timing, the same two-timing I'd have to tolerate, because Ángel was a waste of space. So why did you sleep with me? I yelled, pushing him in the chest. His reply was to yell back that he liked me; he wasn't going to marry anyone and was free to sleep with whomever he damn well pleased. The bastard was right, wasn't he? I was the one who'd been messing around where I shouldn't, and that made me so furious that I told him he was a bastard and a liar, and then tears started to well up in my eyes and I went on saying that he'd used me to score a point over his rival, and that he was the one going after Barbara because she was a foreigner, and he had the document because Margarita had given it to him after he'd fucked her, and he was the biggest liar of all and, to top it all, he'd lulled me with all those untrue stories, because he'd never left Cuba, never once travelled anywhere. I can tell you, Leo went crazy when he heard that. He looked at me like a wounded wild beast and screamed: Never travelled anywhere? Never travelled...? Then he took a book down from the shelves and showed it to me, saying: What about this? It was Victor Hugo's *Les Misérables*. And this? Cortázar's *Hopscotch*. And he threw them onto the bed, saying: Paris. He turned back to the bookcase, pulled out two more volumes and flung them onto the bed as well: Are you going to tell me that I've never been to St Petersburg? I only managed to catch a glimpse of the author: Dostoyevsky. Leonardo continued his frenzied throwing of books onto the bed. Thanks to Eduardo Mendoza, he'd visited Barcelona, and he'd been to New York with John Dos Passos and Paul Auster, Buenos Aires with Borges, he knew the whole of the Caribbean through Carpentier and Antonio Benítez Rojo. I don't know how many books ended up on the bed but, when he eventually tired, he looked at me again like a madman, stating that you didn't need physical displacement to travel, he had the whole world in his head and was capable of describing it. If anyone's lying, it's them, Julia, it's the books that are telling lies, not me, he concluded before turning and walking out of the garage, leaving me standing there like an idiot who doesn't know what to do next. It occurred to me that Leonardo could get a job in Immigration; when people applied for permission to go abroad, he'd give them a book and tell them not to be so fucking hung up on the idea of physical displacement. I liked that image, and my laughter helped ease the tension that had built up during our argument.

A short while later, I went outside. Leonardo was smoking on the low wall by the door to his garage. I sat beside him, but he didn't so much as glance in my direction. I didn't look at him either. When he finished his cigarette, he tossed the butt to the ground and only then spoke, still staring straight ahead. He said that he'd loved Margarita very deeply, but she'd fallen for Ángel and that was the cause of the rift between the two men. At first he'd liked Barbara, although not that much, they never went to bed together; she promised things, publications, travel, and to tell the truth he wouldn't have minded getting to know the Italy beyond his bookshelves. He liked me, he said, and that was why he'd slept with me and, yes, it irritated him that I preferred Ángel, and that was another reason why he'd slept with me. As a child he'd been to the centre of the Earth, had travelled with Captain Nemo on the Nautilus, and that made him want to become a writer. But he didn't have Meucci's document; Margarita had told him that stuff about Ángel. Then he finally turned to look at me: I swear on my son's life, Julia. I turned to him, sighed deeply and stood up. Below me, I heard his voice saying that he supposed our pact was a thing of the past now. I asked if he'd heard of the butterfly effect and he shook his head. Then I told him that Ángel didn't have the document: apparently Margarita had been amusing herself with these stories, telling each of them that she'd given it to one of the others. Margaritabutterfly, I concluded before saying bye and walking away. Leo asked if I wanted a ride to the nearest traffic lights to wait for a lift, but, without stopping or turning back, I waggled a finger to indicate no. Then he shouted that he'd call the next day if that was all right. That stopped me in my tracks and I looked at him with a smile, saying he could call me whenever he liked. Havana telephones were almost always out of order when you needed them. Then I continued on my way.

Poincaré said something along the lines that there are problems a scientist chooses to pose and others that pose themselves. By this stage, the problem was who the hell had the document. That night, when I arrived home, the apartment was in darkness. I could hear my stepfather snoring on one side, the creaking springs of my brother and sister-in-law's bed on the other. My sheets were laid out on the sofa. In the kitchen, there was a note from Mum saying that my dinner was in the fridge. I tried to eat, but between the stink of the chickens on the rear balcony and my own discomfort, I could barely manage a bite, so I poured a glass of water and went to drink it on the front balcony, gazing out, as usual, on the clothes lines strung outside the buildings on the other side of the street.

I didn't understand a thing. If Leonardo had the document and hadn't yet sold it to Barbara, it must be because he actually hoped to get a trip to Italy out of it, an international publication or something like that; whatever the case, that paper was a guarantee, a bargaining chip. Bastard. If Euclid had it, I'd just handed him over to Barbara, the ideal purchaser, and he'd be able to negotiate the deal on his own, without my input; I mean, he'd already stabbed me in the back by publishing my work as his own. Bastard. And if Ángel had it, his reason for keeping in touch with Barbara was the money because, he insisted, I was the one who mattered to him, that Italian woman was just a source of cash. Bastard. I didn't understand a thing. My only point of clarity was that, whatever was going on, Barbara and I were being used. Do you see? I suddenly felt a strange sense of female solidarity, or something like that, something new for me. Barbara with her giggles, her boobs, her invitations to dinner, had become the goose that lays the golden eggs. OK, she was on the trail of the document, but she'd kind of half fallen in love with Ángel and he was taking advantage of the situation. That wasn't right. As far as I was concerned, it just wasn't right.

That was when I came to the conclusion that things had to change. Barbara didn't know about my relationship with Ángel, and there was no doubt that he hadn't taken the trouble to enlighten her, but then neither had I. And even though he'd promised to stop seeing her, that wasn't enough, at least it wasn't enough for me because Barbara was still calling him her boyfriend. So, it would be the most natural thing in the world for me to tell her to forget about him, to tell her that he and I were engaged to be married, and that she was completely out of the picture. Ángel might or might not get in touch, but when another woman tells you to keep your hands off her man, the effect is usually instantaneous. And in addition, I was feeling a tad guilty because she'd confided in me, told me about her relationship with Ángel but I, despite calling her on the telephone, greeting her warmly, taking her to meet Euclid, accepting the meals and taxis she paid for, had been incapable of telling her the truth. It was like I was using her too. And that was awful. Like I too was taking advantage of the goose who lays the golden eggs.

As I told you, I'm both sensitive to the feelings of those around me and have a great sense of justice, which must be why that burst of female solidarity was later repaid by Barbara's friendship. And what's curious is that it's a friendship rooted in our liking the same man, but which then transformed and grew. That's unusual for me, you know I don't usually go in for female friends. I generally prefer the company of men and not just because I like them; women have always seemed competitive to me. Some of them seem to think that everything reflects back on themselves: the clothes you're wearing, the few extra kilos, the flirting in the street, everything. You think she's your friend and cares about what's happening to you, when in fact she cares about what isn't happening to her. Talk about boring! And then there are the hopeless cases who ooze that thing about the rib and the weaker sex from every pore. That sort cling to you as an equal, a member of the tribe, and the problem is that they can't bear (not out of spite but because it's stronger than they are) for the other (me, for instance) to be doing fine, and then you stop being a point of reference, one of the tribe, and become something that has to be constantly badgered. It's like a drowning person who, instead of reaching out a hand so the other can pull her out of the water, clutches the head of her would-be rescuer and sinks it into the water: just-like-that; if I'm fucked up, you have to be too. More boring still. However, with Barbara, a situation that could have become an idiotically fierce battle over a man ended by becoming something else. And she actually turned out to be not at all the barbarian I'd imagined.

That night, leaning against the balcony wall, I decided I'd tell her about my relationship with Ángel and make it clear who was the queen bee in that hive. I also wanted to prevent her from being the goose who lays the golden eggs. I finished my glass of water and, with the last sip, pursed my lips and let the liquid fall like a fountain from the fifth floor. Well, everyone's dead to the world at that hour.

21

Barbara sounded truly pleased to hear from me. She said that she'd been working the whole day and wanted to see a movie but couldn't get in touch with anyone, so it was perfect that I'd rung. I remember it was a Friday, and I'd originally intended to spend the night at Ángel's, but that afternoon he'd come to see me at work to say Dayani was back and it would be better to postpone my visit. I'd phoned Barbara immediately, just in case, and was relieved to discover that Ángel's story wasn't merely a ploy to see her.

We met at the Coppelia to have a quick ice cream before going into the cinema. That year, instead of selling the marvellous confections everyone eats in *Strawberry and Chocolate*, the famous parlour was offering tropical ice cream, the tropicality of which consisted of the fact that it was mostly water with very little flavouring, as light as the sweat running down our backs. When we later emerged from the cinema, Barbara bought pizza and beer and we went to sit on the Malecón. Some kids with guitars were singing nearby, and she thought that was so lovely. I guess that as her departure date drew closer she was becoming nostalgic, feeling more deeply in love with our island than ever. She said it was a while since she'd seen or heard anything like that, and she was going to miss Havana so much; Italy was a beautiful country but it was slowly degenerating. Money, she said, ruins everything. I didn't make any comment because, given my lack of financial resources, my best option was to keep looking out to sea and listening to her. Italy seemed a wonderful country to me, famous not only for its artists but also its great scientists: Galileo, Volta, Galvani, Marconi and Meucci himself. What a nation! But that Italian woman was feeling nostalgic about our island, and went on speaking about the strange Caribbean light, and the street sounds, and the people, and how easy it was to get to know them and speak to them. She was going to miss everything, miss everyone, and she was also going to miss Ángel. At that, I re-arranged my dreamy-sea-gazer expression and took advantage of a pause to say that I had something to tell her. As her expression showed curiosity, I went on to remind her that she'd once asked me about Ángel, and I'd told her that he was in love with someone else. Well, I said, he's still in love with that other woman. As you know, Barbara wasn't the sort to beat around the bush. Without batting an eye, she responded: With you, right?

I have to admit, I wasn't expecting that, but before I could reply she smiled and said that she'd always had her suspicions. The witch! I felt awkward and said I hadn't wanted to hurt her feelings, Ángel had met her at a moment when we weren't really talking, but everything was back on track now and we were even planning to get married; he loved me and going with her had been a way of taking revenge on Leonardo, it was a complicated story, but since Leonardo was interested in her, and the two of them had always been locked into a type of male rivalry, Ángel had seduced her just to spite Leo. She let me rattle on without interrupting and when I'd finished, asked: So why are you telling me now? I imagine I was grinning like an idiot as I explained that it must be from female solidarity. Barbara, for her part, smiled mischievously and assured me that, yes, that's what it must be, but it was also to get her out of the way, which meant it was female rivalry too. I could only agree, she was absolutely right. Anyway, she thanked me for my solidarity and rivalry. While thoughtfully opening a can of beer, she said that I mustn't worry, she'd be leaving soon and Ángel was obviously in love with me; she finally understood why he'd been a little elusive lately but, getting back to the female solidarity, she suggested that I keep a closer eye on my own affairs because she had, in fact, seen him again.

Wham! Do you see what I'm saying? Rivalry, pure and simple. That blow hit me so hard I got mad and, after opening my can of beer, said that it wasn't really Ángel she was interested in: I knew she was after the Meucci document. She hadn't seen that coming and so opened her eyes wide in surprise, but before she could respond, I added that, given my decision to speak to her, I'd tell her everything: Euclid didn't have the document. Leonardo had claimed that simply to draw her away from Ángel, because Leo knew that she'd been sleeping with him. Barbara gazed at me with an astonishment I can't even come close to describing. When she finally asked who had it, I said I didn't have the faintest idea. The only thing I did have clear was that they had all been using her, she'd become the goose that lays golden eggs because she was a tourist. Couldn't she see? We were living through a damn awful situation and someone from abroad meant money and other possibilities, I couldn't swear to it, but both Ángel and Leo might be hoping to get something from her, a trip, marriage, European nationality, anything. She could believe whatever she chose but if I was saying all this, it was from nothing other than female solidarity. The expression on Barbara's face began to change slowly, the tensed muscles relaxing into a smile, she bit her lip, shook her head and finally responded: 'As my grandmother used to say: When you're about to shit yourself, it's too late for green guavas.'

I know that a few seconds went by because, while my brain works fast, it took it a while to comprehend that enigmatic phrase, which, being Cuban, I naturally understood; what my brain couldn't do was to form the image of an Italian grandmother uttering those words. Do they have guavas in Italy? my brain went on asking until Barbara's voice broke in on its vacillations: I'm not Italian, Julia. Problem solved.

I don't know how it happened, but without warning my facial muscles, which had also been tensed, began to relax, and the expression on Barbara's face seemed so comical – just as mine must have looked comical to her – that we found ourselves laughing our socks off, as if the beer had gone straight to our heads with apocalyptic effect, as if the sea were tickling our ribs. Yeah, we really did laugh, and when our laughter finally died down, she told me her story.

Barbara Gattorno Martínez was from a town in the centre of Cuba, near Santa Clara, and was of Italian descent. Her great-grandfather had arrived on the island in the late nineteenth century as part of a group of young people who, under the influence of the Italian branch of the Cuban Liberation Committee, came to fight in the 1895 war. What do you think of that? After the war, he decided to stay on; he married and decades later his great-granddaughter Barbara was born. In the early eighties, she'd fallen in love with an Italian man, married him and decided to make the return journey to his country. Barbara had settled in Milan and become an Italian national, which is why she no longer used her original surname. After the couple divorced, she moved between several Italian cities, working on small magazines and trying to make a name in journalism. When I met her in '93, she was dating Leo's Italian freelancer friend but was already tiring of him, tiring of the failures in both her personal and professional life, because she still hadn't managed to break through into the quality press. So when she heard the story of the Meucci document, it occurred to her that she could take a hand in the affair. Everything seemed to fall into place: her boyfriend had been refused a visa, she was Cuban and hadn't been back to the country for ten years. The boyfriend, who believed that she wanted to help him, gave her the articles he'd promised Leo and financed the trip. But she had other plans: she intended to get hold of the document. Leo could then write the book, but the journalistic scoop would be hers. And since everything was easier for a foreigner in Cuba, she'd invented the character of the 'Italian woman', which she'd interiorised to the point of attending the May Day parade as a tourist. As if she'd never been to one before.

I enjoyed listening to her. If in the past I'd thought of her as an Italian who spoke Spanish well, now she was like a Cuban who spoke it badly, with a different music, confusing words, mixing up set phrases. In fact, she had no need to disguise the way she spoke; so much time spent in Italy had erased a great deal of her Cuban accent. Ten years is a long time. Or that's my opinion.

Of course, Barbara hadn't counted on the emotional side of things, she hadn't expected to find the country in such a lousy state or to meet Ángel or recover so many personal memories and aromas, everything she was, and had hidden along with the surname Martínez. She was staying with an aunt who lived in El Vedado, but had already spent a fortune on necessities like soap, tooth-paste, deodorant and food, things we didn't have that year. And now I'm broke, Julia, she told me. So the goose that lays the golden eggs had neither gold nor eggs and, if you'll forgive me saying so, was scrawnier than the chickens we kept at home. Brilliant, right? I promised not to say a word of what she'd told me to the others. We would each play our own hand. She promised not to see Ángel again and even attempted to apologise. But what was she supposed to apologise for? Barbara had been lying too, lying to all of us except, fortunately, me.

So, what do you think? You can laugh if you like, because that's what I wanted to do: bust a gut laughing at us. It was so absurd, chaos raised to the nth power, until I reached my bifurcation point.

On Saturday, I went to our scientists' meeting. We waited a long time for Euclid, but he never turned up. I finally decided to phone him. He said that he couldn't come but asked me to call by afterwards and he'd fill me in on what was happening. Naturally, I was worried and so raced off to see him the moment the meeting ended. Euclid received me with a truly mournful face. As his mother was resting in bed, we sat in the living room and he told me that a friend of his son, a young man of twenty, had died. Euclid's eyes misted as he said that he'd known the boy well because he'd been friends with Chichí for years and was a good lad, a good lad, he repeated, one of the friends who'd criticised Chichí for dropping out of university, but who was always close and had sometimes stayed overnight in the days when Euclid still had a family and used to make breakfast for them all, waking them with the cry of: You're sleeping your lives away! And that boy's life had slipped away, but from a ridiculous illness. Euclid paused before saying that Chichí was heartbroken, and so he'd spent part of the morning in the apartment and that afternoon was going to the funeral home to be with his son. His mum had also been really upset; even though she didn't know the lad very well, it was still awful news. Euclid had decided to give her something to calm her and help her to sleep for a while. As soon as she was feeling better, he'd leave for the funeral home, although he had to confess that – his voice broke again at that point – he was heartbroken too. A child of twenty, Julia. Just twenty.

I took my friend's hands in mine so that he wouldn't have to cry alone and offered to go with him to the funeral home. He had to support his son, but it was my duty to support him. That's what friends are for, right? For being there, always, absolutely always. Euclid gave me a hug and expressed his thanks. When his mother appeared, we had something to eat and she made a thermos of lime tea to take with us.

I don't know if you've ever been to a funeral here in Cuba. It's a strange experience. There are all the grieving mourners, but there are also all the other people who are there from a sense of duty. I was one of the sense-of-duty guests and that undoubtedly allowed me to be an observer. When we arrived, I tactfully positioned myself to one side, Euclid went to embrace his son, his son's friends, the family and acquaintances. I was simply a crutch who was there watching the rocking chairs move back and forth, swaying with the bodies of twenty-year-olds saying goodbye to their friend. There's no doubt that a funeral is a sad affair. But the funeral of a young person is sadder still. No one should have the right to die at that age. No one, not that boy or anyone else. I really have no words to describe the sadness I felt, it was like something pressing here on my chest. Then suddenly, when I was lost in thought, a voice said: Prof. I turned my head and saw that former student from the CUJAE, the one with the curly hair whom I'd met at Euclid's place. Do you remember me mentioning her? Chichí's friend, one of that group of aspiring young writers. With a sorrowful expression and in a quiet, almost non-existent voice, she asked if I'd known her friend. I shook my head and she, standing beside me, staring straight ahead, thanked me, sincerely thanked me for coming. He likes parties, she added; he likes people, he always has something interesting to say, he adores conversation, he's wonderful. Then the girl turned to look at me with her strange, large, yellowish eyes, full of hate and impotence − sort of like someone going downhill on an enormous toboggan who doesn't know whether she'll find water, sand or a void at the bottom of the slope − and, with that vacant, frightened expression in her eyes, muttered: They say he's dead, but they're lying. And with that, she moved off towards the chairs and sat down next to Chichí and the others, all rocking back and forth, back and forth, back and forth. I had to go outside. I needed fresh air.

I walked through the door and the sun suddenly slapped me in the face, forcing me to stop in my tracks and turn my head aside. There was a flight of steps down to the street. I began to slowly descend them, but the sun was blinding. It seemed to be burning brighter than ever that day. So weird, as if it were trying to prevent me going on. And I didn't go on. I sat on one of the steps and, just at that moment, decided to let it all go to hell. Go to hell and stay there.

They're lying, the girl had said, and it was the first time those words seemed to have any real meaning. I asked myself how you continue living after seeing a friend of only twenty die. I guess life goes on, like the rocking chairs, but what happens when the chair rocks backwards? I don't know. Do you ever stop crying? I don't know. The only thing I can say is that, sitting there on the steps of the Calzada & K funeral home, everything felt absurd. Inside, broken lives; outside, just down the street, the office of the United States Interests Section with a long queue of people applying for visas. And all around me, the Havana of 1993, of Year Zero. That night would be the witches' Sabbath, but I wouldn't be there to attend it. I was stuck in the instant when the sun blinded me and, naturally, I had no shades to protect me – not from that sun, not from the terrified gaze of my former student, not from the faces in the queue or the apparent absurdity of the whole story of Meucci's document.

We were searching for a document that someone had once seen. A sheet of paper, almost nothing, a scrap we had all pinned our hopes on. Do you see what I mean? We were living in a country being screened in slow motion and sometimes in black and white, where the only things that weren't an uphill struggle were a smile, making love and dreaming. That's why we're always smiling here in Cuba, why we make love and dream all the time. We'll dream of anything. Nowadays I'm aware that knowing who invented the telephone isn't so important, and nor is the possession of a piece of paper that proves it; but give me a crisis and I can tell you which illusion to cling to. That's what Meucci's document was: unadulterated illusion, pure delusion. Our lives were revolving around it because there was nothing else, it was Year Zero. Nothingness. Smiling, making love. We were fractals reproducing the worst of ourselves.

In the group that morning, we'd studied a very interesting article about fractals and society. I haven't told you about fractals yet, have I? I'll give you the for-dummies version. Fractals are geometric objects whose dimension doesn't fit with classical conceptions, they are neither one, two or three dimensional; they are something else. Take clouds, coasts or trees, for example: natural elements that can be described using classical theory. But one of the most common characteristics of fractals is that they reproduce identical or self-similar structures on a variety of scales. Think of a fern: the smallest frond branching from the stalk has the same form as the whole fern. That tiny part is exactly the same as the small one, which is exactly the same as the big one. Get it? Due to this characteristic, fractals have been applied in music, the visual arts, finance and even the social sciences.

What we studied that morning was the idea that in society, negative emotions disseminate with fractal growth. It's as if they were branching out, reproducing themselves, growing and growing. You wake in the morning, the power is off, you breakfast on sugar-water, leave the house feeling grumpy, you push me as I'm trying to get on the *guagua*, shout at me when I protest, I push another woman to get off at my stop, I get to school, hate my students, speak to them roughly, they all seem thick as planks, classes finish, they leave, and when they get home, one has an argument with her mother, shouts at her, behaves badly and the mother cries, wondering what's wrong. She doesn't understand that, like fractals, we reproduce the worst of ourselves and aren't even aware of it, we just follow the flow. That's what had happened to us. See? Each of us holds within us the discontent of society and every one of us reproduces it. I swear, I had the urge to jump up and cry, Shit! Shout it good and loud, so the whole world could hear, but I was on the steps of the funeral home and inside sadness had taken up residence. Inside was shatteringly real life.

That was why I decided to get myself out of this story. I'd never set eyes on Meucci's document, had no idea who had it, and to be honest, I didn't give a fuck. All I really wanted was to live with Ángel. That had been my objective right from the start and I was about to achieve it, so I didn't want any more mix-ups or lies. As far as I was concerned, it was a closed book.

The only problem was that I felt I had to do something, I wasn't sure what, make a small movement that would in some way counteract the spread of the negative emotions. For an instant I considered following Margarita's example and becoming a Juliabutterfly, rearranging the variables, telling Leonardo that Euclid had the document, and Euclid that Ángel had it, and Ángel that it was in Leonardo's hands; not a bad game for a puppeteer. Only I no longer wanted to be a puppeteer. Moving the variables around would just mean that the game would go on ad infinitum, that the positions of the cannons would change in order to prolong the attack and allow all the negative emotions to continue multiplying. No way. None of that made sense. What's more, both Leo and Ángel still considered Barbara to be the hypothetical purchaser they didn't want to lose, while for Euclid she was the hypothetical purchaser he wanted out of the way. It was absurd. Do you see? Barbara, who had no money, who wasn't going to invite anyone to Italy, who was just pure bluff, was still a source of hope. Ridiculous.

Something had to be done. When I was arguing with Leo, I'd ended by telling him that Ángel didn't have the document. I'd also told Barbara that Euclid didn't have it. Correct. Don't rearrange the variables; clearing them away is the better option. I decided to tell Euclid that the author didn't have the paper, and Ángel that Euclid didn't have it. In this way the negative emotions would slowly disperse and I'd be content to have done something sensible, maybe not for Meucci, but at least for us. That was my decision, and I don't regret it. Our equation needed to be finally solved. Meucci's solution would soon follow, although his variables were different from ours.

22

And that was our story. I managed to convince them that Margarita had been secretly enjoying herself, having a joke at their expense, giving them all false information. If anyone wanted to continue the search, they would undoubtedly have to go back to square one, but without my involvement, because I'd decided to quit.

Barbara returned to Italy a few days later. I went to her aunt's house to say goodbye and received a warm welcome, as I was the first of her niece's friends to visit. Naturally, Barbara had made sure not to invite anyone else because that provincial aunt wouldn't have agreed with her niece passing herself off as an Italian. That afternoon, Barbara gave me her cosmetics and almost all her clothes: I think she only kept the two-sizes-too-small bras. Ángel found it pretty weird to see me wearing her clothes but I thought up some story and he ended up believing it; anyway, he'd given me some of Margarita's things and all that saved me from wardrobe-shortages during those difficult times. Deep down, I know that what he found strangest was Barbara's sudden disappearance, with only a last-minute phone call to say goodbye. But we never mentioned that.

Curiously enough, not long after Barbara's departure, Ángel announced that his sister had moved in with the diplomats' son. So I was able to bid farewell to the sofa in Alamar and became a true El Vedado girl. The day I brought Ángel to meet the family, my stepfather killed two chickens and no one went hungry that evening. Soon afterwards, we were married. Euclid gave me away. In the end, I decided not to tell him that I knew what he'd done with my thesis: the money he'd earned from it was lost in the mists of time. Why embitter our lives further? Once we were officially living together, I got to know Ángel better and, by tacit accord, we decided that he would never speak about Margarita, at least not in my presence. With Leonardo, on the other hand, things had been more complicated, so we only rarely met. We once ran into each other at a set of traffic lights. I was waiting for a lift, he for the lights to change. He had a young woman on the back carrier and in a little seat at the front was the small boy who looked at me with those disquieting eyes. I only had time to tell Leo about my wedding and he wished me happiness before I walked on. I thought I'd never see him again, but we still had one more encounter to come.

At times I had to bear Dayani's histrionics: when she had an argument with the diplomats' son and installed herself in our apartment for a week; when she made it up with her father; when she fell in love with someone else; when she stopped talking to her father again. My sister-in-law and her new boyfriend finally decided to leave during the Rafter Crisis of '94, when the Cuban government opened the gates to the sea, allowing anyone who wanted to leave. The only problem was that they set out too late, when the United States government had put a halt to the mass migration by sending the rafters to the Guantanamo Naval Base. Dayani ended up there and it was a hard knock for her family, especially for my poor Ángel, who was heartbroken. Fortunately, an aunt and uncle of the boyfriend claimed them and they wound up in Miami. Ángel took it badly, but at least he knew that his sister was settled somewhere.

As for Meucci, we knew that his story hadn't yet finished. After her experiences in Havana, and even though she was aware nothing more could be done, Barbara continued to take an interest in the subject and whenever she came across even the smallest piece of news, cut it out to post to me. And that was how, in 1995, I received an article by the famous Basilio Catania in which he revealed that a year earlier, in the Washington archives, he'd found an unpublished document which would finally allow him to demonstrate the priority of Antonio Meucci in the invention of the telephone. Barbara had taken the trouble to translate the whole article for me. Do you see? An unpublished document written by Meucci had been found. It was like a pitcher of cold water hitting us in the face.

This is how things stood: Do you remember that there were two lawsuits? In one of them, the Bell Company won against Meucci and the Globe. The verdict was published, which meant that Meucci's defeat went down in the history books. The other was the United States Government versus the Bell Company, which was discontinued without any verdict and, as the statements and proceedings were never published, no details were in the public domain. But it was in 1994, in those papers, that Basilio Catania found the unpublished document.

The evidence presented in both cases was practically identical, with only one small difference: Meucci's notebook. The original one, in which Antonio wrote in his own hand, with the addition of sketches and designs, wasn't submitted in evidence because it was in

Italian. What was offered in both cases was an English translation. Well, in the Bell versus Meucci case, the English version of that notebook only included the text explaining his experiments, with the word 'Drawing' where the designs should have been. As this notebook was published with the rest of the documentation, it was freely accessible to anyone. Alternatively, the case of the United States Government versus Bell included a sworn statement by the lawyer Michele Lemmi. Do you remember Lemmi & Bertolini? Lemmi redacted a sworn statement, signed by Meucci, in which appeared the English translation of the notebook, with the explanations plus all the designs drawn by Meucci long before Bell had ever dreamed of inventing anything. The translation was never published, and lay buried among the piles of papers in the growing archive. But that very document changed history.

A while ago, I told you that the sciences can't be explained with words; they are for art and philosophy; in science what matter are numbers, formulas, diagrams or designs. Before speaking, a scientist picks up a pencil and draws things. And there's an interesting detail related to this. Without Meucci's designs, his explanations are just words open to interpretation: froth, smoke, nothing. Aristotle understood that: Some people pay no attention to a speaker unless he offers mathematical proof. And Meucci's words were carried away on the wind; it was his designs that, over a century after his death, achieved justice for him. Do you see?

As Catania explains in his articles, which I was able to read thanks to the translations Barbara sent me, the discovery of the document was a surprise because it demonstrated that Meucci was technologically ahead of his time. But the researcher's surprise was even greater when he began to tease out the threads of the story and uncover the forgotten details of the lawsuit the United States government brought against the Bell Company. Basilio Catania started his research in 1989, the centenary of Meucci's death, and visited archives in Florence, Havana and Washington. The discovery of the unpublished document and, later, other equally important evidence, allowed the case to be taken to the Supreme Court in New York and then to Congress. At that point, many Italian-American associations joined the cause, particularly OSDIA – the Order Sons and Daughters of Italy – which is the group responsible for the Garibaldi Meucci Museum on Staten Island. They issued a press release, officially recognising the importance of Basilio Catania's role in the investigation.

On June 11th 2002, they won the battle: the United States Congress passed resolution 269, officially recognising Antonio Meucci as the inventor of the telephone.

Applause.

Whenever I think of this, I want to applaud and I imagine Meucci beaming, and Alexander Graham Bell asking if he'd like a beer. Two great scientists: yes, indeed. But Antonio got there first. It's as simple as that. He got to the telephone first, yet recognition came long afterwards. Justice sometimes travels by bicycle, but better late than never, right?

Naturally, I wanted to share the pitcher of cold water that had hit my face with the news of the discovery of the unpublished document. Leonardo was surprised when I turned up at his office, although my visit pleased him enough to invite me to go out for a coffee, and then we sat together in Plaza de Armas. When I showed him the article, he asked if I knew that Barbara was Cuban. He'd received that information from his freelancer friend. She had us all fooled, he said. I nodded and he took the pages from my hands. When he'd read them, he heaved a sigh and lit a cigarette. I'm still going to write my novel, he insisted. With or without Margarita's document. That seemed logical to me; it was important for him to finish the book and, what's more, I told him that he could photocopy the article and that I'd pass on any further information as it reached me. Leonardo looked at me over his glasses with his comical expression. And how's your little angel? he asked with a smile. I replied that he was fine, and knew that there was little else for us to say. That was the last time we spoke. I spotted him in the distance in 1999, when they laid the stone in honour of Meucci in Havana's Gran Teatro to celebrate the 150th anniversary of his earliest experiments. It was there that I had my first glimpse of Basilio Catania, the man who had made Euclid's dream a reality. I know that Leonardo later published a few things, but I've still to hear anything of the Meucci novel.

The moment Euclid learned of the New York document, he screamed the house down. In his opinion, it was a tragedy, they had got there ahead of us, but we could still do something. He'd written a very serious letter to Margarita and was hoping that her stony heart would be melted by it; his own daughter couldn't do something like that to him, he'd been on the trail of that piece of paper for too long. I listened as he paced from one side of the room to the other, exactly as he used to in class, and it amused me to see him that way, but also saddened me. What could we do? Nothing. The story had come to an end, even if my dear tutor refused to accept that fact: good scientists are stubborn. And that's how he still is: a stubborn scientist, looking after his aged mother, taking old Blot's successor for a walk, more absorbed in his scientific books than ever. Chichí, who is now an author and has even been published abroad, continues to support him financially. And Barbara occasionally sends him gifts and money. Euclid still believes that she's Italian and I don't have the least intention of disillusioning him. What would be the point?

When I showed Ángel the Catania article, his first reaction was to make a jocular comment about my correspondence with Barbara, but as soon as he saw the title he plumped himself down on the sofa and began to read. I watched him out of the corner of my eye. When he'd finished, he set the pages aside, saying that he'd put that whole affair out of his mind. Do you want a drink? he asked. He was just beginning to develop a belly thanks to the beer he bought with the money his mother began to send after Dayani had contacted her in the United States.

In the end, Leo had been right when he said I was an intelligent woman and would eventually tire of Ángel if he didn't do something to stop that happening. He did nothing, simply allowed his beer gut to grow and became addicted to movies on DVD after our video player gave up the ghost and even the cassettes belonging to his unknown woman were put away in a drawer. Our marital idyll slowly decayed and I ended up bored with my angel, really bored. Luckily for us both, two years ago he won the *bombo*: you know that visa lottery for permission to enter the United States. He's in Miami now. From time to time he calls, drunk, homesick, saying that he'll come back, but to be honest, I hope he doesn't. I've already had long discussions with his father about the apartment because, naturally, he doesn't want to admit that the residence in El Vedado isn't his, but he's wrong. Ángel takes my side: the place had belonged to his mother's family and in his absence, it's now mine.

So this is where I live. I left the Tech some years ago and now give private classes in maths and rent out one of the rooms. But I pay my taxes, right? Barbara sends Italian tourists to me, so I get by. And I have a boyfriend who spends the occasional night with me, but not every night. I know what they're like. They start by leaving a toothbrush and before you know it, they've moved in. No way. This apartment is mine.

Have you been out onto the balcony yet? Even though I've never travelled anywhere, I'm certain that this is my favourite road in the whole world, with its trees, its streetlights and its shadows. Even in the dark, it's beautiful. Always beautiful. It's the main artery of the city. I like to go out onto the balcony at night to breathe the cool air and dream. Didn't I say we're all dreamers here? Many things have changed since 1993. And although we're still stuck in that sort of eternal limbo, if you look outside, you'll see the past and the present pass by on Calle 23: there are fewer bicycles now, but there are both old and modern cars; the power doesn't cut out so often and we're even allowed mobile phones. Yes, things are undoubtedly better, we keep smiling, keep making love and dreaming, even if many of our dreams have changed. The crisis of the nineties finally convinced us that we're not all equal and the world is divided into those who have money and those who have none. That's the way it's always been. Everywhere. Aren't I right? We'll slowly begin to look more like normal countries, where you're fine if you have money and fucked if you don't. That damned normality is no surprise to anyone. It's the changes that surprise you, the uncertainty of the bifur-cation point. Don't you think so?

I've often asked myself what would have occurred in 1874 if Antonio Meucci had had the ten dollars he needed to renew the provisional patent. History would have been different. On the other hand, what would have happened in 1993 if one of us had found Margarita's document? Nothing. I'm certain absolutely nothing would have happened. We were hanging on to our illusions, living one more dream, in a state of chaos, and chaos is a vortex that sucks everything in.

But better late than never, right? What happened was that when Ángel left the country I decided to rearrange the apartment in El Vedado to suit my own tastes. I had a pile of boxes with all my work stuff, so I set about classifying them and throwing out the things that were no longer useful. New house, new life. One of the boxes contained things from my years at the Tech, and that was where I came across a folder containing the stories Chichí had given me to pass on to Barbara. Remember? It was the day Euclid had gone out with her and, while I was waiting for him to return, his son turned up with the folder. He had to leave, Euclid and Barbara showed no sign of appearing and I needed to get home. The folder of stories was buried under my other papers in Alamar and eventually ended up in a box in El Vedado. To tell the truth, I'd never really liked Chichí's stories, but that night, when I was putting things in order, I opened the folder out of curiosity and began to read one, hoping to find something marvellous. And I did. The stories were written on the reverse side of a variety of documents: telephone bills, school tests, diplomas. It was impossible to buy paper in '93. Year Zero, remember. The sheet of paper on which the last page of the story was written was thick, and it had another, yellowing sheet taped onto it. Clumsily taped. I forgot the story. There were sketches. Symbols. Diagrams. I had such an urge to laugh aloud that the only thing I could do was cry. Honest. I cried the whole night long. I cried for months. I cried until I found you. What would have happened if Euclid and Barbara had come home earlier that day? I don't even want to think about it. How did Meucci's document get into Chichí's hands? I don't know and I don't care, but it's possible that it never left Margarita's family home

– Euclid can't have been aware of that – and the boy had no idea of the importance of those drawings. He wanted to write a story, and for that he needed a sheet of paper. Long live the creatives.

And that's it. I've told you everything. In this folder, which has lain on the table during our conversation, is the document containing the designs Meucci made here in Havana in 1849, in this marvellous country where we go on smiling, and making love and dreaming. But between the smiles and the sex and the dreams, you have to make a living, so turn off the tape recorder and we'll get down to business. I know this document isn't worth as much now as it would have been in '93, but shall we talk money?

Acknowledgements

First and foremost, I would like to thank Dr Catania, who is no longer with us. His tenacity and meticulous research underlay the fact that, in 2002, Antonio Meucci finally received the recognition that was denied him during his lifetime. It is due to his kindness and to all the information he offered me, that I was able to write this novel.

I also wish to thank all those who helped me in one way or another: my parents, my sister and my aunt, Josefina Suárez; Armando León Viera; Patricia Pérez (thanks, Prof); Leonardo Padura; The Centre National du Livre in Paris; Anne Marie Métailié; Amir Valle, José Ovejero, Antonio Sarabia, Alfredo Rey, Rafael Quevedo, Pierpaolo Marchetti, Bárbara Bertoni and Juan Pedro Herguera. I would finally like to thank José Manuel Fajardo and Silvia Bastos Agency.

CHARCO PRESS

Director & Editor: Carolina Orloff
Director: Samuel McDowell

www.charcopress.com

Havana Year Zero was published on
80gsm Munken Premium Cream paper.

The text was designed using
Bembo 11.5 and ITC Galliard.

Printed in December 2020 by TJ Books
Padstow, Cornwall, PL28 8RW using responsibly
sourced paper and environmentally-friendly adhesive.